HE COURTED HER WITH PUNCH LINES.

Middle-aged stand-up comedian Josh Steinberg, formerly the star of his own popular TV series, finds himself struggling to keep his career alive, playing seedier and seedier clubs. Plump, balding, and plain-looking, he has never had much luck with women. That is, until Josh meets Holly Brannigan while performing his stand-up act in a comedy club. Holly, an attractive, intelligent, and divorced 50-year-old businesswoman, becomes instantly smitten with Josh and even finds his unconventional looks wildly sexy.

"... a surprising novel ... Filled with characters that seem as if they just walked out of a sitcom, *Love Is the Punch Line* might just tickle your funny bone."—*Anne Clinard Barnhill, author of The Beautician's Notebook, At the Mercy of the Queen, and Queen Elizabeth's Daughter*

"Outside observers might wonder what middle-aged romantics Josh Steinberg and Holly Brannigan see in each other, beyond the mirror image of their mutual loneliness ... Fireworks onstage. Fireworks off-stage. Fireworks in the bedroom. Then come the duds..."—*B.A. East, author of Patchworks*

"... Author Kathleen Jones successfully brings readers into the gritty, often brutal worlds of stand-up comedy and the Hollywood film industry, where talent means little unless it is combined with youth and beauty, and where love is often an illusion."—*Kathleen Duhamel, author of the Deep Blue Trilogy*

"When aging comedian Josh meets businesswoman Holly, sparks fly, but it's not an easy road to happy ever after … a sweet love story with lots of twists and turns that will take you on an emotional rollercoaster ride."—*Alicia Montgomery, author of the True Mates Series*

"…relatable and relevant, edgy and witty. It is clearly well sequenced and flows as a good piece of writing should, with plenty of moments to pause and chuckle along the way."—*Chris Sellars, personal trainer, BRM, NSCA-CPT, CSCS*

"… an authentic romance novel … love builds not in a linear way, but in a realistic, fragmented pace. … I liked how Jones treated the story and how the romance follows a different path. An enriching reading."—*Lisa Torquay, author of The Lass Defended the Laird*

"… fascinating and different … There are sorry-for-themselves male characters and strong women … lots of sex and also a religious theme … a page turner for sure. It ends somewhat happily. "—*Marika E. Tamm, freelance editor*

"… reminds you that 'love conquers all', and that … love will go a long way to ensuring success. In this case, Holly's love for Josh carries him through his personal crisis to a new beginning."—*David Iggulden, former editor, Wolters Kluwer Canada*

"Holly and Josh aren't your typical young, beautiful lovers. They are real people with real feelings, and come complete with flaws that I can identify with. As I was reading, I was rooting for them to make it."—*Charlene Watters, editor, Wolters Kluwer Canada*

"A well-written novel of turbulent love and the catastrophic happenings of a Jewish comic. It is fast moving and very descriptive. The characters are easy to remember."—*Gordon Calvert, former employee, Wolters Kluwer Canada*

"... unforgettable and touching ... a story about disappointment, failure, and shame ... but also a story about faith, courage, hope, and triumph. ... The path to true love can be a treacherous one indeed, stretching the human character to its limit ... "—*Sheila Mitchell, author of I Love You, Grandma!*

"Brilliantly humorous, fun romance! ... Kathleen Jones is not only brilliant with her storylines, but she is also amazing at her imagery and scenes. *Love is the Punch Line* will keep you thoroughly entertained, and I bet you even laugh out loud a few times!"—*Stella Knights, author of The Dusty Rider Series*

Love is the Punch Line
Kathleen Jones

Moonshine Cove Publishing, LLC
Abbeville, South Carolina U.S.A.
First Moonshine Cove edition April 2018

This book is a work of fiction. Names, characters, places and incidents are products of the author's imagination or are used fictitiously. Any resemblance to actual events, locales or persons, living or dead, is entirely coincidental.
ISBN: 978-1-945181-33-7
Library of Congress PCN: 2018938528
Copyright 2018 by Kathleen Jones-Lepidas
All rights reserved. No part of this book may be reproduced in whole or in part without written permission from the publisher except by reviewers who may quote brief excerpts in connection with a review in a newspaper, magazine or electronic publication; nor may any part of this book be reproduced, stored in a retrieval system or transmitted in any form or by any means electronic, mechanical, photocopying, recording or any other means, without written permission from the publisher.

Book cover design by The Book Design House
www.thebookdesignhouse.com

About the Author

Kathleen Jones is a former book editor and technical writer. She graduated from the University of Toronto with a degree in English literature and completed Ryerson University's Certificate in Publishing program. Kathleen writes for a number of popular book blogs, including Romance Junkies and the blogs of Jane Friedman and British novelist Tony Riches. She also contributes monthly book reviews to Goodreads. Kathleen lives in Toronto, Ontario, Canada. Visit Kathleen online at https://kathleenjones.org/ and on Twitter at https://twitter.com/joneslepidas and sign up for free updates at http://eepurl.com/ceSobT

For my second grade teacher, the late Mrs. Eleanor Campbell, the first person who told me that I could write.

Acknowledgments

I would like to thank Gene D. Robinson of Moonshine Cove Publishing for his valuable support, as well as my substantive and stylistic editor, Jenny Govier, for her knowledge, guidance, and patience. Without her, I would never have been able to complete this project. I would also like to thank my copy editor, Allister Thompson, for his eagle eye, and my proofreader, the late Marika E. Tamm, for her meticulous work.

Finally, I would like to thank my friend Elissa (Lisa) Berger, who reviewed the Jewish references in the novel and provided valuable insight.

Kathleen Jones

LOVE IS THE PUNCH LINE

Chapter One

Josh Steinberg's mission in life was to make other people laugh, but these days, he could barely make himself smile.

"Good evening, everyone," Josh said, starting his act in a halting voice, his eyes sweeping the half-empty, dimly lit room.

Holy shit, what a dive. The Yahoo Comedy Club in Toronto? Never heard of it before. God, why does Greg keep lining up these crappy gigs? And how did I end up with an agent who knows nothing about the comedy business? Serves me right for hiring someone who used to be a roadie with a rock band.

Josh smiled at the half-drunken faces before him, then launched into his routine — the usual *shtick* about his hopeless love life.

"My looks have helped me in life. I mean, no women are filing paternity suits against me."

Deep down inside, Josh knew that his looks had done absolutely nothing for him. He had never really been a hunk: five foot nine; slightly plump — always plump, even when he was young; a plain face with a big nose; thinning and graying brown hair; receding hairline; double chin. Josh especially hated his big, protruding belly; he had tried for years and years to get rid of it, with no success.

As if his aging looks weren't bad enough, Josh now had some unwelcome competition from his new twenty-eight-year-old agent, Greg. Despite his short stature, Greg was darkly handsome — and Italian — with brilliant, piercing blue eyes and perfect features. On more than one occasion, Greg had stolen the woman that Josh tried to pick up. Each and every time it happened, Josh vowed to fix himself up through the magic of drastic diets and plastic surgery.

"I have to be realistic about my expectations. I mean, if I were a woman, I wouldn't date me."

Josh had always known he wasn't great-looking, but he had never dreamed that he would still be alone at the age of fifty-four. He believed that once women got to know him, they would see the beautiful heart under his less than gorgeous exterior. All he had ever wanted was a soul mate, one special woman who could love him as much as he could love her. Josh knew that he would make a great husband, unlike most of the other comics on the road, who often cheated on their wives.

"Anyhow, don't feel too sorry for me. I've slept with lots of gorgeous women. They simply can't resist us paunchy guys."

Over the years, Josh had managed to pick up a fair number of tall, thin, young, and beautiful models and actresses. But he had never been able to hold on to them; as far as they were concerned, Josh was nothing but a useful celebrity name who could get them auditions with producers, escort them to movie premieres where they could be photographed, or just satisfy them in bed until their far better looking Prince Charming came galloping along. Once they got what they wanted, they always disappeared.

"I remember one gorgeous blonde I asked out through a dating app. When I turned up at her door for a date, she took one look at me … and threw up."

They barely laughed at that one. In fact, they've barely laughed at any of my punch lines.

"I guess she had the stomach flu. And who could forget the flawless Asian beauty I met on a movie set? When I asked her out, she actually laughed at me."

Out of the corner of his eye, Josh spied a woman seated alone at a table in the corner, her chestnut hair styled in a chin-length bob that perfectly framed her delicately pretty face.

She hasn't laughed at any of my jokes. But for some reason, I can't stop looking at her. The woman Josh kept staring at wasn't his type at all. Oh, she was pretty enough, but she was hardly young. If she didn't laugh at him, so what? She was only one woman out of billions, a total stranger that he would never even see again.

The "total stranger" couldn't take her eyes off Josh either.

Holly Brannigan's gaze trailed Josh onstage. *He's not bad looking.* She had always found Josh somewhat repulsive whenever she saw him on TV; as far as she was concerned, he was just a fat, ugly guy with a nasal voice. But when he stepped out on the stage tonight, she found him wildly sexy. He wasn't Holly's type, and he was far from handsome, but … there was *something* special about him. Maybe it was his big, cuddly body … or his eyes. Yes, it had to be those warm brown eyes of his. Holly had never seen kinder eyes on a man's face.

"I should join Daters Anonymous. I've become a love-a-holic."

Holly didn't find Josh funny at all. She couldn't possibly laugh at a man who had been badly hurt by so many women. In fact, he depressed her… and she came to the club tonight to cheer herself up.

"Believe it or not, I was engaged once. Of course, she stood me up on our wedding day …"

A phone rang. Very loudly.

It's my phone, Holly thought. *I forgot to turn it off. Shit!*

As she reached into her handbag to silence the offending phone, she could see a shadow looming over her. She looked up timidly into the glaring, unfriendly face of Josh Steinberg.

"What the hell are you doing, lady?" he said.

The audience tittered. Holly's heart started to pound.

"This happens to be a comedy club. Why haven't you laughed at any of my jokes?"

"I'm sorry," Holly said in a soft voice, blinking back tears.

"Not only did you not laugh at me, but you had the nerve to pull out your phone during my set. What right do you have to do that? Answer me!"

"I said I was sorry. Please leave me alone!"

"Why should I leave you alone? You're ruining my act. Get out of this place right now!"

That was the last straw. She felt horrible about her phone, but she couldn't believe he had the nerve to accuse her of ruining his unfunny act. And now he was trying to kick her out, too. Infuriated, Holly stood up, grabbed a glass of water off the table, and tossed it into Josh Steinberg's face. Then, without missing a beat, she snapped up her handbag and bolted down the hall.

The audience — finally — gave Josh the heartfelt approval he'd been seeking, punctuating their roaring laughter with loud applause and lusty whistles.

Stunned, Josh blindly picked up a napkin from a nearby table and mopped his face, his eyes trailing Holly as she disappeared into the women's washroom.

She locked herself into the nearest stall. Hot tears coursed down her cheeks. *Why did he upset me so much?* Holly had always been a tough businesswoman; it was unusual for her to crumble like this. Was she touchy because Eric just dumped her … or did she have a crush on this big prick?

Ten minutes later, Holly emerged from the washroom to find the big prick himself standing outside, his eyes slightly downcast, his angry face transformed by a kind expression.

"Excuse me, dear," Josh began in a humble voice. "I want to apologize for yelling at you."

Maybe he didn't mean to hurt me. Maybe he needed to lash out at someone, and I just happened to be there.

"I know I interrupted your act, but you had no right to yell at me."

"Look, I'm sorry. I was having a rough night, and I took it out on you."

He looked so sad on that stage. She really felt sorry for him ... even though he was a celebrity.

"You think you're better than me because you're a celebrity, don't you?"

"No, I don't. I'm sorry, really." Josh sighed. "What else can I say?"

I guess he's sincere. After all, he didn't have to apologize to me.

"Okay," Holly said, her voice softening. "You don't have to keep apologizing."

"But ... you really didn't laugh at me. Why? Was I terrible or something? Please tell me."

He might be an asshole, but he did notice me. Maybe there's more to him than I thought.

"I couldn't laugh at you because you just seemed so ... sad."

"Sad?"

"Yes. All of those mean women rejecting you, treating you like crap."

"Oh. Well, it was supposed to be funny."

But Holly really hadn't found Josh's act funny. And she couldn't understand why all the women in Josh's past were so cruel to him. He wasn't that bad-looking ... and he was actually sweet.

"I'm sure it was. I'm sorry I didn't laugh."

"Lady, you have nothing to apologize for. Well," Josh glanced at his watch, "I'd better call it a night."

It's now or never, Holly. Go on and ask him — you'll never get another chance.

"Oh, uh, Mr. Steinberg?"

"Yes?" Josh looked up, puzzled.

"Can I buy you a drink?" Holly asked, her heart pounding. "It's the least I can do after I ruined your act."

"You didn't ruin my act. You helped me get a big laugh," Josh said, a playful smile spreading across his face. "You should join my act — and I should buy *you* a drink."

"No, I should. I'm the one who asked you out."

"Oh, okay." Josh chuckled. "But you really don't have to. Now," he said in a more businesslike voice, "can we get out of this place and go somewhere decent?"

"I know just the place," Holly said, smiling back at him. "Follow me."

Chapter Two

What a crazy evening, Josh thought as he sat down in an old wooden booth at the back of Paddy O'Connor's, an Irish pub down the street from the comedy club. The cheerful room was small and cozy, its walls covered in colorful travel posters bursting with blue skies and sandy beaches, its floor covered with a soft carpet. *One minute, I'm depressed and lonely and pouring my heart out onstage; the next minute, a pretty lady is asking me out. Though who knows why — you can't really trust women.*

"What'll you have?"

Josh looked up. A heavy-set young woman in tight black jeans glared at him.

Josh smiled at her. "I'll take a pint of the house draft. And you?" he asked, turning to Holly. "Perhaps you'd like a glass of water to replace the one you spilled at the club?"

"Uh, no. I'd like something a bit stronger than that. I'll have a pint of the house draft, too."

"My kinda woman," Josh said, a grin spreading across his face.

The server scribbled on a notepad and disappeared.

Holly glanced around the room, which was full of young couples and a smattering of middle-aged men perched on stools at the bar, hoping that they wouldn't be bothered by a bunch of autograph seekers. And Holly hoped that Josh hadn't agreed to go out with her just because he felt guilty about yelling at her. But that was probably the only reason he was here; she knew that he wouldn't have asked her out on his own. *After all, he is* the *Josh Steinberg and I'm nobody special.*

"So, why did you bring me to an Irish pub? Are you Irish? And Catholic?" There was a twinkle in his eye.

"Sort of."

"Sort of? What's your name?"

"Holly Brannigan."

"Holly ... Brannigan? Sounds Irish to me. Unless Brannigan is your married name."

"It's an Irish name, but my family hasn't been Irish or Catholic for several generations. I'm Protestant — and mostly English — thanks to intermarriage. And it's *my* name. I'm divorced."

"I'm Jewish. I guess that's pretty obvious. Does that bother you?"

"Of course not. Jewish men are gorgeous ... and sexy." She smiled warmly at Josh.

"Oh," Josh said, looking down at the table. "And what exactly do you do for a living? Do you have any kids? Or a serious boyfriend?"

"I own an event planning business called An Affair to Remember. I have a grown son named Kyle. And I don't have a boyfriend anymore. My ex-boyfriend, Eric, dumped me a couple of months ago after five years together. I guess it would have happened sooner or later — he is seven years younger than me — but it still hurts." Holly sighed. "Look, Mr. Steinberg — Josh. I hope you didn't agree to go out with me just to be polite. I mean, I'm a boring person and nothing special to look at."

"Holly — "

"You're Josh Steinberg. You can have any woman you want. Actresses, models — "

"Josh Steinberg is just a *schmuck*. I didn't go out with you just to be nice, and I can't have any woman I want. A lot of women turn me down. And you're not a boring person at all — you're a smart, capable woman with your own business. And you're pretty."

"Maybe for my age. I'm old, Josh."

"How old are you? You can't be older than me. I'm fifty-four."

"I just turned fifty today."

"You're ancient. Anyway, you've held up a lot better than me."

"That doesn't matter. Men your age only date younger women."

"Maybe some other old guys do, but I date anyone I want."

The server appeared and set two frosty mugs of beer on the table.

"A toast!" Josh declared, picking up his mug. "To Holly! Happy birthday, Holly!" They clinked their mugs together. "Speaking of looks," Josh continued, lowering his voice, "I've always hated mine. Holly, if you were me — if you looked like me — what work would you have done? Would you reshape my nose, get rid of my double chin, do a hair transplant? Or something else? Please tell me, and be honest. Be brutal!"

Holly stared at Josh, dumbfounded. "Well, I don't know. Are you planning to have some work done?"

"I want to, but I don't know where to begin."

"Don't, Josh. Please don't do anything to that beautiful face of yours." She picked up his hand from across the table and tenderly kissed the palm. Now it was Josh's turn to look dumbfounded. "You shouldn't have any work done. You're gorgeous, Josh. Really."

"Oh." Josh reached across the table and gently stroked Holly's hair.

"All those women you talked about in your act, they really did treat you like crap, didn't they? And that's why you feel bad about your looks."

"It's the other way around. They treated me like crap because I'm fat and ugly. Women have always used their beauty to hurt me." Josh paused. "But don't you think your questions are getting a little too personal?"

Holly flinched, stung by this sudden verbal attack. "But you just asked me a bunch of personal questions. And you talk about your personal relationships onstage."

Josh considered Holly's words for a moment, a sober expression on his face.

"Maybe you've been chasing the wrong women. You need — you deserve — to be with someone who really appreciates you."

"There's no such woman."

"Sure there is. You're sitting across from that woman right now. I think you're very sexy, Josh."

"Oh."

That word again! What's he's really thinking?

"I really wish I could take away all of the hurt those mean women inflicted on you. You didn't deserve it."

Josh looked tenderly at Holly and smiled. "Thank you, dear."

The next two hours flew by. Josh found himself pouring out his heartaches to this lovely stranger: His loneliness on the road and empty sexual encounters. His bouts of depression and suicidal thoughts, always unpredictable and scary. His stalled career and his fruitless search for work — any work.

"It wasn't always like this. Not long ago, I was a superstar on the stand-up circuit, and I had starred in a hit TV show and several popular movies. Lately, though, I have to scramble for work, and the clubs keep getting smaller and smaller."

"Why don't you create your own work? You could write your own screenplay, then get some studio to produce it — "

"Oh, sure. The movie studios don't want anything to do with me. They're not interested in producing another dumb Josh Steinberg comedy."

"You don't have to write a screenplay for another dumb Josh Steinberg comedy."

"What would I write about?"

"Real life. Real people."

"I couldn't do that. All I know is comedy."

"Yes, you could! You're more than smart enough, Josh. Challenge yourself. Reinvent yourself — "

The server returned to the table. "Excuse me, folks. Closing time in five minutes. Sorry to kick you out."

"I can't believe how late it is," Josh said, glancing at his watch. "It's already midnight."

"I hope I didn't take up too much of your time. Or bore you," Holly said as she paid the bill.

"Not at all, dear." Josh smiled. "I had a wonderful evening."

"So did I." Holly smiled back. "Even though it didn't quite start out that way."

Thirty minutes later, Josh's compact black car pulled into the driveway of Holly's small townhouse near High Park. Holly had expected to get roaring drunk at the comedy club to blot out the pain of her breakup, so she'd left her car at home, planning to travel by cab. But Josh, concerned about Holly's safety, insisted on driving her home.

As Holly climbed out of the car, a cool late-summer wind whipping across her face, Josh pulled her close to him a bit awkwardly, then, pressing his lips against hers, kissed her deeply and passionately. Holly wrapped her arms around his big, solid body and buried her face in his chest.

I never want to let him go. I feel so safe in his arms. I don't think I've ever felt this way about anyone else.

He lifted her face and brushed his lips against hers. "I love the way you taste. And I love the way you feel, baby. You're so soft."

"It's a little late to drive back to the hotel," Holly said as he kissed her neck tenderly. "You're welcome to stay here for the night. There's room on my couch … or in my bed."

Oh my God! Did I just invite him to have sex with me? He must think I'm really ballsy.

"Are you sure?" Josh asked as he nibbled her ear. "I don't want to put you to any trouble."

"It's no trouble at all. Of course, you don't *have* to stay if you don't want to."

"Of course I want to. I'll take the bed over the couch. But where will *you* sleep?"

Holly laughed.

"What do you know? I finally made you laugh. I guess you can't hate me too much."

"I don't hate you at all, Josh." Holly fumbled with the key as she tried to fit it into the lock. With a jerk, she flung the door open, then reached blindly for the light switch in the front hall.

"Don't turn it on," Josh said in a voice scarcely louder than a whisper. Before she could reply, he scooped her up into his arms and carried her down the dark hall and up the stairs. Somehow he managed to find the bedroom on his own.

***

Early the next morning, as the bright August sun streamed through the front window of Holly's townhouse, a rumpled but happy Josh, a contented, lazy smile gracing his face, stumbled into the front hallway. A few seconds later, Holly, dressed in a short-sleeved navy shirt and faded jeans, followed him, clutching a small brown paper bag.

"Homemade peanut butter cookies," she said, handing the bag to Josh. "Just in case you get hungry on the road."

"Do I look like I need cookies?" Josh patted his rotund stomach.

"Don't worry. They're low-fat."

"Thanks. And thanks for the most romantic evening of my entire life."

"Thank *you*, sir. And just for the record, you were the best lover I ever had. You're a fabulous lover, Josh."

"So are you, dear. You really know how to please a man."

"That's a real compliment from a guy who's bedded so many young and beautiful — and tall — models."

"You're way better than them in bed. They just lie there and expect to be serviced. And you're smart. There's nothing hotter than a brainy lady."

"I don't think so," Holly said in a flat voice.

"Look, honey, smart ladies like you are hot. The brain is the biggest sex organ."

"Sure, Josh," Holly muttered. Then she burst into tears.

"What's wrong, dear? Did I say something to upset you?"

"No, of course not. It's just, well … you live in Los Angeles. I'll never see you again."

"It doesn't have to be that way. We can always see each other. I'll call you."

"No," Holly said, shaking her head. When Josh shot her a puzzled look, she continued. "I hate it when men promise me that they'll call. They never do, and I end up getting hurt. I can't stand it when men and women play games with each other. So please don't promise to call me, Josh. Okay?"

"Oh, okay." Josh chuckled softly. "I can't stand it when people play games, either. But does this mean you'll get mad at me if I do call you?"

"No, of course not."

"Then do I have your permission to call you?"

"Of course. Don't be silly."

"Maybe I will, then." Josh smiled at Holly. "Well … goodbye, Holly the Brain."

"Goodbye, Josh, the … Jewish Comedy King."

"Jewish Comedy King? That's quite a claim! You must be sucking up to me."

Holly laughed. Josh pulled Holly close to him and kissed her — hard.

Holly kissed Josh back, taking in his sweet taste and musky scent for several deliciously long minutes.

And then, in a flash, Josh thrust open the front door, hopped into his car, and drove away.

Chapter Three

Josh's romantic one-night stand with Holly raised his sexual confidence — just a notch. But once he had been on the road for several days and the hard daily grind had again set in, all of the old, familiar hurts came flooding back.

Why did she sleep with me? She must have had some hidden reason; women always do. She's middle-aged, lonely, and insecure about her looks ... or she needed to feel good about herself after her younger boyfriend dumped her ... or maybe she just wanted to bed a celebrity and I happened to be an easy mark. That must be it. Why else would she sleep with someone who looks like me?

The end of the day was the worst time for Josh. That was when he was unable to run away from the loneliness that always lurked just below the surface, masked by the constant hard work and the relentless travel. That was when Josh missed Holly the most. And that was when Josh, dozens of times over the following month, tried to reach out to Holly by picking up the phone and punching in her number.

But he never spoke to her. Instead, he disconnected the call each and every time she answered the phone.

Josh knew that Holly really didn't want to talk to him. And he didn't want the risk of getting hurt again. Besides, she wasn't really his type. He was into tall, beautiful blondes, not short, unbeautiful brunettes.

But Josh was trying to fool himself; he didn't really feel that way. The truth? He was just not attractive enough for Holly. He would have to forget that he had ever met her, keep himself busy, and concentrate on his work.

But he couldn't concentrate on his work, and he couldn't stop thinking about Holly. He soon started performing a new stand-up routine about a small woman, an "Irish midget," who had "assaulted" him at a comedy club in Toronto by throwing a drink in his face. And, taking Holly's advice to heart, he started writing a screenplay about "real" people: a comic romance between a fat, plain-looking Jewish man, a computer sales rep who traveled from city to city, and a slim, petite, non-Jewish businesswoman who just happened to have an Irish background.

***

Holly couldn't stop thinking about Josh, either. She kept hoping that he would call her; the voiceless calls, which she hoped were from him, always left her crushed. But she knew that she had no reason to feel hurt. Josh never promised to call her, and she had even told him not to. Besides, Holly meant nothing to Josh. She wasn't famous, wasn't beautiful, wasn't young. And contrary to what he told her, she knew that celebrities like Josh are always surrounded by beautiful women just panting to jump into their beds.

Holly's self-scolding didn't work; she still couldn't stop thinking about Josh, no matter how hard she tried.

I must forget about him, she told herself sternly one evening, after a long, hard day spent struggling with clients. *I have to get on with my life. And the only way I can forget about Josh — the only way I can stop caring about Josh — is to dig up some dirt on him. Maybe he cheated on his ex-girlfriends or beat them up or had a child with one of them that he refused to support financially.*

But Holly, after searching online for hours, found no dirt on Josh, no fatal character flaws, no evidence of cruelty to past lovers. She did, however, uncover dozens of photos of him from his high school days into his fifties, images from movies, television shows, star-studded charity events, and red carpet movie premieres. Holly printed off every photo of Josh she could find, then stuffed the growing stack of images into large, brown — and increasingly plump — envelopes. That big pile of pictures only made Holly miss Josh even more.

After two weeks of searching online, Holly knew that she had to see Josh again. And if he didn't call her — and she was sure that he never would — she would have to make things happen.

That evening, she purchased a ticket for Josh's show at the One Liners Comedy Club in Denver the following Saturday night, along with a plane ticket and a hotel reservation. She would just have to tell the office that she would be going on a business trip. None of Holly's employees, or her business partner, would ever know the truth … or so she hoped.

***

That same evening, another former lover of Josh's — Jill Boudreau, a blonde, blue-eyed model in her late twenties — also purchased a ticket for his upcoming show in Denver. Jill had dumped Josh only a year before and married one of his best friends, a popular young stand-up comic. Hurt and deeply embarrassed, Josh had sucked up his feelings, even agreeing to serve as the best man at their wedding, trying hard not to look at the beautiful young couple, trying hard not to cry.

Jill's marriage had lasted a mere six weeks, with her complaining to the ever-present paparazzi that her former husband was "neglectful." Several months later, Jill picked up the phone and called Josh, crying and begging for his forgiveness … and asking for his help in starting a career as a stand-up comic.

"I can't get much work, Josh. The bad publicity from the divorce — my ex has gone out of his way to spread lies about me in public — has hurt me. A big modeling contract

I had for a major cosmetics line got canceled; some movie parts I was up for went to other people. I need to try something else."

"Uh-huh."

"I've always loved comedy, and I'd like to try stand-up. I've written some material, but I don't know if it's any good. Maybe you could take a look at it, since you're such a great comic …"

Flattery will get you everywhere.

"… and I know I'm asking a lot …"

Aha! An almost-apology!

"Look, Jill, I can try to give you some pointers, but I want you to understand that we're not getting back together again. You and I just don't mesh. But if you're really serious about a stand-up career, why don't you catch my gig in Denver this Saturday, and then I can take a look at your stuff the following day? You just might learn something."

"Sure, Josh. I'll be there. And don't worry about the … the … personal stuff. I'm engaged."

"Anyone I know?"

"His name is Jacques Von Graff. He's Belgian. A billionaire. Made his fortune as a futures trader."

"Haven't heard of him. How does Mr. Moneybags feel about you becoming a stand-up comedian?"

"Oh, he doesn't know about it."

"Doesn't know about it? Why?"

Jill paused. "I don't think he'd want me to work in a club." She sighed. "Let's just keep this a secret for now, okay?"

The following Saturday night, Jill drove to the One Liners Comedy Club in Denver, arriving fifteen minutes before Josh's gig. Dressed in a tight black nylon mesh tank top and a skimpy black leather miniskirt with a fringed hem, she stepped into the noisy and spacious room, cleanly furnished with white walls, white wicker chairs, and small, glass-topped tables, and scanned the faces in the crowded room for Josh. Unable to find him, she seated herself on a stool at the long, sleek bar at the front of the club, ordered a glass of white wine, and then turned to the darkly handsome young man who was sitting beside her, his ear glued to a smart phone.

Gorgeous guy. Looks like an agent.

The man turned off his phone and stuffed it into the pocket of his black leather blazer.

"Excuse me. Do you know where I could find Josh Steinberg? He's a friend of mine."

"Is he?" the man responded, smiling at her. "Well, I happen to be Josh's agent. I'm Greg — Greg Fanelli."

"Jill Boudreau."

"Nice to meet you, Jill. Come with me and I'll take you over to Josh."

Greg rose from his stool at the bar and stood up — all five feet seven inches of him.

Jill stood up, tall in her silver heels, and looked down at Greg, sighing. "You know, Greg, you're really handsome. If someone could stretch you out, you'd be perfect for me."

"Well, you're far from perfect for me. I don't date bony giraffes."

"I was only trying to be funny."

"Oh, sorry. Well, Ms. Boudreau, I happen to be busy, so if you don't mind …"

"Jill."

Jill turned around to see Josh standing behind her, a cautious smile pasted on his lined face.

"Josh," Jill smiled, hugging him a little too tightly.

"I see you've met my new agent," Josh said, pointing at Greg.

"Unfortunately," Greg said.

Josh tossed one arm around Jill's shoulders and pulled her toward the far end of the room. Laughing and talking excitedly, they passed table after table filled with customers, young couples on dates, groups of co-workers from nearby businesses, middle-aged men engaged in loud, passionate conversations.

And, at a table near the stage, Holly Brannigan. Josh didn't notice Holly, since she was cowering under the small table, deeply embarrassed.

I knew I shouldn't have come here! He doesn't want me — not when he can have her — and I'm just making a fool of myself by chasing him. I'll have to get out of this place before he sees me.

"Excuse me, miss?"

Holly looked up. A small and pretty Asian woman with a friendly face looked down at her.

"Did you lose something?"

"Uh, no," Holly said, trying hard to smile at the attentive young server. Out of the corner of her eye, she saw Jill sit at a table at the opposite end of the room and take out a small notepad.

As Holly pulled herself upright, the stage in front of her was suddenly flooded with blinding lights as loud, aggressively cheerful pre-recorded music filled the air. A young man stepped onto the stage and picked up a microphone.

"Good evening, folks!"

It was too late for Holly to sneak out of the club.

"Here he is, the one, the only ... Josh Steinberg!"

Josh bounded onto the stage, beaming, as the audience greeted him with thunderous applause.

Her hands shaking, Holly shielded her face behind a large plastic menu.

"You really meet some colorful characters on the road," Josh began after the applause faded. "I met one of them in Toronto about a month ago."

Holly's heart sank.

"This woman, this clueless loser, had her cell phone on during my act. I mean, what woman talks on a cell in a comedy club — unless she's trying to pick up a client for the evening?"

Mild titters from the audience.

"But she wasn't *that* type of woman; she was just some bimbo."

Is he talking about me? Of course he is. What an asshole!

"So anyhow, I told this loser to shut off her phone, and this little woman, this pathetic midget, actually beat me up. A big guy like me!"

That's not true at all. You provoked me, you liar.

Holly couldn't take it any longer.

"Screw you, asshole!" she cried, rising to her feet. "You have real nerve to say that!"

Josh wheeled around, startled, and stared dumbly at Holly.

"Well, look who's here," he began, a mean smile spreading across his face. "It's my wee friend, the leprechaun."

"How dare you call me that? You … you big fatso!"

"Fatso? Is that the best you can do? I thought you were cleverer than that." In an even louder voice, he added, "I can always lose weight, but you, leprechaun, won't grow any taller. In fact, you'll never grow up."

"Hell will freeze over before you lose an ounce. And you have no right to insult me in public. I should sue you for defamation of character."

"Defamation of character? Listen, honey, this is a *comedy* club. There's no reason for you to feel hurt."

"But you're picking on me. You're making fun of my size. You're acting like a bully, not a comedian."

Josh glared at Holly. "What makes you think I'm even talking about you? You can't exactly prove it, can you?"

"It's obvious you're talking about me."

Josh ignored Holly's reply. "Listen, Holly the Brain — Holly the Shrimp — I have no reason to talk about you. I have no interest in you. You're not really my type. I rarely date anyone who can shop for clothing in the children's department."

Enraged, Holly snatched a slice of chocolate cake off a nearby table, jumped onto the stage, and smeared it down the front of his white polo shirt. Then she ran out of the club. Her heart beating wildly, she dashed through the crowded parking lot, searching for the small blue car she rented that afternoon.

What if she couldn't find the car? What if the security guards at the club stopped her? What if Josh caught her? She was afraid to think of what he would do to her.

Shaking and out of breath, Holly finally found the car, slipped inside it, and turned on the ignition. A few seconds later, she could hear someone shouting.

Holly glanced up. Josh was standing outside the car's passenger-side window, yelling at her and gesturing broadly. A large crowd of people — customers and employees from the club, as well as curious onlookers — was standing behind Josh, laughing and jeering.

Terrified, Holly backed out of the parking lot, praying she wouldn't hit another car, and drove off down the highway, the car's tires screeching.

Josh couldn't move. He stood in the parking lot and stared at Holly's car until it became a speck in the distance, the cool fall breeze ruffling his hair.

Oh my God, what have I done? She didn't get my act at all, and I've just driven away the one woman on this planet that I can't stop thinking about. Shit, I really hate myself sometimes!

Chapter Four

The next few days were hell for Josh. When he wasn't working — when he wasn't trying to make other people laugh — he kept to himself, holed up in cramped and moldy motel rooms, beating himself up with painful thoughts.

Josh felt guilty about the fiasco in Denver. He'd finally met a really nice woman — someone classy and smart and pretty and down-to-earth — and he had treated her like crap. But he knew that he himself was no catch — he was old, fat, ugly, and washed up. He also knew that he couldn't go on like this; he had to fix things. He had to call Holly today, tell her that he didn't mean to hurt her, beg for her forgiveness …

Josh pulled out his phone from the front pocket of his navy nylon jacket and punched in Holly's number.

"Hello?" Holly said.

What can I say to her?

"Hello? Hello!"

Josh turned off the phone, trembling.

He didn't have the guts to speak to Holly. But he couldn't keep calling her and hanging up. What could he possibly do?

The calls made Holly angrier than ever.

"I have a perfect right to be left alone," Holly said to her business partner, Diana Atkinson. "I'm getting those pesky calls again." She glanced out the window of her office, located in an old four-story brown brick building on Adelaide Street in downtown Toronto, at the dozens of people milling around on the sidewalk below, the cold October wind blowing decayed leaves and soggy newspapers into their paths.

"Maybe you should call the police," said Diana, a dark-haired, genial fifty-year-old with a handsome face, as she sat down on a white plastic swivel chair in the corner, the early morning sunshine casting playful shadows on the pale blue walls of the dusty and cluttered small office. Diana, a happily married mother of three adult daughters, had co-founded An Affair to Remember with Holly, her best friend since childhood, over twenty years before.

"What can the police do? My whole life sucks. The only men who even know I'm alive are this pervert who keeps calling me every night and Josh."

"Look, Holly, you've got to make the effort to meet a nice man. You can't just give up and get depressed like this."

"There are no nice men." Tears filled Holly's eyes. "I'm fifty years old. Men my age want younger women, and younger men don't want a serious relationship with someone as old as me. Oh, Diana, why was Josh so mean to me? What did I do to deserve being treated like that?"

"You didn't do anything, honey," Diana said, rising to her feet and hugging Holly. "Josh Steinberg is just a pig, a big, fat loser who can't relate to women. You can do a lot better than him, and I know just the guy for you. He's a neighbor of mine whose wife died a couple of years ago. He's a bit older than you, a stable man with his own business — he owns a garage. Ed's a good guy, Holly; you'll really like him."

"I appreciate your concern, Diana, but I don't really want to bother with dating anymore."

"Just go out with him once. If it doesn't go well, you don't have to see him again. And he might get your mind off what's-his-name."

"Okay," Holly replied, her voice heavy with reluctance. "Give him my number and my email address."

A few days later, Ed Walton sent Holly an email suggesting that they meet for drinks some night after work. Holly sent him an email back, inviting him to dinner at her townhouse the following Friday evening ... without mentioning that her son Kyle would be home from university for the weekend.

"Do I have to dress up for this Ed guy?" Kyle, an easygoing, tall young man with curly, sandy brown hair, asked Holly from his perch on the couch, his eyes glued to a football game on TV.

Holly surveyed her son's red cotton pullover and scruffy blue jeans and sighed. "No, you look fine. Just answer the door when he comes. I have to check on dinner."

As soon as Holly disappeared into the kitchen, the doorbell rang. Groaning, Kyle pulled himself off the couch, strolled over to the front door, and opened it.

"Hi, I'm Kyle, Holly's son," Kyle smiled, extending his hand. "You must be Ed."

Ed, a slim, moderately attractive man with thick gray hair and chiseled features, neatly dressed in a navy-and-white checked shirt and navy twill pants, walked past Kyle without shaking his hand or even speaking to him.

Holly, who had dressed up for the occasion in a knee-length camel wool shirtdress, a thin dark brown belt, and camel high-heeled pumps, felt uncomfortable around Ed from the moment he entered her home.

The three of them sat down on the cranberry leather couch in the cozy family room, surrounded by soft, pale pink walls. *He's not bad-looking*, Holly thought. *But there's something "off" about him. I just know it.*

"So," Ed began, helping himself to a handful of salted nuts from a small glass dish on the coffee table, "what happened to your marriage? What happened to Kyle's father?"

Holly sipped her glass of Perrier and gave Ed a hard stare. She wondered why Ed would care so much about her marriage to Kyle's father. The thought made her squirm. It seemed odd that he would ask her such personal questions. After all, he didn't even know her.

"I divorced Kyle's dad almost twenty years ago. He's not part of our lives anymore."

"Mom and I have done all right without him," Kyle said, pride creeping into his voice. "She has established a successful business, and I'm not exactly a deadbeat —"

"You mean Kyle grew up without a father? Did Kyle's father at least visit him or provide some financial support?"

Financial support? From Kyle's father? He couldn't even hold down a job.

"No, I've had no contact with him since Kyle was a baby. He was an alcoholic, and he wasn't able to take care of himself, let alone provide any financial support to me and Kyle. Besides, I haven't really needed it."

"Why did you marry someone like that? Did he knock you up or something?"

Holly sighed, exasperated with Ed's rude questions. "Why are you even asking a question like that?"

"Hmmm," Ed paused, munching slowly on a mouthful of nuts. "I guess everyone can't be as lucky as I was. My wife Barbara — she died a couple of years ago — was really special."

I don't care. You're supposed to be on a date with ME.

"She was everything a man could possibly wish for," he continued, his eyes misting over. "Beautiful, even in middle age ..."

Even in middle age? You think old guys like you are hot?

"... gave up a promising career as a nurse to stay home and raise our four children ..."

I suppose us employed women are selfish, neglecting our kids just to pay those pesky bills.

"… there will never be anyone like her ever again."

Thank God for that.

"I suppose all this is boring to you."

"Oh, no, not at all," Holly responded, her voice betraying her annoyance. "Can I get you a drink?"

There was no point in trying to be polite to this jerk. Holly wished that she had the nerve to tell him to get lost instead.

"Sure," Ed replied in a cold voice.

Rising from the couch, a fake smile pasted on her face, Holly made her way to the kitchen. As she pulled a tall glass off a shelf, something dark caught her eye: the clingy black knit dress she had worn the last time she saw Josh, now wrinkled and shapeless, tossed over a kitchen chair.

Why did Josh hurt her? Why did he hate her? Holly's eyes filled with tears. Why didn't he reach out and apologize? Did she really mean that little to him?

***

Josh also longed for Holly, longed for some way, any way, to heal the hurt festering between them. He knew that he had to find some other way to tell her how he felt. He couldn't keep letting his feelings eat him up from the inside, and he couldn't keep calling her and hanging up.

A few days after her miserable date with Ed, Holly arrived at work to find a long message on her voicemail.

"Greetings, Holly the Brain," a familiar male voice began.

It's JOSH! Holly's face broke into a smile.

"Please hear me out before you erase this message," the voice continued. "I never wanted to hurt you, Holly, and I only made fun of you in my act to get a laugh. And just in case you were wondering, I'm no longer dating Jill, that model at the club; our relationship is strictly business."

Bullshit. Jill's your type; I'm not.

"Anyhow, if you really want to understand what happened at the club, you'll watch Skip O'Neill's talk show on TV tonight."

Holly never watched Skip O'Neill's show; she hated the way he insulted his guests.

"Please watch it, Holly. Please, honey."

Holly stared at the cold, blinking green light on her phone and sighed.

She wondered why he wanted her to watch it. Was this just another dumb joke of his? She shouldn't waste one more second on him. She should just delete the stupid voicemail and forget about this loser, once and for all.

But she couldn't. And, despite her best judgment, she found herself sitting down, alone, at 11:00 that night to watch *The Skip O'Neill Show*.

"We have a real treat for you tonight," said Skip O'Neill, a tall, blond, blandly attractive man in his mid-thirties, dressed in a navy pinstripe suit and a red tie. "A real comedy legend ... Mr. Josh Steinberg!" Thunderous applause followed.

A rumpled-looking Josh, clad in a black suit, black shirt, and black tie, his face creased with worry, bounded onto the spare set and sank down into a light gray leather sofa beside the host's desk.

"So, Josh, you've been having some run-ins with a certain lady from Canada." Josh responded with a sheepish grin. "Why have you singled out this poor woman, Josh? Is she really as ugly as you've made her out to be?"

"I haven't been singling her out," Josh began in a sober voice, sweat forming on his brow. "And she's not ugly at all. It's just that ..." He paused, groping for the right words. "Guys like me — guys who aren't handsome — know that we can't hang onto attractive women like her, even if we can get them to go out with us in the first place. So we try not to get too serious about them."

"So that's why you've been making fun of this woman. Makes perfect sense, doesn't it?"

"No, you don't get it. Fat guys like me don't make fun of these women to be mean. We only make fun of them because we know they aren't really attracted to us. Sooner or later, they always leave us for some thin and gorgeous young hunk."

Holly snapped off the TV with the remote.

Maybe she had overreacted at that club. Maybe she hadn't understood Josh's act. Maybe she had taken his words the wrong way. Maybe, just maybe, Josh was really insulting *himself.*

Four nights later at Nit Wits, a small, dingy club on the outskirts of Buffalo, Josh found himself trotting out his old routine, the one about his long string of ex-girlfriends and miserable dating history.

Josh scanned the sea of faces in the sparsely furnished room, its walls covered by old, faded posters of rock bands. *I can't talk about Holly anymore. If she really cared about me, she would have watched the show and called me or emailed me by now. All I did was make a fool of myself over a woman in public. I'll never perform that routine on her again, and I'll destroy that stupid screenplay I was writing.*

Josh was five minutes into his routine when he was interrupted by a woman's voice.

"Hey, Josh!" Holly shouted from her front-row table. "Why don't you do that routine on the little lady who beat you up?"

"Holly?" Josh paused, his eyes focusing on Holly's face.

Holly stepped toward the stage and peered up at him. "Yes, it's me."

Josh smiled, then his face grew solemn. "I didn't think you were such a big fan of mine," he said in a small voice.

"Look, Josh. I-I came here to say I was wrong about you. I didn't understand you — or your act — and I took your words the wrong way."

Josh smiled again. "I guess you saw me on *Skip O'Neill?*"

Holly nodded.

"Holly, you have nothing to apologize for. I'm the one who should apologize to you. All the cruel and stupid things I said about you at the club were just part of my act."

Holly's eyes filled with tears. "Then you didn't mean what you said about me? And you're not mad that I went to see you at that club?"

"Of course not," he responded in a gentle voice as he reached out and pulled her onto the stage. Holly looked up into his tender brown eyes, her heart beating wildly. "You have every right to be mad at me. I never wanted to hurt you, Holly. You don't know how sorry I am. And if you don't want anything to do with me ever again — "

"Shut up, Steinberg. I didn't travel all the way here to dump you."

Josh smiled. "Crazy lady." Then he wrapped his big, strong arms around Holly and kissed her. The audience cheered and applauded wildly.

Chapter Five

"Who were you thinking about when you climaxed?"

You were thinking about that hot model at the club in Denver, weren't you?

Josh, startled by Holly's words, shot a puzzled look at her. They had just made love on the lumpy bed in Josh's room, surrounded by the deep, shapeless shadows of midnight and the dank, musty smelliness of old hotel rooms. The sex had been hot, passionate, rough but sweet, the urgent hunger of two people who had been denied each other for too long.

"Who was I thinking about?" Josh said, loosening his arms, which had been wrapped snugly and protectively around Holly.

"Admit it, Josh. You weren't thinking about me, were you? You were thinking about someone else."

"That's not true."

"Sure it is. You even told me, 'You're not really my type. I rarely date anyone who can shop for clothing in the children's department.' Don't you remember?"

"Yeah. But that was before I knew what your type is like. I'm now learning to appreciate the, shall we say, special pleasures of small women."

"Sure, Josh."

"Look, honey," Josh said in a gentle voice, drawing Holly closer to him, "I said a lot of very stupid and untrue things about you in my act. I guess I never understood why a woman as pretty as you slept with a fat guy like me." He paused and stroked Holly's hair with his soft, plump fingers. "I'm sorry. I never wanted to hurt you, baby."

Holly shook her head. "That's bullshit, Josh. You don't really think I'm pretty. You said some very vicious things about me onstage."

Josh sighed, "You don't understand."

"I don't. Okay, I do understand that you didn't mean to hurt me with your act, but sometimes, you seem to forget that I have feelings. All you care about is getting a laugh."

"You can't prove that."

"Sure I can," Holly said, blinking back tears. "If you really cared about me, you would have called or sent an email or text. Instead, all you did was exploit me in your stupid stand-up act."

"That's not true! I *did* call you, Holly. Many, many times." When Holly glared at Josh, he continued, "I called you dozens of times, but I didn't speak to you. Haven't you been getting a lot of late-night calls from someone who keeps hanging up on you?"

"You mean *you* were the one calling me? I thought it might be you, but I wasn't sure." Josh nodded. "But … but why did you hang up on me? Why didn't you speak to me?"

"Because I lost my nerve. I was afraid you weren't serious about me, Holly."

"But what have I done — or said — to make you feel that way?"

"Nothing. The truth, Holly, the real truth, is that I'm not attractive enough for you, and I know it. And that's why I poked fun at your size. I felt intimidated by you, and your size was the only 'flaw' I could use to bring you down to my level."

"So you *do* find my size unattractive!" Holly exclaimed, recoiling from Josh.

Josh chuckled softly. "Stop it, Holly. You're beginning to sound as neurotic as me." When Holly glared at him, he added, "Why can I make everyone else laugh but you?"

Holly didn't respond.

"Look, honey, I do find your size — and you — very attractive."

"But you made fun of me!"

"Holly, I only wrote all those jokes about you because I just couldn't get you off my mind. I kept thinking about you, day and night, ever since I left Toronto. In fact, you should feel flattered, not insulted — I only make fun of women I care about."

"That doesn't make sense."

"Sure, it does … from a comedian's point of view. A comedian's sense of logic is totally different from a normal person's."

"So you *were* making fun of me."

"Holly, look at me." When Holly reluctantly raised her eyes, Josh continued, "I never in a million years wanted to hurt you, honey. But I've been badly hurt myself in the past by too many other women. When I met you, I had feelings for you, but I was scared of getting hurt again, so I had trouble expressing my real feelings …"

Holly lifted Josh's hand and lightly kissed his palm. "It's okay, Josh, I understand."

"But … wait a minute," Josh said, withdrawing his hand, his voice suddenly hardening. "You called *me* a big fatso in public. *You*, lady, have trouble with *my* size, not the other way around."

"That's not true. I love big men."

"Bullshit!"

"Well … I was just defending myself. You attacked me first. I-I had to bring you down to *my* level."

Holly and Josh looked at each other and laughed.

"This is so silly. We're acting like a couple of kids," Josh sputtered between laughs.

"I'm really sorry I hurt your feelings, Josh. And you are more than attractive enough for me — you're hot."

"I feel the same way about you, dear."

"Sure, Josh."

Josh sighed. "You have absolutely no idea how depressing it is to be fat."

"I do know. I used to be fat myself."

Josh looked at the wand-slim Holly and shook his head. "Sure you did."

"No, really. I'm just a slimmed-down fat person. I was fat all during high school, and I never had a single boyfriend. And to top it off, I wore thick glasses and had severe cystic acne. I hated myself and would eat and eat and eat — always the greasy, fatty, salty stuff — to numb the pain inside me."

"Really? Hard to believe."

"It's true," Holly said. "I have the photos to prove it."

"But you're so thin now."

"Yes," Holly nodded, "but I had to go on — and stay on — a very strict diet. But even after I lost all that weight, I still hated my looks. Deep down, I was still a fat girl."

Josh stroked Holly's hair, a thoughtful expression on his face. "I know exactly how you feel."

Holly smiled. "See, Josh, you're not the only person who feels bad about their looks. Oh, by the way, what happened to that screenplay of yours?"

"Oh, that. Forget about it. I'm not going to bother with it anymore."

"Not going to bother? Haven't you written anything?"

"I wrote a film treatment. I even approached all of the studios. None of the movie people will even meet with me; to them, I'm just another has-been comic who died decades ago."

"But you can't just give up. You can't!"

Josh sighed. "Do I have to spell it out for you? I'm washed up, Holly, kaput. My career's on life support, I'm broke … and I'm old and ugly. Why should I waste my time on something that will only fail? Just so I can feel more depressed and hopeless?"

"But you could make a comeback! Other people have done it … you're so talented, Josh."

"You think I'm talented? Since when? I never seem to make you laugh, only cry. Anyhow, talent means nothing, only looks … and youth … and I have neither."

Holly shook her head, determined to ignore Josh's dig. "I could help you raise the money for your film. I have lots of business contacts, and I'm sure some of them would be happy to invest in it." She paused. "What's your screenplay about, anyway?"

"It's about a couple — " Josh began, then abruptly stopped himself. "Holly, look, it's late, and I'm tired. We can talk about this some other time. Let's get some sleep, okay?"

"Okay. But don't destroy that screenplay. Promise?"

Josh looked at Holly through heavy, sleepy eyes and grunted, "Okay."

I don't care about this stupid screenplay, Josh thought, as his head hit the pillow. *Why does she have to keep bugging me about it? Just let it go, lady, let it go.*

But Josh was lying to himself; his screenplay meant a lot to him.

It's the most deeply personal piece of writing I've ever created, Josh mused one afternoon when he checked his laptop for messages. The screenplay mirrored his life. It was the love story of a plain but big-hearted Jewish man — computer sales rep Howard Greenberg — and a petite, pretty, part-Irish businesswoman — Hannah O'Leary. It was Josh's heart, in cold type, on display.

Still no messages from Greg about the screenplay.

Why won't they consider my screenplay?

He had poured his soul into that screenplay, crafting a *real* story with *real* people. People the audience could relate to. It was nothing like the ones he had written in the past; those so-called screenplays had just been bunches of dumb gags strung together. But it was still a Josh Steinberg screenplay, and no studio wanted anything to do with him.

The movie studios' refusal to even consider his screenplay hurt Josh deeply. But his public image as a "washed-up" comedian would — ironically — soon help him land some lucrative jobs.

***

"Has-Been Comic Attacked in Club!" trumpeted the headline of one Hollywood gossip site that Greg found a few days later when he searched online for Josh's name.

Greg clicked on the link to the site.

"You are visitor number 30,010," read the first page, the words set in small white type against a stark black background. "Click on the link below to enter."

Could this have something to do with Josh? Greg wondered, as he clicked on the link.

A few seconds later, a grainy video popped up on the screen. An irate Josh — obviously working in a comedy club — yelled at the top of his voice, "Why should I leave you alone? You're ruining my act! Get out of this place right now!" A few seconds later, a woman's hand tossed a glass of water into Josh's startled face.

Someone in the audience of the Toronto club had captured Josh's first run-in with Holly on video. And over thirty thousand people had watched the clip in a short period of time. As far as Greg was concerned, the video's popularity was an amazing opportunity for Josh.

A few days later, Greg visited the site again ... then a few days later ... then a few days after that.

65,000 views ... 87,510 views ... 103,026 views ... 172,002 views ... 215,056 views ...

320,000 Fans Visit Site of 'Washed-Up' Comic! blared the subject line of Greg's email to the executives of TV networks, cable networks, and production companies. *320,000 fans can't be wrong. Book the legendary Josh Steinberg today!* the email urged, ending with a helpful link to the much-watched video at the club.

The television people ate it up. Josh suddenly found himself busier than ever before, as his calendar filled up with guest appearances on sitcoms and talk shows and even a commercial for a sticky-sweet breakfast cereal, which Josh had to force himself to swallow. And, of course, stand-up gigs at more prestigious comedy clubs. But some club owners were less than enthusiastic about Josh's online video. In fact, the owners of the Toronto and Denver comedy clubs — who had both chewed Josh out after his confrontations with Holly, tossing customers' complaints at him and threatening to cancel his future bookings — begged Greg to take the video down. Josh himself was deeply embarrassed by the video ... and terrified that Holly would see it and get hurt, yet again.

Josh decided to phone Greg.

"There's nothing I can do," Greg told him. "I don't have the power to take the video off the site."

"But can't you threaten legal action? Sue the bastards?"

Greg sighed. "You can't afford to sue them — and why would you? This is *free* publicity, the type of publicity that will save your career, the type of publicity that money can't buy. Besides, look at all the great gigs you've been offered. Most stand-up comics would *kill* for these opportunities."

***

But at least one of Josh's "great" new comedy club gigs went badly. One night, a few weeks after his latest romantic encounter with Holly, Josh called Jill about a job in Boston.

"I have a gig at a club in Boston next Thursday night, and I need someone to open for me. Do you want it?"

"Sure, Josh. I'll take it, on one condition."

"One ... condition?"

"Yes. Just don't promote me as your opening act."

"Why not?"

"My boyfriend might find out."

"Are you talking about the Belgian billionaire?"

"Yes."

"Why would you want to keep this a secret from him?"

"Because ... he looks down on people in showbiz. He's a control freak, and he'd go nuts if he knew I was doing stand-up. Please, Josh."

Jill's concerns about her wealthy boyfriend turned out to be the least of her troubles that night. Jill arrived at the swanky club, filled with polished marble tables and mirrored walls, looking sexy in a clingy white cotton shirt, tight black leather pants, and high-heeled black sandals — and then tripped on her way to the stage. Once she got onstage, Jill's act fell flat: her timing was off, she forgot some of the punch lines, and the audience barely laughed at her.

"I'm sorry, Josh," Jill whispered, as she limped off the stage at the end of her act, rubbing her sore leg.

"Don't worry, honey," Josh whispered, patting her on the shoulder. "You just need some practice."

Jill nodded, then dragged herself into a small lounge at the back of the club. Its walls were covered with dark oak paneling; the room's dim lighting was punctuated by tall, white flickering candles on each table.

"Boy, you really sucked up there tonight!"

Jill glanced up, startled. Greg, who had flown into town to discuss a contract for a new comedy series with Josh, was sitting across from her.

"You have absolutely no talent. What makes you think you can do stand-up comedy?"

"Lower your voice. You're embarrassing me."

"You *should* be embarrassed after giving a shitty performance like that."

Jill scowled and looked away.

"Why don't you go back to modeling, or to your rich boyfriend, and leave us alone? Josh doesn't need your crap. Stop screwing him around."

"Screwing?" Jill laughed. "That really bugs you, doesn't it? I've screwed your boss in the past, and now I'm screwing Jacques Von Graff, but you're not getting any action. Poor thing."

"God, lady, you're really full of yourself." Greg shook his head. "I told you before that I'm not interested in you."

Jill laughed again. "Oh, come on, Greg. You want me, I know you do. *You* know you do. Admit it."

Greg stared at Jill blankly. Without speaking another word, he got up from the table and stumbled out of the room.

Josh didn't fare much better than Jill that night. The audience, soured by Jill's half-hearted stand-up act, was in a nasty mood, and Josh, dressed sloppily in a worn red polo shirt and scruffy blue jeans, could sense it from the moment he stepped onto the stage.

Struggling to compose himself, Josh picked up the microphone, his eyes scanning the hostile faces in the audience. His regular material was not going to work tonight. He just had to try something different. But what?

He caught his reflection in a mirrored wall.

That's it! That's my answer.

"Hi, everyone," Josh began, forcing himself to smile. "I know you guys came here to listen to the same old stuff, but I'd like to try something different tonight."

The rowdy audience fell silent, still hostile but now curious.

"I'm a middle-aged guy who works in a youth-obsessed business where appearance means everything. I can't get jobs — movie jobs — unless I look a certain way. As you can see, I have a lot of stuff to fix."

Mild titters from the audience.

"Anyhow, there are too many things for me to fix, so I'd like you guys to vote on the first cosmetic procedure I should do. Should I fix my nose first? Cut my chins down to one? Fill in my receding hairline? Go on some drastic diet and get rid of this big, fat belly once and for all? Or something else?"

Josh's questions were met with a cold, awkward silence.

"Come on, guys, tell me. Don't be shy! Just tell me what I need to do first."

More awkward silence.

Then a drunken man's voice shouted, "There's too much to fix, Steinberg! You couldn't even begin to afford it all."

Too much to fix.

Shit, am I really that ugly?

***

Josh was still asking himself that same question hours later. It was keeping him awake, torturing him, filling him with feelings of shame and worthlessness. Finally, at around two in the morning, Josh forced himself to pick up his phone and ring Holly's number.

"Holly, I can't sleep."

"Josh? Why are you calling at this hour? Is something wrong? Are you okay?"

"No, I'm not okay," Josh said, starting to cry. "I can't stomach this anymore. The movie studios won't look at my screenplay, my stand-up gig bombed, I'm old and fat and ugly and broke …"

"What happened? I thought things were going well. You've been getting a lot of TV appearances and more bookings at bigger clubs."

"My act bombed tonight, big-time. And I've only been getting the TV work because I made a big fool of myself on the Internet — "

"What do you mean, you made a fool of yourself on the Internet?"

She doesn't know about the video!

"Never mind, honey. I just called because I needed to hear a friendly voice."

He just called to hear my voice? Holly's heart soared. *And he's confiding in me, too. I must mean a lot to him.*

"One bad gig is nothing, Josh. Everyone has bad days. Even me."

"You deserve someone a lot better than me. Not only do I stink as a comic, I've actually hurt you with my act."

"You didn't hurt me. I took your act personally, but I understand now that you didn't mean it that way. You are a wonderful man, and I love you with all my heart. And you're very funny. Please don't get so down. Please get some help."

"You love me? But Holly — "

"Who cares what some stupid audience or brain-dead studio head thinks? Anyhow, take it easy and get some sleep. I'll fly down to your next gig in a couple of days. Then we can sit down and talk things over calmly. Okay? Promise me, Josh?"

"Oh, okay. Thanks, Holly. I really appreciate your support."

Holly sighed. "And, Josh?"

"Yeah?"

"Don't give up on that screenplay of yours. I'll find some way to raise the money for it."

Holly turned off her phone, her mind reeling.

She had just told him she loved him. She wondered how he felt about that. And she wondered how she would raise the money to produce Josh's screenplay. Should she contact people she knew? Get a loan from a bank? Or use a crowd funding site?

Then, seemingly out of nowhere, the answer popped into Holly's head.

A party! I'll throw a big party.

Chapter Six

A week and a half later, in late November, Holly hosted a fundraising dinner for Josh and four dozen of her well-heeled business contacts at the Emperor's Court, a large, luxurious Chinese restaurant in Toronto. Holly chose the restaurant because most of her business colleagues lived in Toronto ... and because the Emperor's Court was across the street from Paddy O'Connor's, the pub she took Josh to on their first date.

Maybe this neighborhood will be lucky for us again, Holly thought as Josh steered his car into the parking lot behind the restaurant.

Tonight, Holly wore a strapless slim, floor-length gown in a rich emerald green silk that hugged her small curves. Her delicate face was framed by a pair of long, sparkly emerald earrings. Josh was smartly dressed in a navy wool suit, a crisp white cotton shirt, and a silk tie with red and navy diagonal stripes.

Holly smiled warmly at Josh as they entered the restaurant together. *He's so handsome.* But Josh didn't smile back. *Maybe he's just nervous.*

"Why didn't you have the party at Paddy O'Connor's?" Josh asked, surveying the elegant room, its white walls adorned with Chinese brushstroke paintings of flowers in soft hues of pink and lavender, the floor covered with polished black and white ceramic tiles, the lighting dim and intimate. "This looks like a snobby place. Are you trying to impress a bunch of boring old suits?"

Holly glared at him. "Josh," she said in a loud whisper, "drop the attitude. You're here to sell your screenplay, not to tick these people off."

Josh ignored Holly's protests, sniffing the air, which was full of the earthy scents of lively spices. "At least it smells good in here," he said. He smiled briefly at Holly and gently squeezed her hand. "Do you really think this will work?" he asked. "What if it doesn't?"

"Holly!"

Josh looked up to see a tall, trim, white-haired fifty-something man approaching them.

"Hello, Tom," Holly responded, hugging him.

"Thanks so much for inviting me here tonight." Turning to Josh, he began, "Is this — ?"

"Tom," Holly said, "this is Josh Steinberg. Josh, my friend Tom Jackson."

"Oh, hi," Josh said, sweat beading on his brow. He shook the man's hand limply. "Have you — you know — heard of me?"

"Of course I've heard of you!" Tom laughed. "You were my favorite comedian when I was in university, Josh."

Josh noted Tom's white hair and deeply lined face. *Holy shit. Am I really that old?*

"And this is Mary Hui," Holly said, smiling at a young woman who had just entered the restaurant. "Mary, this is Josh Steinberg."

"Hello, Josh," Mary said, smiling warmly. "I've always loved your work on *The Peterson Family*." Josh stared at Mary blankly. "The sitcom."

"Oh, uh, I wasn't on that show. You must be thinking of another comedian."

Mary smiled sheepishly, then turned and headed for the bar at the back of the room.

Josh frowned. "I can't give my spiel in front of these people. Most of them have probably never even heard of me. They're certainly not going to invest their hard-earned money in my movie."

Holly looked at Josh tenderly. "That's not true, honey. Maybe not all of them will invest in your movie, but I'm sure some of them will."

Josh shook his head. "You're dreaming."

Holly sighed. "I'm not," she insisted, prying open the clasp of her small crystal-encrusted evening bag. She pulled out a piece of paper and handed it to Josh. "Here's a start."

Josh stared dumbly at the paper. "Holly ... this is a check for $50,000. *Your* check for $50,000."

"It's for your movie, Josh. I've decided to invest my money in it." When Josh failed to respond, she added, "I threw this party to get other people to invest in your movie. I'd be a hypocrite if I didn't invest in it myself."

Wow! She must really be serious about me to give me this much money.

Impulsively, Josh gently kissed Holly's cheek.

"Holly, this means a lot to me. I really appreciate your support ... but," he handed the check back to her, "I can't take it. I can't take your money."

Holly handed the check back to him. "Why can't you take it? Is this some sort of ego thing? Is my money not as good as someone else's? Is my — "

"Stop it, Holly! It has nothing to do with that. Look, honey, the movie business is risky. And you're not rich. If I take your hard-earned money, you might never see it again."

"But don't you believe in yourself?"

"Holly — "

"You're bound to succeed. I know you'll succeed. You're so smart and talented."

"Talent doesn't really matter. *I* don't really matter. The whole movie business is a crapshoot, Holly. Lots of great movies lose money. But I don't want you to lose *your* money. You worked so hard for it. I really appreciate your support, honey, but if you lost that money, I could never live with myself. You understand that, don't you?"

Holly nodded reluctantly. "But I still want to invest in your movie, Josh. It's your *dream.*"

Josh sighed. "Okay, I'll keep your check ... for now. But I won't be spending it." He stuffed the check into the inside front pocket of his suit jacket.

Holly hugged him warmly. "Thanks, Josh. I know you'll put the money to good use. Now, get up on that stage and sell your screenplay. Go get 'em, Josh!"

Still nervous, Josh willed himself to walk toward the front of the room, climb onto a small platform, and pick up a microphone.

The room fell eerily silent.

"Good evening, everyone. Thanks for coming here tonight," Josh began, a wobbly smile pasted on his face. "I guess you folks want to know why I'm begging for your money. Well ... I need a job."

The audience laughed politely.

"What I mean is, I'm trying to create a job for myself. I've written a screenplay for a movie I hope to star in. It's a comedy with some romance in it, but it's not one of those silly romantic comedies." He paused, then glanced quickly around the room. "It's about a romance between two people with absolutely nothing — and I mean *nothing* — in common. The man is a Jewish computer salesman who travels from town to town. He's been unlucky in love ... and, oh yeah, he's a real geek."

The audience laughed again.

"Anyhow, this computer geek pays a visit to one of his customers, a businesswoman who lives in another city. This woman is lonely, also unlucky in love, and not Jewish. The problem is, this woman falls for the guy, but she's not the type he usually goes for. He has a thing for tall, blonde, model-types, but this woman is short and dark-haired. But they — "

Out of the corner of his eye, Josh saw Holly squirm in her chair, a crestfallen expression on her face.

"Anyhow ... th-they — these two characters — they fall in love ..." Josh's voice trailed off as his eyes frantically scanned the audience.

Holly's chair was empty.

Josh nervously cleared his throat. "So," he continued hesitantly, "that's the basic story. Thanks for coming tonight."

Sick with worry, Josh abruptly dropped the microphone, jumped off the platform, and rushed out of the restaurant.

***

Half an hour later, Josh's car pulled into the driveway of Holly's townhouse. Glancing up at the darkened windows, searching vainly for signs of life, Josh walked up to the front door and rang the doorbell.

No answer. No sound, except for the loud and harsh whistling of a cold wind.

Josh rang the doorbell again. No answer. He was about to ring the doorbell one more time when he was hit from behind by a powerful beam of brilliant white light. Turning around, he saw a car back into the driveway of the townhouse across the street. A few seconds later, a man and woman got out of the car.

"Who are you and what are you doing here?" shouted the man.

Josh didn't respond.

That was all he needed. A couple of busybodies who would report him to the cops — or to some celebrity rag.

Dispirited and defeated, Josh quickly walked back to his car, got inside, and drove off into the inky night.

Why does she have to be so pissed off at me? Josh fumed as he turned his car onto the nearest expressway. Because he had written a screenplay about a Jew and a *shiksa* who fall in love? Did she think they were the only ones? And didn't she tell him to write about "real people"? Well, he did! God, why did women have to personalize everything? And why did they have to hate him? He was a decent guy. He didn't beat women up. He didn't drink or smoke or take drugs. He never cheated on his girlfriends. What the hell did women want from him?

Overwhelmed by painful thoughts and unanswerable questions, Josh found himself unable to sleep that night. But as night faded into the welcome dawn of a new day, he was struck by a brilliant idea.

A few hours later, Holly arrived at work to find a new email on her computer with the unusual subject line "This is my peace offering." Holly hesitantly opened the email.

Greetings, Holly the Brain, the email began.

It was from that asshole Steinberg! All he wanted to do was exploit her. He was selfish and sneaky, and he'd proven that he couldn't be trusted. Why was she wasting her precious time reading his email? She should delete it right now.

But Holly couldn't. Instead, she found herself glued to the screen, deeply curious.

Please don't erase this message before you read it. And please don't be so mad at me. You can't judge a movie by a comedian's spiel, and you can't hate a screenplay you haven't read. Attached to the message was a file with the title *It Only Hurts When I Laugh.*

It's Josh's screenplay! Holly gasped. Before she knew it, she had printed out the entire document and bound it together with the largest elastic band she could find. She tossed the hulking block of paper onto the backseat of her car. *I'll have to read this when I get home tonight.*

***

Several hours later, in a dark and shabby hotel room in New York City, Josh was roused from a deep sleep by the insistent ringing of his cell phone. Groggy and sleep deprived, Josh snapped on the bedside lamp and plucked the phone from the pocket of his jeans.

"Whoever you are," he began, "it's 3:00 a.m. and — "

"Josh, it's me!"

"Holly?" *Am I dreaming?*

"Yes, it's Holly. I'm so sorry I woke you up, but I had to tell you, I loved your screenplay. I've been up all night reading it."

"Have you?" Josh asked, warm tears filling his eyes. "Did you really read it? Did you really like it?"

"Yes, I read the whole thing. It's brilliant — so funny and so real."

"Oh." Josh paused. "But why were you so mad at me? Why didn't you go home from the party with me?"

"Because I thought you were just exploiting me — exploiting our relationship — by writing that screenplay." *Because I've been hurt by your so-called comedy act too many times in the past.*

"If you want, I can change the main female character in my screenplay, make her different from you. I can also stop telling jokes about you in my stand-up act. It's not okay for me to keep telling them if they hurt you."

"No, you can keep telling them. And you don't have to change your screenplay, either."

"Are you sure, Holly? I don't want you to feel exploited by me."

"I'm sure. And I don't feel exploited by you, not anymore. After reading your screenplay, I think I understand you a lot better, and I now know how you really feel about me." She paused. "I'm sorry I got so upset."

"It's okay. I understand, dear."

"And Josh?"

"Yes?"

"Are you ... crying?"

"Of course not," Josh responded, trying hard to blink back the tears in his eyes. "Anyhow, the screenplay doesn't matter anymore. No one will ever produce it."

"Sure they will. We'll just have to keep trying to find investors."

"But no one at that party — except for you — wanted to invest in my screenplay. Right?" He paused. "I guess I did a pretty lousy job of selling it, didn't I?"

"Look, Josh, you tried your best. Okay, nobody at the party invested in it, but we can't just give up. I'm sure someone will be interested in financing it."

Holly's words turned out to be prophetic. A few days later, Josh got an email from a stranger, someone who had, presumably, learned about his screenplay from one of the guests at the ill-fated party. The stranger was Paul Cohen, a newly minted film school graduate — and the nephew of a powerful Hollywood studio executive.

Chapter Seven

"I thought you said you weren't exploiting me," Holly said. "And you have the nerve to claim that men can't trust women."

That morning, while casually trolling the Internet for tidbits of gossip on Josh, Holly had been rudely confronted with the video in which she had tossed a glass of water into Josh's face at the Yahoo Comedy Club.

"We're both being exploited. Welcome to the wonderful world of celebrity."

"What do you mean?"

"I mean, celebrities — even faded celebrities like me — are exploited by other people all the time. And we also have very little privacy."

"But I'm not a celebrity," Holly sighed into the phone. "I'm just a normal person."

Josh laughed. "That doesn't matter. Once you became involved with me, you gave up your privacy. Better get used to it."

Better get used to it? Does that mean — could it mean — that Josh wants to have a serious long-term relationship with me?

"Okay, Josh. Has something come up?" she asked, probing Josh to disclose the reason for his early-morning phone call.

Josh told Holly about the email he received from Paul Cohen.

"This guy has fabulous connections, honey. The Cohen family has been a major force in Hollywood since the 1920s. They've written, produced, and directed a slew of classic Oscar-winning movies. And Paul's uncle heads a major studio. We've just got to meet him."

"But where does he live?"

"In Los Angeles."

Holly paused. "That's a long way for me to travel."

"Don't worry, honey, I'll send you the money for your flight, and I can make reservations at a hotel. Of course, you're welcome to stay at my house. That is, if you want to." He sighed. "I know I'm asking a lot, but it would mean so much to me if you came."

Holly smiled. "Okay. I'll get there as soon as I can. No need to book a hotel."

The following week, Josh arranged a lunchtime meeting for himself, Holly, and Paul at a low-key restaurant in Los Angeles. Arriving early, Josh and Holly seated themselves in a corner of the restaurant's patio, their white cast-iron table shaded by a large red-and-white-striped umbrella, the cool December sun beaming down on them. Both Josh and Holly dressed up for the occasion. Josh wore a navy wool suit, white cotton shirt, and yellow silk tie, while Holly was neatly attired in a black wool skirted suit and a ruffled white cotton blouse. A few minutes later, a tall, slim young man with rumpled sandy brown hair, dressed in a pale blue polo shirt and khaki chinos, his eyes covered by a pair of sunglasses, walked up to their table. He pulled off the sunglasses and smiled shyly at Josh.

"You must be Josh Steinberg," he said.

"You actually know who I am?" Josh asked, startled by Paul's youth.

"Of course I do. I'm a showbiz buff. Showbiz is in my blood. Maybe you've never heard of the Cohens?"

"Look, kid, I was in this business long before you were born," Josh scoffed. He gestured to Holly. "This is Holly Brannigan, my — business partner."

Holly tried hard not to frown. *Your business partner? Is that all I am to you?* "Hi, Holly," Paul smiled as he lowered his gangly frame into a large white wicker chair. A middle-aged woman in a black knee-length shirtdress, her short, graying hair precisely styled, promptly appeared and placed three long menus on the table.

Josh shot a slightly challenging look at Paul from across the table. "Prove that you know who I am."

Without missing a beat, Paul launched into a recital of one of Josh's old stand-up comedy routines. He then sang the theme song from *Guys Like Us*, the TV comedy series that had made Josh famous back in the 1980s, in a slightly wobbly, off-key voice. As Paul finished singing, the other diners on the patio applauded loudly.

"Very impressive!" A broad grin spread across Josh's face. "So, Paul, it seems like you know a lot about Josh Steinberg ... but have you ever made a movie?"

Paul frowned. "Well, I am a film school grad."

"Yeah, but have you made a real film?"

"I've made films — student films."

"And I'll bet they're good," Holly said, smiling at Paul. "Give the guy a chance. At least take a look at his student films."

"I didn't say I wasn't going to give him a chance," Josh said. He actually liked this geeky kid.

"Of course I can show you my student films," Paul said. "And I can probably get some financing for your movie from Paragon Studios. My uncle Ari Cohen runs it."

Josh nodded absently. "Show us your films; I'll show you my screenplay." Turning to Holly, he asked, "Is that okay with you, Holly the Brain?"

"Sure, Josh — the Jewish Comedy King."

Paul laughed.

Two hours later, Josh and Holly found themselves sitting in Paul's tiny and cramped bachelor apartment, just a few miles from the restaurant, watching one of Paul's quirky student films on his big-screen TV, a documentary about a homeless elderly woman who collected discarded toys from garbage cans and recycling bins and then resold them at inflated prices to wealthy collectors through the Internet, using a computer at her local library.

"You certainly have a lot of talent," Holly told Paul as the closing credits rolled on his 45-minute film. "I've never seen anything like this before."

Paul glanced at Josh. "What do you think?"

"Well," Josh said, a teasing smile playing on his face, "I'm not quite sure."

"Not … sure?"

Josh laughed and extended his hand. "Look, kid, if you really want to produce my masterpiece and you think you can find the money to bring it to life, then the producer job is yours."

"Of course I do," Paul grinned, shaking Josh's hand. Turning to Holly, he asked, "Are you okay with my becoming the producer of your movie?"

Holly smiled warmly at him. "Of course."

Deep down, however, Holly wasn't smiling.

"I still can't believe that Josh introduced me as his *business partner*," she complained to Diana and Kyle when they sat down to dinner at Holly's townhouse in Toronto two days later. "I understand why he did it, but I feel a bit hurt."

"Get away from this bastard, Holly," Diana said, sipping a glass of red wine. "These comics are notorious womanizers."

"Listen to Diana, Mom," Kyle urged as he polished off a slice of crusty French bread. "And try to get your money back. Fifty grand is a lot of money. You'll need it when you get old."

Holly looked at Kyle, then at Diana, and sighed. "Are you sure?"

"I'm sure," Diana said. "He doesn't care about your feelings, and he's no great catch, either."

"He's kinda ugly," Kyle added. "I know you're old, Mom, but why settle for a fat guy like him?"

"He's *not* fat and ugly!" Holly exclaimed.

Kyle and Diana exchanged puzzled looks.

"What makes you think he's into you?" Diana asked in a quiet voice. "Men like him pick up lots of women."

"Well, he told me that he found me attractive … and that he didn't mean to hurt me."

"But he made fun of your size in public, so obviously he didn't find you attractive, and he also didn't care about hurting your feelings as long as he got a big laugh from the audience. He's actually proven that he doesn't respect you."

"But Josh didn't mean what he said. It was just part of his stand-up act. Besides, he's been hurt in the past; he has trust issues with women."

Kyle shot a withering look at Holly and shook his head. "Forget about this fat loser. Just get your money back. Don't put it off any longer."

***

Several hours later, in a small, moldy motel room outside of Chicago, Josh woke up to the loud ringing of his cell phone. Grumpily, he flicked on the bedside lamp, then snatched up his jeans from the floor and pulled the phone out of the front pocket.

"Look, whoever you are, you have no business calling me at this hour."

"Josh?" Holly said.

"Holly? Are you okay?"

Holly paused. This wasn't going to be easy.

"Look, I'm tired of being just another notch on Josh Steinberg's bedpost. If you're not serious about me — "

"What brought all this on? It's the middle of the night, for God's sake!"

"You told Paul Cohen I was only your business partner. Plus, there's tons of pictures of you on the Internet with beautiful women."

Josh sighed. "Old pictures. Besides, what was I supposed to tell Paul? 'This is the woman I'm currently sleeping with'? Look, honey, I care about you. And as for those other women … well, you're the only woman I can really talk to. Honest."

"But do you love me, Josh? Yes or no?"

Josh sighed again. "Look, Holly, I'm tired. I have a couple of shows to do tomorrow. You mean a lot to me, I care about you, you're the only woman I can really be myself with. Isn't that enough?"

"Sure. And I care about you, too, Josh."

"Then let me sleep, lady," Josh said and ended the call.

She's nuts to bother me at this hour. What the hell does she want? Why can't she just leave me alone?

But that was the last thing Josh really wanted. As his semi-successful comedy club tour limped to its end, he started to look forward to Holly's late-night calls. And sometimes Josh called Holly first, usually after performing at a half-empty club to an audience that was hostile to his unique style of edgy humor.

"Some half-stoned asshole heckled me tonight," a distraught Josh told Holly when he called her after one disastrous show in Phoenix. "Then he actually had the nerve to piss all over the floor …"

Holly sighed. Josh kept complaining about the same thing over and over again. She was worried about him; he got hurt far too easily whenever audiences failed to laugh at his jokes.

"I mean, if he hates me so much, what was he doing at my show in the first place?"

"I don't know, honey." Holly paused. "Josh?"

"Yeah?"

"I think you should find a new line of work. Quit the stand-up comedy business."

"Quit stand-up comedy? You must be kidding, Holly. It's my whole life. It's all I'm good at."

Holly paused again. "But you're so vulnerable when you talk about your personal life onstage. And when a show doesn't go well, you get so *hurt.* I'm really worried about you."

"Don't worry about me, honey. I can take care of myself. Anyhow, it doesn't matter if my comedy club gigs are going well or not. It looks like my TV and movie career is starting to make a comeback."

But it wasn't. To his surprise, Josh received only one job offer, one that was far from lucrative: a small role in a new comedy series about the staff of a Detroit pizzeria. The low-budget show, *Pizza Heaven,* was scheduled to run on an obscure and little-watched cable TV network.

"I wouldn't touch this piece of crap with a ten-foot pole!" Josh yelled when he met with Greg in late December at Greg's tiny, dusty, and perpetually messy New York office. "Did you even *read* the script for the pilot?" Josh sat on a rickety, uncomfortable white plastic chair. Greg sat across from him behind an old wooden ink-stained desk overflowing with press releases, books, and towering stacks of paper.

"It's not that bad — "

"Read the script, asshole!" Josh hurled it at Greg.

Greg ducked. The script struck the wall behind him and fell on the threadbare beige carpet with a thud.

"Now, Josh, that wasn't very nice," Greg said, as he retrieved the script from the floor. "Okay, maybe this show isn't as good as the other ones you've been on, but your career isn't quite what it used to be."

"All you care about is your stupid commission!" Josh exclaimed, pounding Greg's desk with his fist. "Well, it's about time you actually earned your commission by finding me something better than this piece of trash."

"Look, Josh, you have to be realistic. There are no other offers for you right now, and you need the money. Your last tour didn't exactly sell out."

"But this show will end my career. The pilot isn't funny at all — it's horrible."

"Well, then, why don't you try writing some scripts for the show? I'm sure you could make it a lot better."

***

"Just listen to Greg and take it, honey," Holly told Josh when he called her later that night. "And take his advice about writing some scripts for the show."

With great reluctance, Josh swallowed his pride and joined the cast of *Pizza Heaven*. He quickly wrote and submitted a script to the producers … only to see it mysteriously vanish. Josh then submitted a handful of suggestions to improve the unfunny show's dismal scripts … only to see them ridiculed by its hostile producers, directors, and staff writers.

I can't take this any longer! Josh fumed in an email to Greg after the first frustrating week. *Get me out of my contract NOW! I'm quitting this show.*

But Josh didn't need to quit the show.

"The network decided not to pick up the show," Greg told Josh in a phone call one gray and icy morning in late February. "No need to draft a resignation letter."

At first, the show's failure hardly seemed to upset Josh at all.

Thank God he was no longer chained to that garbage. And he had his dream movie to fall back on.

Except he didn't. Paul Cohen's attempts to win financing for Josh's movie fell flat. He spoke to his uncle, only to be told that Paragon Studios was "under severe fiscal constraints and unable to even consider financing any new projects at the present time."

At least that's what Paul told Josh. But that wasn't what had really happened.

"You're wasting your time and expensive education on a big loser," Ari Cohen said when Paul pitched Josh's screenplay to him. "Josh Steinberg is old and washed up — he was washed up years ago — but he doesn't know when to quit. Nobody's going to pay money to see him in a movie, and the young kids who buy most of the movie tickets don't even know who the hell he is."

Paul didn't have the heart to tell Josh the truth. And he didn't have the nerve to tell Josh that he had been unable to even make contact with people at other studios.

"I'm still looking into possibilities," Paul said whenever Josh pumped him for progress reports. "These things take a bit of time, you know."

Josh wasn't fooled by Paul's vague, reassuring words. His screenplay — his comeback dream — was going nowhere. He was going nowhere, fast.

Even before he checked on the progress of his screenplay with Paul, Josh knew that his career was doomed. Shortly after the fiasco of *Pizza Heaven*, while rummaging through the discount bin of a neighborhood record store, Josh had found a DVD of a movie he had starred in over twenty years before, marked down to 99 cents.

That was all his career was worth now. That was all *he* was worth now.

With a heavy sigh, Josh pulled his phone out of his jacket pocket and called Greg.

"Looks like I'll have to get back on the road to keep up with my bills," he told Greg's voicemail. "How quickly can you line something up for next week?"

Okay, maybe my comeback plans are going nowhere and most of my fans have forgotten me, but at least I can still get bookings. For now.

Chapter Eight

The following week, on a cool and sunny morning in early March, Josh, already exhausted from too many long, hard days on the road and more lonely for Holly than ever, drove his car into the parking lot of a shabby but homey roadside diner in New Hampshire.

I just have to see Holly again, he told himself as he pulled his phone out of the glove compartment and punched in the number of An Affair to Remember.

"Mr. Allan Kesterson here," Josh announced to the young woman at the other end of the line, infusing his words with a plummy English accent. "I'm the CEO of one of the world's largest garbage disposal companies — you know, the folks who pick up junk from people's homes and dispose of it."

"Y-y-yes," replied Rachel Thomas, the brown-haired, freckle-faced young woman who had started working for Holly and Diana three months earlier.

"Anyhow, I'm coming to Toronto to look for Canadian franchisees, and I need to book a launch party at a local venue."

"Oh," Rachel replied, typing frantically on a computer keyboard, "what size of venue do you need? And on what date?"

Josh drew a deep breath as he tried to gather his thoughts. "I can't answer those questions now. I have to discuss the event in person with your president first."

"Sure. Let me check Ms. Atkinson's schedule."

"*No!* I need — want — to meet with your *other* president, Holly Brannigan. Next Friday night at seven."

"I'm afraid Ms. Brannigan will be at an event that evening, but Ms. Atkinson will be happy to meet with you."

"Well, I wouldn't be happy to meet with her. Unless I can meet with Ms. Brannigan next Friday night, I'm prepared to take my business someplace else."

"Mr. Kesterson — "

"I really must meet with Ms. Brannigan. Couldn't Ms. Atkinson take care of that other business next Friday, whatever it is?"

Rachel sighed. "I'll see what I can do."

"Thanks so much. Tell Ms. Brannigan to meet me next Friday night at seven sharp. I'll make reservations at a restaurant and call you back with the details."

***

The following week, Holly, bleary-eyed and burned out, reluctantly forced herself to walk to a tall, imposing office tower in the heart of Toronto's financial district.

It's Friday night. All I want to do is go home, eat a quick supper, and crawl into bed, she thought as she entered the lobby. The last thing she wanted was to have dinner with some asshole, especially at one of the most expensive restaurants in the city. Whoever he was, he better pick up the tab or at least bring in a lot of business.

Holly squeezed herself into an already crowded elevator filled with a dozen business people, men and women of various sizes, ages, and shapes dressed in serious gray, navy, and black business suits, all of them talking non-stop about multi-million dollar deals, company mergers and takeovers, and court cases being fought over ridiculously huge sums of money. Holly blended in effortlessly, dressed in her usual work uniform of a black wool pantsuit and ruffled white cotton blouse.

Fifty-four floors later, the elevator ground to a halt. The mass of business people, still lost in their conversations, streamed into Canoe, eager to hash out their deals and cases in the restaurant. Holly, following hesitantly behind them, approached the maître d', a sandy-haired man in his mid-30s, who was standing near the entrance.

"I'm meeting a Mr. Kesterson here. Has he made reservations for seven?"

"I believe he has," the man smiled. "Are you Holly Brannigan?"

Holly nodded.

The man reached behind a table and pulled out a single long-stemmed red rose. "For you," he said, handing the rose to Holly.

"Thanks," Holly said, taking the rose. She wondered what kind of business this Kesterson guy had in mind.

"This way, please," the man said, leading Holly to a small table in the corner. The walls, full-length panels of clear glass, provided a breathtaking view of the setting sun. Below, the lights of the city twinkled in the fading daylight, the outline of Lake Ontario a soft blue shadow in the distance. A heavy-set middle-aged man dressed in a handsome navy wool suit was seated at the table, his back turned to Holly.

"Mr. ... Kesterson?" Holly said, as she approached the table.

The man rose from the chair and turned around to face Holly, his face covered in a broad grin.

"Good evening, Holly," Josh said, as he pulled her chair out for her.

Holly ignored the polite gesture. Instead, she grabbed Josh, wrapped her arms around him, and kissed him. Josh kissed her back and held her close to him for several long minutes before releasing her so they could sit down at the table. Seated across from each other, they spoke only with their eyes, gazing longingly and intimately.

"Would you care for anything to drink?"

Holly looked away from Josh, turning her gaze to the waiter.

"I'll have a bottle of Perrier. What'll you have, Josh?"

"You," Josh said, his eyes still fixed on Holly's face.

"Excuse me?" the waiter asked Josh. "What did you say?"

"Oh," Josh moaned. "Sorry. I meant …" He paused, his eyes scanning the menu. "Bring us a bottle of champagne. The best one you have. Forget the Perrier." He smiled at Holly. "Okay?"

"Okay," Holly smiled back. "But not the best one. Bring us a half bottle of your least expensive champagne," she told the waiter.

"Are you sure? I'd be happy to pay for the best."

"I'm sure. You can buy it for me when your career picks up again." Taking Josh's hands in hers, she gently kissed his palms. "You're very sweet."

Almost three hours later, two cars pulled into the driveway of Holly's townhouse.

"Your son isn't at home, is he?" Josh asked anxiously, eyeing the half-dark townhouse.

"No, he's away at school," Holly said as she walked toward Josh's car. "Let me help you carry in your bags."

Josh shook his head. "You don't have to," he said as he opened the trunk of his car.

"I can carry at least one bag. I'm actually a very strong girl. You'd be surprised."

Josh sighed. He handed Holly a small overnight bag and picked up his heavy battered black leather suitcase. Together, they carried the bags into the house.

As they reached the darkened front hallway, Josh said, "Drop that thing. Now." Without missing a beat, he scooped Holly up in his arms and carried her up the stairs to her bedroom.

He's so sexy. She covered his neck with soft, tender kisses, delighting in his musky scent. *No other man on earth comes close to him.*

Josh gently lay Holly down on the large bed, guided by a small green night-light plugged into the opposite wall.

"You're so yummy," he said, rolling down his pants and boxers to his ankles.

Hastily, Holly pried off her shoes, pants, and cotton briefs and flung them onto the floor, then pulled him down into her, deep, both of them moaning with exquisite pleasure.

***

The following morning, as the sun slowly broke through the white lace curtains, Holly awoke to find Josh beside her in bed, stroking her hair with his thick fingers.

"You're a real genius in bed, baby," Josh said. "You're so beautiful and soft." His eyes drank in her sweet, pretty face, her small, delicate body, the earthiness of her curves.

"You're gorgeous, too," she responded sincerely, delighting in his cuddly plumpness, his large, masculine nose, his gentle vulnerability and sensitivity, and, above all, his kind brown eyes. The dark stubble on Josh's face — and the dark, thick hairiness of his body — made him even sexier.

"You don't have to go to work today, do you?" Josh asked, anxiously eyeing the digital alarm clock on the bedside table. "Please tell me you don't."

"But Mr. Kesterson, we have very important business to attend to. We simply must start planning that conference for garbage aficionados."

"Shut up." He pulled Holly close to him, kissing her lustily on the mouth. "I didn't travel all the way to Toronto to talk about trash."

Holly laughed … but Josh didn't.

"What happened to your sense of humor, Steinberg? Oh, okay, I think I can spare the time for you. The garbage business will have to wait for another day."

"Are you sure? I wouldn't want to waste the time of an important businesswoman like you."

"Don't be silly." Holly sat up in bed and peered through the curtains. "It'll be warm today. Perfect weather for a day in the sun. And I know just the place to spend it."

***

A few hours later, Josh and Holly drove to a park in the Beach neighborhood, nestled in the east end of Toronto, and set out a picnic lunch on the grassy lawn facing the beach, the old wooden boardwalk, and Lake Ontario. The late winter sun was unseasonably warm; a gentle breeze blew across the park, creating soft ripples in the lake. A group of teenagers was caught up in a lively game of volleyball on the beach, shouting at each other, while a dozen dogs of various sizes, shapes, and colors chased each other in an off-leash area, barking joyously. Both Holly and Josh wore blue jeans and puffer jackets.

"I'm actually glad you got me away from the office today," Holly said between bites of a fragrant, freshly made pizza they had purchased at a nearby restaurant. "I'm constantly worried about the business; the competition is so tough, and all of my employees depend on me." She sighed. "And I worry about Kyle, too. He's a smart boy, but he has no idea what he wants to do with his life. Maybe I should tell him to try stand-up comedy."

"Don't tell him that," Josh groaned, as he sipped lemonade from a Thermos. "It's a hard and unstable life, Holly. And it's lonely."

"Do you still get depressed on the road?"

"All the time. It's disheartening to constantly travel from place to place, knowing you're getting nowhere in life."

"Maybe you should see a therapist, get some help."

Josh shook his head. "I tried that. It's a big waste of time and money."

"Maybe you should try again, find a better therapist."

"The worst part is going home after a tour to an empty house." His eyes misted over. "I can't tell you how lonely that is."

"Josh, please promise me something. The next time you get depressed when you're on the road — or when you come home to an empty house — call me. Okay?"

"I can't," Josh said, gazing at the dogs playing together. "I'm already calling you several nights a week. If I called you whenever I got depressed, I'd be calling you every single day and all hours of the night."

"I don't care. I still want you to call me, no matter what. Promise you'll call me."

"Okay, dear. I'll try."

Sqwaaaaak!

Josh turned to find himself face to face with a seagull, its beady eyes fixed on the remnants of Josh and Holly's pizza.

"Get lost!" Josh yelled, as he tossed a handful of pizza crusts to the bird. The seagull greedily gulped down the bits of crust, then, bobbing its head up and down, began squawking for more. This time, Holly threw the scraps of pizza crust to the bird.

"I think he's trying to tell us something," she said to Josh as she rose to her feet. When Josh responded with a puzzled look, she added, "I think he's telling us it's time for a walk."

Josh and Holly tossed the remains of their lunch into a garbage can, then joined the throngs of people crowding the boardwalk: young couples pushing strollers, teenagers holding hands, elderly people using walkers. A few minutes later, Josh saw several huge trucks parked beside the road, large lights, and cameras, signs of a movie set. He noticed a familiar face.

"Holly," Josh said, pointing to a muscular man with graying hair, "that's Richard Feeney, the Hollywood director."

"I'm not surprised. Lots of movies are made in Toronto."

"You don't understand. I actually know Richard. He directed me in one of my first movies."

Josh strode across the field toward him.

"Richard! Richard!"

Feeney, engrossed in a lively discussion with a thin, dark-haired young woman dressed all in black, didn't respond.

"Josh," Holly said, running behind him, "he's busy right now."

Josh ignored her. "Richard," he said in a louder voice, "do you remember me?"

Richard Feeney stopped talking to the woman and looked up at Josh. "Remember you?"

"Y-y-yes. Josh Steinberg."

"Josh … Steinberg?"

"You directed me in *Big Bad Bart Rides Again*. Almost twenty-five years ago."

"I remember the movie. Were you in it?"

"Yes, I was in it. Josh Steinberg — the big, fat Jewish guy?"

"Oh, now I remember."

No, you don't. You really have no idea who I am.

Richard glanced down at his watch. "I'm running late today. I don't have time to talk right now. Sorry."

With that, he turned away from Josh and continued talking to the young woman.

Josh slowly made his way back to the boardwalk, his steps wobbly and unsteady, his mind reeling, his spirit crushed.

"What an asshole," Holly said when they were out of Richard's earshot.

Josh stopped walking and gave Holly a long, hard stare. "I've been in this business for thirty years, Holly, and what have I amounted to? Nothing. I'm a nobody, a loser. That's the truth."

"No, it isn't. You are *not* a nobody, Josh. You're a kind, intelligent, caring human being."

"No, in this business, I'm a nobody. He didn't even remember me."

"You still have lots of fans. Who cares what some senile old coot thinks?"

"That old coot is doing well in this business. I'm not. I can't even sell my screenplay."

"Well, then, you should just quit this stupid business. I'm tired of always seeing you unhappy and stressed out whenever your act doesn't go well. You go onstage night after night, making yourself vulnerable to strangers … for what? Why do you keep doing it?"

"Holly, I told you before. It's all I know. It's the only way I can make a living."

"Maybe it isn't. Maybe I could sell my business and we could open a new business together. A restaurant maybe, or a bed and breakfast, a food shop … or how about a comedy club?"

"Maybe. I can't live like this forever. There has to be something better. There just has to be."

Three days later, Josh finally made up his mind.

I'm going to quit the comedy business for good, he told himself while holed up in yet another drab motel room, this time in Syracuse. Life was way too short to keep putting up with this crap. Besides, there had to be more to life than working at an endless series of tacky comedy clubs, and Josh had been missing out on real life for far too long.

Josh felt his cell phone vibrate in his pants pocket.

Greg Fanelli, I've played my last stand-up gig. And as of now, you are no longer employed by me.

Buoyed by this bold new resolution, Josh answered the phone.

"Josh," Greg said, "I have a great job lined up for you next month. It's a soft drink commercial …"

Tell him. Tell him, Josh. No more gigs.

"Well, what do you think?"

I think it sucks.

"Are you interested? Yes or no?"

Josh sighed. He needed the money. The bills weren't going to go away.

"Josh? Are you interested?"

Josh drew a deep breath. "Where and when do I show up?"

Chapter Nine

The soft drink commercial gig wasn't as bad as Josh feared. The director, a down-to-earth, big-boned, thirty-something woman named Kelly was a big Josh Steinberg fan.

"Go ahead and improvise," she told Josh. "Toss the script. I'm sure you can come up with something a lot funnier."

So Josh did.

"I can't stand Limefresh!" Josh said, visibly grimacing as he guzzled a can of the sugary green pop on camera. "It's fatal to my sex life. My ex-girlfriend dumped me over it — she has a real *fetish* for this stuff."

"Brilliant! Brilliant!" Kelly shouted. "Edgy stuff! Only you could dream up something this provocative."

But most of Josh's gigs weren't as pleasant, and soon, worn down by the long hours of travel and sheer loneliness, he once again found himself sinking into depression. And he once again found himself picking up his phone and turning to the one and only person on the planet he could truly talk to.

"I don't know how much longer I can take this," he told Holly one warm and lazy early spring afternoon while relaxing at a small roadside diner in Toledo, Ohio. "Maybe I should give up my stand-up career and open a bed and breakfast with you."

"Is that what you really want?"

"I don't know. I mean, I love doing stand-up comedy and making people laugh. But once I'm off the stage, I feel like a big, fat loser."

"Why do you feel that way?"

"Because I'm going nowhere. I mean, just look at what happened to my screenplay. Paul can't get any of the studios to look at it, let alone buy it. Writing it was a big waste of my time."

"Josh, you didn't waste your time. You wrote a brilliant screenplay."

"It doesn't matter how brilliant it is. No one will ever buy it. No one will ever make it into a movie."

"Someone will buy it, Josh. Just hang in there. Your screenplay will become a movie, even if I have to raise all the money myself."

"You've done enough, honey. It's now up to me. I guess I just have to keep trying, no matter how long it takes." He paused. "See," he added in a mischievous voice, "I told you it was a bad idea for me to call you every day. You just keep getting the same old crap from me over and over again."

"That's okay. I love getting your crap."

"Masochist." Josh smiled then turned off his phone and glanced at his watch. *It's getting late. I better head toward Michigan for that club gig tonight*, he told himself as he ducked into the washroom to change. A few minutes later, dressed in a white polo shirt and crisp blue jeans, Josh pulled out of the diner's parking lot and pointed his car toward Michigan.

On the way to the club, Josh stopped at an old motel off the highway called The Shamrock Isle, a row of small, identical concrete boxes covered in peeling pale green paint and surrounded by decaying grass. A young Japanese-American man, dressed in scruffy blue jeans and even scruffier sneakers, approached Josh's car, a nervous smile on his face.

"Are you Josh?"

Josh nodded. "You must be Henry Otu."

The young man smiled, the tension draining from his face. "Yeah, I'm Henry."

Josh smiled back. "Get in the car, kid."

An hour and a half later, Henry stepped out onto the stage of the comedy club — frightened and elated at the same time — as the opening act for Josh Steinberg. The spacious club, located just outside Detroit, was half-full of politely enthusiastic middle-aged couples. The walls of the room were covered with fishing poles, seashells, and nets; the lighting was bright but not glaring; the hardwood floors were polished to a dull sheen.

Josh watched Henry's act from a table at the front of the room. *I really like this kid*, he thought. Henry was different from most of the stand-up comedians on the comedy club circuit, especially the older ones. He was naive, not jaded, fresh, just a bundle of positive energy radiating from the stage. Josh thought that his timing was sometimes a bit off, but he knew that Henry had enough talent and chutzpah to win over the audience. Henry was a lot like Josh used to be when he started out in the business. Before he got ground down by bills, lost dreams, and loneliness.

"Hey, Josh!"

Josh looked up, startled, to see Henry grinning playfully at him from his perch on the stage.

"That lady you make fun of in your act — are you sleeping with her?"

"I beg your pardon? Why are you talking about her?"

"I just wanted to know — "

"Don't steal my material, kid!" Josh said, rising to his feet and taking the stage over from Henry as the audience filled the club with laughter.

An hour later, exhilarated and drunk on applause, Josh and Henry sat down at a tall wooden booth in a quiet corner at the back of the club and ordered two beers.

"Great show, kid," Josh said, smiling at Henry after the server took their order.

"Thanks, Josh. That means a lot coming from someone like you. I've always been a big fan of yours."

Before Josh could respond, he felt his phone vibrate in his pants pocket.

"Excuse me," Josh said as he pulled out the phone.

"How did the Jewish Comedy King fare tonight?" asked Holly.

"Great. My opening act more or less told the audience that we're sleeping together."

"Just where did your opening act get such a strange idea?"

"Well, hmmm, I don't know where it came from." Josh smiled and winked at Henry, who appeared to be listening intently to Josh's half of the conversation. "What's so strange about that idea, anyway?"

"Don't you think it's odd for a comedian to sleep with his punch line?" She paused. "I thought you were going to stop exploiting us in your act."

"Look, honey, he just threw that line at me from the stage. I didn't tell him to do it."

"Oh, okay. Anyhow, I just wanted to know if you'll be in the Michigan area for the next few days. Because tomorrow I'm meeting a client across the border in Windsor. I was thinking that maybe you could meet me at my hotel there tomorrow night and we could have dinner together."

"And I could supply the after-dinner entertainment."

"If I need it."

"Oooh, mean one! Okay, whether or not you need or want it, I promise to be there."

***

The following evening, just as the sun was fading and shadows were starting to creep through the sky, Josh drove over the Ambassador Bridge into Canada and the small, sleepy city of Windsor, Ontario. Below the tall, majestic suspension bridge, he could catch glimpses of a hulking black cargo ship as it moved slowly down the Detroit River. Exiting from the bridge, Josh turned onto Riverside Drive, a narrow highway hugging the shoreline, dotted with small parks filled with colorful gardens, trees, benches, and clusters of people.

Josh pulled his car into the parking lot of Holly's hotel. He promptly fished out his sunglasses from the glove compartment and put them on, their large, black frames nearly covering his entire face. Josh then snatched a wide-brimmed navy cotton sun hat from the backseat and plopped it onto his head.

He passed through the front doors of the hotel. *I hope nobody recognizes me.* He was starting to think that Holly was right to keep telling him they needed their privacy.

Josh headed for the lobby, where, dressed in a navy and pale blue color-blocked shirt and navy chinos, he blended in easily with the dozens of vacationing families and businesspeople checking in at the front desk. The lighting in the room was low-key and muted, the walls covered by dark brown mahogany paneling. Sinking down into an armchair, he picked up a magazine from a small table and tried to read it.

Peering above the magazine, Josh kept his eyes glued to the front doors, his heart beating wildly as he wondered whether Holly would show up.

A short, middle-aged woman with dark brown, above shoulder-length hair styled in a bob entered the lobby.

It's not Holly. When is she coming? He hoped he had the right hotel.

Twenty minutes later, he finally saw her. But she wasn't alone.

Holly entered the room dressed, as usual, in her work uniform of a black wool pantsuit and a crisp white cotton blouse. Behind her was a stunning thirty-something man, his immaculately tailored outfit highlighting his muscular build.

Josh's face felt hot. This man was definitely Holly's type. She had always gone for gorgeous young hunks like him. Josh knew that he could never begin to compete with a guy like him, even if he was still young.

Holly and the young man sat down in two wing chairs at the opposite corner of the room, talking animatedly.

It was a mistake for me to come here today. Josh tried to hide his face behind the magazine. *She doesn't want to bother with me. I'd better get out of here.*

As quietly as possible, Josh rose from the chair and started walking through the lobby toward the front doors. He pulled the handle. A split second later, he found himself covered from head to toe in gooey pink icing.

"My cake!" a woman yelled. "You ruined my cake."

Josh pried off his sunglasses and peered through the curtain of icing at a small elderly woman, her deeply lined face contorted with a mixture of anger and worry.

"I'm sorry. I'll pay for it."

"Josh?"

Josh wheeled around to see Holly staring at him. The younger man was standing behind her, an impatient expression on his face.

"I had a small accident." Turning to the elderly woman, he said, "I had no idea you were on the other side of the door."

"You could have been more careful."

Holly pulled out a wad of bills from her handbag and handed them to the elderly woman. "He didn't mean to wreck your cake."

"I'll pay you back later," Josh told Holly in a weak voice.

"No rush. Anyhow," Holly continued, pointing to the younger man, "this is my client, Lyle Davidson."

"Your boy toy," Josh smirked.

"Don't be silly. Lyle, this is Josh Steinberg, the comedian."

"Comedian, huh?" Lyle stared at Josh, trying hard not to smile. "I guess some comedians will do anything for a laugh."

"Or some boy toys will do anything for a screw."

Holly gave Josh a sharp look. "Stop it, Josh! You're not onstage right now."

Lyle chuckled meanly. "Well," he said, looking at his watch, "I've got another meeting. I'll be in touch."

"Okay, thanks, Lyle," Holly said, shaking his hand. "That was very rude of you," she snapped at Josh after Lyle left the building. "And why did you call him a boy toy? You didn't think I was fooling around with him … did you, Josh?"

"Of course not, honey. I was just joking."

"Were you really? Do you trust me?"

"Of course I do."

I do trust you. What a fool I was. What came over me?

Twenty minutes later, having showered off all of the sticky icing, Josh emerged from the bathroom in Holly's hotel room, naked under a large, white fluffy towel. The moderately luxurious room was warm and intimate, its walls dressed in delicate yellow and pink floral wallpaper, its floors covered by thick pale-yellow wool carpeting that blotted out the harsh noises of the outside world.

"I sent your clothing out to be laundered," Holly said, lounging on the bed, dressed in a fetching ivory silk satin teddy, its thin spaghetti straps highlighting her taut, muscular shoulders, and the thigh-length shorts flattering her long, slim legs. "I can throw on some clothing and grab your suitcase from the parking lot, if you want."

"Don't bother," Josh said. "I can wait for the cleaners to return my clothing."

Holly smiled at Josh, a long, feline smile. Rising from the bed, she sauntered over to him and ripped off his towel.

"Give it back!" Josh exclaimed, reaching for the towel. "I'm too fat. I'll only gross you out."

"No, you won't." Holly tossed the towel on the floor. "You have a big, beautiful, sexy body."

"Holly — "

"Shut up, Steinberg!" She pulled him down on the bed. "Shut up and kiss me."

"Kiss you? Is that all you want?"

"You know what I want." Holly pulled off the silky teddy and dropped it onto the floor then climbed on top of Josh.

Josh smiled. "You think I can just put out whenever you want me to? You think — ?"

Holly kissed him on the mouth, hard.

"I'm not ready yet," he said, gasping for breath.

"Bullshit. You're as hard as a rock."

"I tell you, I'm not ready."

"Then satisfy yourself," she said, as she started to sit up.

Josh chuckled. "You're silly enough to believe anything a comedian tells you." Before Holly could respond, he had pulled her roughly into him, two hot and aroused bodies merging into one.

Just as Josh climaxed, someone knocked hard at the door.

"Maybe you should have brought in my suitcase after all," Josh grumbled, reluctantly pulling out of Holly and covering his body with the thick, floral comforter. "Worst possible time."

Holly sat up, pulled on the teddy and a white terrycloth robe, stepped into a pair of fluffy slippers, and padded to the door. She reappeared carrying two bulging paper bags, fragrant with the aroma of freshly cooked food.

"It's our dinner. I had a local deli bring in kosher food."

Reaching into the bag, Holly began to set out the food on a small table: matzoh ball soup; thick smoked meat sandwiches on light rye bread, smothered in tart yellow mustard; crisp dill pickles; pillowy potato latkes.

Just as Holly finished putting the food on the table, there was another loud knock at the door. This time, Holly emerged carrying a silver ice bucket, a small bottle of champagne, and two long, tapered crystal glasses.

"Mmm, Jewish soul food," Josh said, sniffing the air, as he got up from the bed and wrapped his body in the white towel. "What a marvelous idea."

"Do you really think so? I read your blog to find out which Jewish foods you liked best."

"I do, honey, but you shouldn't have gone to so much trouble for me," Josh said as he sat down at the table and picked up a sandwich.

"No trouble at all." Holly uncorked the bottle of champagne with a resounding *pop*. "I just wanted to make you happy. If anyone deserves to be pampered, it's you."

But I really don't deserve it. I was rude to you today when I saw you with that young hunk, even though you were planning a romantic dinner for the two of us. Shit, I really hate myself sometimes.

***

Josh wasn't the only person who was angry with Josh. Early the next morning, with Holly fast asleep beside him in bed, he got a less than friendly call from Greg.

"Where the hell have you been?" Greg asked when Josh answered the phone. "Have you suddenly stopped checking your messages?"

"Listen, asshole, I happen to have a personal life, unlike someone I know."

"Very funny, Steinberg. Anyhow, Ivan Bronkov, the legendary movie director, wants to speak to you about your screenplay."

"Ivan Bronkov! He was my mentor when I first came to Hollywood decades ago. Did he really call?"

"No, stupid, I just made it up. Anyhow, I'll text you his contact information and you can take it from there. *If you're interested.*"

"Okay, thanks."

"So, he finally called."

Turning off the phone, Josh wheeled around to see Holly sitting up in bed, a triumphant smile on her face.

"Finally called? What do you mean?"

"I researched your career and uncovered your connection to Ivan. I found out he was once a big supporter of yours. Just for the heck of it, I asked Greg to track him down and send him a copy of your screenplay." She paused. "I hope you don't mind."

"Why would I mind? Holly, you're much more than a brain, you're a *mensch*."

"A ... *mensch*? Is that good or bad?"

"It's very, very good," Josh smiled, hugging Holly. "The best."

"See, Josh? I knew you were going to sell your screenplay. And I'll bet Ivan Bronkov will end up directing it, and he'll probably talk some big studio into buying it."

"Calm down, Holly, he hasn't made any promises yet. For all I know, he might even hate my screenplay. But I'll call him later today for sure. It can't hurt to try."

Chapter Ten

"Josh! What a wonderful surprise!" Ivan Bronkov's voice was warm but slightly ragged, the sound of a tired old man.

"I heard you were interested in my screenplay," Josh said. He glanced around the quiet, sparse room in the brightly lit diner, located in a small town off a Michigan highway, only to see a brown-haired, freckle-faced boy of about four or five staring at him from a booth across the aisle. Josh stuck out his tongue at the boy and then returned to the phone.

"Yes, your agent sent me a copy of it. I haven't read anything this good in a very long time; it's so funny and smart. Quite a bold and courageous departure for you."

"Thanks." From the corner of his eye, Josh could see the small boy sticking out his tongue back at him.

"Let's set up a meeting at Summit Studios. Would next week work for you?"

"Sure. I should be able to make it. Just let me know when and where."

A week later, back in Los Angeles, Josh found himself battling early morning traffic on the way to his meeting at Summit Studios.

Josh drove through a narrow street thickly carpeted with cars, trucks, buses, and taxis. *I can't believe I'm going to work with Ivan again. And we're going to work together on my dream project!*

It had been eighteen long years since Josh last worked with Ivan. Fearing that his former mentor would be shocked by his aging face and pudgy body, Josh had made an effort to dress as splendidly as possible: a finely tailored black wool suit and a crisp, open-collared black cotton shirt, the stark color emphasizing Josh's brown eyes and olive skin.

Josh maneuvered his car around a work crew repairing a fallen hydro line. *Ivan might not even recognize me. After all, I'm no longer the young comedian from* Guys Like Us.

Guys Like Us had been a silly and forgettable TV sitcom from the mid-1980s, but it had been wildly popular and had transformed Josh into a star overnight. Ivan saw the show and thought that Josh had great potential. Josh was thrilled when Ivan contacted him at the end of the show's first season to offer him a flashy supporting role in a big-budget comedy movie that he was set to direct, *Mr. Right Is Always Wrong*. Josh snapped up the part, thrilled to be working with such a highly respected Russian director, a man renowned for his deft handling of comedy.

And Josh loved working with Ivan; the two of them had the same crazy, offbeat take on the world. Josh wasn't the star of *Mr. Right*, but Ivan made sure the movie showcased Josh's sarcastic sense of humor. Ivan really took a chance on Josh, but his gamble paid off: the movie made a ton of money, and even the critics fell over each other praising Josh's talent. Josh ended up stealing the movie from the stars, and his fee doubled.

Honnk!

Josh glanced behind him. A bald man in a white minivan was gesturing angrily at him. Josh steered his car down a side street.

After Josh's first big movie success, Ivan commissioned a new screenplay from the same team of writers who created *Mr. Right*. He built the new movie around Josh's quirky personality, and the vehicle the writers created for him, *The World's Smallest Hero?* was a spoof on superhero movies. Josh starred as a bored accountant who donned a black mask and blond wig to fight the sorts of petty, everyday crimes the police usually ignore: people who board buses without paying fares, "friends" who borrow items without returning them, homeowners who keep their neighbors awake until the wee hours of the morning by throwing loud parties in their backyard. In his own clumsy way, Josh's "heroic" character tried to win justice for the parties victimized by these small injustices, but he always ended up making things worse for them.

But *The World's Smallest Hero?* bombed, big-time. Nobody liked it — not Josh's fans, not the critics — and it hurt his career badly. That movie had soured Ivan and Josh's promising working relationship. After that fiasco, neither of them bothered to keep in touch.

The light turned green. Steering his car onto a busy four-lane highway, Josh spotted the studio in the distance.

Maybe he shouldn't let Ivan direct his screenplay. Things hadn't gone well the last time they worked together … and Ivan's last hit movie was fourteen years ago. In fact, it looked like Ivan expected Josh to help him, but Josh was the one who needed help. Maybe he shouldn't even bother to meet with Ivan … but he had to. He had no choice. Nobody else wanted to have anything to do with Josh's screenplay, or with Josh himself.

A couple of traffic lights later, Josh drove into the studio's parking lot. He turned off the ignition, then peered self-consciously into the mirror, forcing himself to smile.

This could work out. This will work out. Just think positive. The two of us struck gold once. We can do it again.

But Josh simply couldn't feel positive. And when he walked into Ivan's office at Summit Studios, a small, nondescript room painted in bluish-gray tones, the old furniture chipped at the edges, the worn wooden chairs squeaky with age, Josh knew that there was no point in even pasting a fake smile on his face.

"Josh! It's been a few years, hasn't it?"

The voice, once so bright and energetic, was faded. The face, once unlined and handsome, was now sagging and covered by a network of deep lines. The once-dark hair was still thick, but it had turned into a snow-white mop. The body, once tall, lean, and muscular, was now shorter, heavier, and stoop-shouldered, clothed in expensive but worn clothing.

Josh, startled by the radical change in Ivan's appearance, tried hard to make himself smile.

"Yeah, it's only been a few years."

"And how is everything with you, Josh?" Ivan asked from behind his desk, the dark brown wood scarred by deep pockmarks.

"Oh, everything's great," Josh said as he sat down opposite Ivan on one of the squeaky chairs.

Josh didn't bother to ask Ivan that same question. He knew that Ivan was doing lousy right now, and he didn't have the heart to force an old man to put on a happy face just for him.

Ivan picked up a stack of paper riddled with hard-to-decipher comments written in red ink in the margins. It was a printout of Josh's screenplay. He wondered what all those comments were. He was almost afraid to ask. And he wondered whether Ivan really liked it. Maybe he didn't. In fact, he wouldn't be surprised if Ivan expected him to rewrite the whole thing for some big star.

"Your screenplay," Ivan said, his eyes rapidly scanning the pages.

Josh suddenly felt his heart pound.

Ivan put the stack of paper back down on the desk and peered up at Josh, smiling.

"This is amazing, Josh. Simply amazing." Josh felt the tension drain from his body. "It's a truly brilliant screenplay. I always knew you had the potential to write something like this."

"Thanks."

"It is ..." Ivan paused for dramatic effect, "it is, in essence, an insightful comment on the human condition ..."

An insightful comment on the human condition? It's only a comedy!

"Nothing like this has ever been attempted before. It's so ... profound."

Profound? How could a mere comedy be profound? He obviously hasn't read my screenplay; for all I know, he's just trying to use my name to restart his career. Shit!

"... and I'm sure I can get Summit to finance it. I just need to tie up some paperwork." Ivan paused and smiled again at Josh. "You do want me to direct it, don't you?"

"Of course."

"Splendid! I would be thrilled to direct your movie. As far as I'm concerned, it has the smell of a real masterpiece. And I should know — I've been in this business for a long time."

As far as Josh was concerned, Ivan had been in the business too long. He wasn't sure he even wanted Ivan to touch his precious screenplay. Josh was seeing a whole new side of Ivan that he had never seen before, and he didn't like it.

"Who did you have in mind for the lead?"

"Why, *you*, of course!" Ivan said, rising to his feet. "You're the only person on this planet who can play this part. It was made for you."

Of course it was. This part is me. I wrote it for myself.

"And that's not all," Ivan continued, as he paced around the room, each step more frenzied than the last. "This is *the* movie, Josh, that will turn you into a big star. And it will force the critics to finally acknowledge the brilliant mind of Joshua Steinberg."

The critics hate my guts. And I'll be lucky if audiences even remember who I am.

Ivan stopped pacing and sat down at the desk. "So, Josh, do we have a deal?"

It didn't look promising, but this was the only real chance Josh had to sell his screenplay.

"Yes, we do." Josh rose from the chair and leaned over the desk to shake Ivan's hand. "I really appreciate your support, Ivan."

"Great," Ivan responded, smiling. "I'll get back to you in about a week. I just have to finish up some paperwork, and then we can bring your brilliant vision to life."

But would Ivan really get back to him? Did Ivan have the power to sell the pet project of a washed-up comedian that no other studio wanted anything to do with?

***

Several hours later, back on the road and holed up in yet another small and drab motel room, this time in northern California, Josh was abruptly awakened by the ringing of his phone. Still half-asleep, he snapped on the bedside lamp and searched blindly for the phone.

"Josh," Holly said, "you didn't tell me how your meeting with Ivan went."

Josh glanced at the digital clock on the bedside table. It was 10:30 p.m. "I was fast asleep. Couldn't this have waited until the morning?"

"Is the studio going to buy your screenplay? Will Ivan direct it? Will you star in it — ?"

"Holly, you woke me up. For nothing. Thanks a lot."

"I'm sorry. Is everything okay? Are you okay?"

Josh sighed. "I'm fine. Look, there's no news. Ivan seemed interested in my screenplay, but the studio might not be. I'll let you know if I hear anything. Okay?"

"Okay. But please call me as soon as you hear something."

"If I hear something. *If.*"

Over the following week and a half, Josh thought constantly about Ivan and the studio, checking his phone and email messages dozens of times a day. Ten days filled with anxiety, fear, anger, bitterness, feelings of powerlessness. No messages from Ivan or the studio. No announcements, online or anywhere else, from the studio or from Ivan, of any plans to buy Josh's screenplay and turn it into a movie.

It's almost like Ivan's forgotten that my screenplay — or I — even exist, Josh thought one morning as he sipped coffee in a small motel room in Buffalo after fruitlessly checking his phone and email for messages. *If the asshole doesn't want my screenplay or can't buy it, why doesn't he at least have the balls to call me and tell me the truth?*

Josh punched Ivan's number at Summit Studios into his phone.

"The number you have reached is not in service," came an impersonal woman's voice from the other end of the line. "Please check the number and try your call again."

Josh checked the number on the screen of his phone.

It was exactly the same number that Josh reached Ivan at a week and a half ago. What the hell was going on here?

Heart pounding, Josh immediately called Paul Cohen. To Josh's great relief, Paul answered the phone right away.

"Paul, have you heard anything from Ivan Bronkov or Summit Studios? Ivan told me he was going to buy my screenplay — "

"Josh, haven't you heard the news?"

"News? What news?"

"Your friend Ivan has been convicted of tax evasion. He's on his way to prison. I thought you knew."

"Tax evasion? Ivan? Are you sure?"

"I'm positive." Paul paused. "I guess we'll have to keep looking for a buyer for your screenplay. It doesn't look like

Summit is interested, and Ivan certainly won't be directing it. Not too many directors work from jail."

Very funny. Josh abruptly ended the call. A moment later, he called Holly, only to be greeted by her voicemail message.

"… just record your message at the tone," Holly's voice said as her message drew to a close.

You should have done some digging on Ivan before you asked Greg to contact him. Why weren't you more careful?

"Holly the Non-Brain, thanks so much for putting me in touch with Ivan. The damn prick is nothing but a crook and a first-class liar. He's been stringing me along with lies and hiding the truth. Meanwhile, you wasted my time and demoralized me by telling me to contact him. From now on, stay out of my career."

Josh turned off the phone and tossed it across the room. It landed on the gray carpet with a soft thud. He felt like the world's biggest loser. That screenplay of his would never be sold. He had to stop fooling himself.

Josh picked up the phone from the carpet and punched in Holly's number again.

"Holly," he told the voicemail in a slightly calmer voice, "as of today, my screenplay no longer exists. As soon as I get off the phone, I will destroy every last copy of it, and I want you to destroy yours. And I'll also call Paul and tell him to get rid of all his copies. I want you to forget that it ever existed."

Josh turned off the phone, his mind racing. He wished that he had also told her to forget he existed. After the messages he left today, she probably would.

Chapter Eleven

The day started out badly for Holly. Early that morning, while checking her email after breakfast, she discovered that Sharon Roussey, the magician she hired to entertain at her client's sales convention, wouldn't be able to make it.

I have to cancel today's booking, the message read. *Part of my act involves interacting with volunteers from the audience, but I can't talk right now, thanks to laryngitis. Sorry for the short notice.*

With a heavy sigh, Holly put down her phone and glanced at the clock on the bedside table.

I only have four hours to find someone else. Her mind raced as she pulled on her usual work uniform. Four hours. How on earth could she find anyone in such a short time?

Holly picked up her smart phone again and called Diana. All she got was a voicemail message promising to return the call "as soon as I can."

"Diana," Holly told Diana's voicemail, "this is urgent. The magician who was supposed to entertain at today's sales conference lunch canceled at the last minute. I'll be tied up in meetings with other clients all morning. Could you please find someone else — pronto — then give me a call on my cell?"

Diana's call never came. Over the next three and a half hours, Holly checked her phone dozens of times for messages — nothing. She tried phoning and texting Diana again and again and again — nothing. She even phoned their assistant Rachel half a dozen times, but couldn't track her down.

What the hell is going on? Holly thought, frantic with worry, as her final meeting of the morning, located in a brightly lit but stuffy hotel lobby in the north end of Toronto, drew to a close. It was 11:30, and she had been calling both of them for hours. The very least they could do was send her a text. She just had to pass by the sales conference to find out what was going on.

Half an hour later, her heart beating rapidly, Holly rushed through the front doors of the convention center, past small clusters of suited businesspeople clutching briefcases and expensive leather handbags, and down a long flight of stairs. As she ran down the carpeted hallway, she could hear a crowd laughing heartily.

Holly nudged open the heavy door of a conference room at the end of the hall, only to be greeted by the sight of Josh Steinberg beaming down at her from a small platform, clutching a microphone in one hand.

"Well, well, well," he said, "if it isn't my little pal, the leprechaun."

"And *my* pal, the big fat jerk," she said.

The audience roared with laughter.

"Now, Brannigan," Josh said, wagging a finger at her, "that wasn't very nice. Anyhow, you probably wonder why I'm up here. I happened to be in town, and I thought it would be fun to spend time with a certain lady, so I dropped by that lady's office for a surprise visit. I was told that the entertainer that lady had hired for today's lunch couldn't make it, so I thought I'd help her out by coming here." He paused. "Is that okay, Boss Lady? Are you mad at me?"

"You bet I am, Steinberg. Didn't you tell me to stop meddling in your career a couple of weeks ago?"

"Look, honey, I'm sorry. I got upset and carried away." He paused. "Are you still hurt, Holly? Are you still mad at me?"

Holly sighed. "I guess not. I appreciate your help. Thank you, Josh."

"My pleasure," Josh smiled.

"Just one thing. I'm not sure I can afford a big-name comedian like Josh Steinberg."

"Don't worry about that. My act is on the house."

"No, you'll get paid like everyone else. We'll discuss your price later on."

"I can tell you my price right now," Josh said, a broad grin spreading across his face. "It's dinner at your house tonight at seven — alone."

Holly smiled. "Okay, Mr. Steinberg, you have yourself a deal. See you tonight."

It was very easy for Holly to keep her side of the deal. Always an excellent cook, she went out of her way to create a first-class meal: a crisp Caesar salad topped with homemade, garlicky croutons; thick, juicy sirloin steaks; small Parisian potatoes, richly seasoned with herbs and baked in the oven; fresh asparagus spears; a fine bottle of champagne; and a sweet and savory carrot cake topped with sour cream icing. Holly also set the stage for romance, dressing her dining room table in a white linen tablecloth, white bone china, silverware, and two long white tapers perched in silver candlestick holders — and dressing herself in a tight black wool sweater and slim, ankle-length black wool pants that perfectly outlined her curvy, womanly figure.

But apparently Josh hadn't bothered to honor his half of the deal.

Holly glanced at her watch, as her carefully prepared potatoes burned in the kitchen. *It's already 7:45. Where's Josh?* The dinner she had worked so hard on was going to waste.

Holly picked up her phone and called Josh. No answer, other than a voicemail greeting. Maybe something bad happened to him. Maybe he was in some terrible accident. Maybe his car conked out, and he ended up stranded by the side of the road.

Once again, Holly peered out the front window of her townhouse at the darkened street. Two or three cars passed by, but not Josh's car.

She had been stood up. She supposed Josh had only been "joking" when he made dinner plans with her.

Then, all of a sudden, Holly had an idea. A bold, twisted idea bursting with the sweet taste of revenge.

I'll call Josh's agent to find out where he's staying in town. Then I'll courier over "his" part of the dinner, the yucky bits and pieces he would actually hate: salad leaves that have wilted, the tough stems from the asparagus, peelings from the carrots I put in the carrot cake, all of that putrid, smelly stuff. On the outside of the box, I'll attach a note that says, "Here's the dinner you missed tonight."

Rummaging through the small compost bin on her kitchen counter, Holly couldn't help but smile, a malicious, Cheshire cat grin, as she pictured Josh opening the box and grimacing at the discovery of its stinky contents. She fished out a slimy pile of small orange carrot shavings, took one quick look at them, and then tossed them back into the bin.

It's no use, Holly fretted, wiping her hands on a red-and-white cotton dishtowel. If she sent this stuff to Josh, she would just give him another opportunity to make fun of her in his stand-up act. That was the last thing she needed or wanted. She was already depressed; she didn't even feel like eating right now. With a resigned sigh, she turned off the stove and then flicked off the kitchen light.

Maybe I'm being silly. He probably isn't late on purpose. I'm just overreacting.

A few minutes later, Holly, now dressed in a black chiffon negligee, its dark color a strong contrast to her pale skin, found herself upstairs in bed with only a big bottle of champagne and a fluted crystal glass to keep her company.

No sense in letting this go to waste, she thought, as she took the foil off the top of the bottle. *Maybe if I drink the whole thing, I'll feel better. Champagne is the best medicine for healing a broken heart.*

Just as Holly began to remove the cork, she could hear the faint ringing of her doorbell.

Could it be him? It must be him. Who else could it be?

The doorbell rang again, several times. Then someone knocked at the door, loudly and insistently. Stepping into a pair of black velvet slippers, Holly padded down the stairs and unlocked the front door.

"Well, hello, Holly."

Josh stood on the front porch, his face clean-shaven, smelling of musky cologne mixed with soap. He handed Holly a brown box trimmed with a wide red velvet ribbon. "For you."

Holly took the box, which was infused with the aroma of fresh chocolate. "Thanks for the chocolates," she said, prying open the box. Inside, she found six bagels, all chocolate-flavored. "Thanks for the chocolate *bagels*."

"It's the least I can do. I'm sorry I'm so late."

"Why didn't you answer your phone when I called you?"

Josh blanched. "I left my phone in my hotel room. I'm sorry. I guess I got distracted and forgot it."

"That's okay, Josh. I understand. But why did you take so long to get here?"

"Some paparazzi were camped out in the lobby of my hotel, and they started to harass me before I could get to my car. Then I got stuck in one traffic jam after another. I'm sorry, dear." He smiled. "You look so yummy."

Holly's face fell.

"What's wrong? Don't you believe I was held up? Are you mad at me for being late?"

"N-n-no. It's not that. I was just worried about you. You could have been in some horrible accident, for all I knew."

"You shouldn't worry about me." He smiled. "You're so sweet, Holly. And you look so hot. Do you always greet visitors like this?"

"Of course not, silly. I didn't hear from you, so I assumed you weren't going to make it tonight and got ready for bed. I'll change — "

"Don't you dare change." Josh leaned forward and kissed her neck. "You look so perfect."

"Thanks, but I'm a bit cold." Before Josh could object again, she grabbed a sweater off the living room couch and pulled it over her head. "Let's eat."

To Holly's great relief, she was able to salvage the remains of her dinner. Seated in the dimly lit dining room, the soft light of the candles flickering and dancing on the walls, Holly tried, over and over again, to start a conversation with Josh.

"So, how are your gigs going?"

Josh didn't respond. Seated across the table from Holly, he stared deeply into her eyes, mesmerized.

"How are your gigs going?"

Again no response.

"What about your screenplay?"

"My screenplay?" Josh asked, his eyes still fixed on Holly's eyes.

"You didn't destroy it, did you, Josh?"

"No," Josh said, his stare unbroken. "I'm sorry I yelled at you about Ivan Bronkov."

"Why did you yell at me? I was only trying to help you."

"I understand that, dear. I'm sorry. I didn't mean to upset you."

"Okay, Josh. Try not to get so angry next time." Holly sighed. "Are you depressed about what happened with Ivan?"

Once again, Josh's only response was a long, fixed stare.

"Are you sad? Are you happy? What's going on with you? Please tell me."

Still no response.

Holly sighed again. She rose from the table and disappeared into the kitchen. A few minutes later, she reappeared, carrying two golden slices of carrot cake topped with white icing, the thick triangles spilling over the edges of the dessert plates.

"I hope you like this," Holly said as she set down a slice in front of Josh. When she leaned toward him, he touched her sweater.

"I'm sure I will." Josh's plump fingers brushed her sweater lightly. "Mmm, so soft."

Don't stop, Steinberg. Keep going.

"You're my *real* dessert," Josh said, his strokes now longer and silkier. "Yum."

Holly yanked the sweater over her head and tossed it on the floor, then sat sideways on Josh's knee. Picking up a silver dessert fork from the table, she proceeded to feed the cake to Josh, wiping his face gently with a white linen napkin as he swallowed each mouthful.

After a few mouthfuls, Josh, now hard as a rock, knocked the fork out of Holly's hand and kissed her lustily. Holly turned to face Josh, wrapping her slim legs around his body and kissing him passionately back. She rubbed his crotch lightly and insistently with her hand until Josh, moaning with pleasure, came. Josh returned the favor, touching Holly with long, teasing strokes, quickly bringing her to climax.

"Was that an orgasm or a hot flash?" Josh asked.

Holly smiled. "You big, sexy prick." Rising to her feet, she grabbed his hand and started to pull him up.

"Naughty girl." Before Holly could respond, he scooped her up into his arms and carried her off to the bedroom.

The next several hours passed in a blur. Snuggled up together in bed, Josh and Holly talked and talked until the early hours of the morning, just like they had on their first date.

"Do you want me to beat up all the assholes who ever hurt you?" Josh asked after Holly had told him about the string of former boyfriends who had dumped her after taking advantage of her love and unconditional support.

"No, of course not," Holly laughed.

"Don't laugh. I'm serious. I really want to teach them a lesson for treating a special lady like you so badly." He paused. "I'd do anything for you, Holly."

"I'd do anything for you, too."

"And I'm nothing like your ex-boyfriends. I'm so sorry I hurt you, Holly. I would never do anything to deliberately hurt you. And I promise I'll never hurt you ever again."

I believe you. I just have to try harder to trust you.

"But ..." Josh began, his eyes suddenly clouding over, "what about you and me? I mean — please be honest with me, Holly — how much time do I have left with you before the novelty of dating a comedian wears off? Before you dump me for some handsome young hunk?"

"You want the truth?" Holly gazed deeply into his eyes. "As far as I'm concerned, we're staying together until you — or I — croak. I'm not going anywhere, Steinberg. Better get used to it."

Josh looked at Holly, his eyes full of tears. Without saying a single word, he kissed her gently on the mouth, then held her close to him for several deliciously long minutes.

***

The morning sun was just starting to stream through the delicate white lace curtains when Holly's phone began to ring on the bedside table. Startled, she sat up, rubbed the sleep from her eyes, and then picked it up.

"Holly, it's Paul," came Paul Cohen's voice. "I have some exciting news for Josh. I haven't been able to track him down on his phone. Is he there, by any chance?"

"I'm not sure." Turning to Josh, who had just opened his eyes, she asked, "Josh, are you here?"

"More than you are," a half-awake Josh retorted as he snatched the phone.

"Josh, Paul Cohen. I have some exciting news about your screenplay."

"You mean the masterpiece I destroyed? And didn't I tell you to destroy all of your copies of it?"

"You did, Mr. Tortured Artist, but I failed to carry out your crazy commands. Anyhow, your so-called masterpiece still exists, believe it or not, and Monumental Studios just might buy it."

"What?" Josh sat up straight in bed. "Monumental wants to buy my screenplay? Did I hear that right?"

"Not quite. I said that they *might* want to buy it. They haven't bought it yet. I'll keep you posted."

Josh hung up the phone, a triumphant smile on his face. "Monumental Studios might buy my screenplay. Can you believe it?"

Holly shook her head. "No, Josh, you're wrong. Monumental *will* for sure buy your screenplay. I just know it. This world hasn't quite heard the last of the talented Joshua Steinberg."

Chapter Twelve

Josh stared at the lifeless, pallid body of Victor Hernandez — his long-time friend and a fixture on the comedy club circuit — lying all too peacefully in the mahogany casket, a mere shell of the vibrant, witty, larger-than-life personality who had once inhabited it.
This can't be him.
But it was him. Victor, a pudgy man with brown eyes, graying dark brown hair, and an easy laugh, died while traveling to a club gig at the youngish age of fifty-one. The official cause of Victor's death was a heart attack.

"Victor really died from a broken heart," Josh had told Holly when he'd called her the evening before. "The hard, thankless life of a stand-up comedian broke Victor's heart, his very spirit. The long, hard grind of the road, constantly traveling from place to place, never really settling down anywhere. The stingy pay and the all too frequent battles to collect that pay from unscrupulous club owners. The greasy, overpriced, less than delicious and less than nutritious food. The rowdy, unsophisticated audiences who fail to 'get' your act. The unrelenting stress of just staying employable in a competitive, cut-throat business."

Not to mention the loneliness that never quite went away. Broken marriages, half-formed romantic relationships, relationships that never quite get started in the first place. Too many times in the past, Josh had approached attractive women in clubs, bars, even department stores, hoping for a date, only to hear them laugh at him, or worse, treat him like he didn't even exist. Josh couldn't forget the snooty blonde who actually said, "That big, fat, ugly guy wants to take me out," to one of her friends. Once in a while, he'd score a few dates with a woman, but she would only go out with him so she could use his show business connections to grab the attention of a movie director or TV show producer. Sometimes women would date Josh for a few months just for the sex. But none of these women gave the real Josh — the man inside the celebrity — a chance.

Josh knew what Victor went through. He knew exactly what that type of loneliness tasted like.

He examined the body again: it was dressed in a drab navy suit, white shirt, and red silk tie, laid out in its casket like a large, grotesque doll.

"Unlike me, Victor was married — twice," Josh had told Holly, his eyes misting over. "Both his wives divorced him, probably because his constant traveling made them lonely and horny enough to seek out more available and attentive male companions." Neither one of them bothered to show up today.

"But the worst thing, for any comedian with talent, has to be the constant, painful disappointment of an unfulfilled career. Both Victor and I struggled for decades, picking up poorly paid gigs in small, seedy clubs, often playing to bored — and sometimes hostile — audiences. And doing it day after day, year after year, decade after decade, unrewarded and almost invisible. Throwing our lives away on the tough, grimy road, chasing an elusive dream with nothing solid behind it.

"Of course, neither one of us would have lasted three decades on the road without some success. Victor's obituary, posted on the funeral home's website, looks pretty impressive: twenty movies and dozens of appearances on TV sitcoms and talk shows … not to mention an uncountable — but unlisted — number of stand-up dates at comedy clubs and other venues across North America. But Victor's list of credits — a long line of dreary movies and dull sitcoms — doesn't really add up to much. When I took a look at them this morning, I felt like I was reading a summary of my own career."

"Josh," Holly had said in a tender voice, "movie and TV credits don't matter. People matter. You and I matter."

Yes, Holly, you're right. But you don't really understand.

"Thank you for coming today." The voice belonged to one of the funeral home's employees, a portly, white-haired man, dressed in a somber dark gray suit. "Please sign the guestbook before you leave."

"I guess Victor reminds me of myself," Josh had told Holly, trying to mask the pain in his voice. "My own career has just been one disappointment after another. Like Victor, I enjoyed some early fame when I landed a co-starring role on *Guys Like Us*. Even though I was a complete unknown at the time, I became the real star of that show — and I was pitted against two handsome young guys, Dennis D'Ofronsio and Jay Anderson, who had once been a model. I didn't think I could possibly compete with two hunks like them. Boy, was I wrong. For some reason, the audience could relate better to a regular-looking guy like me. Almost overnight, I became a hot commodity in Hollywood, courted for roles in movies and appearances on TV shows and offered lucrative stand-up gigs at popular comedy clubs. It didn't last long, though, and most of the movies I ended up making weren't funny … the worst possible legacy for a comedian. That's all I'll be remembered for. A ton of crap. But it's not fair — both Victor and I had so much more to offer."

Josh couldn't forget what Holly had told him before he ended the call. "You've made millions of people laugh. That's quite an accomplishment. Please don't be so hard on yourself."

Josh glanced around the room. Few people bothered to show up, to pay homage to the great man who had entertained millions. Victor's parents were there, of course, frail, delicate, white-haired figures who walked with halting, uneasy movements. A smattering of middle-aged, paunchy, mildly successful stand-up comedians with hard, wrinkled faces who Josh barely knew. No children — Victor never had any — and not even a girlfriend.

Josh walked toward a large green chair in the corner. *What a tense room this is.* Even worse, the suit he wore was extremely uncomfortable. Josh hated gray suits; they always made him look ghastly and washed out. And no matter how much he loosened his tie, it felt like a noose around his neck.

"Thank you so much for coming today."

Josh turned around to find Victor's mother smiling up at him, her hand extended.

"No problem," Josh responded, gamely taking her frail hand in his bigger, stronger one. "Victor was a wonderful guy."

"I guess you knew him a long time," said Victor's mother with a timid smile. "You're that comedian, aren't you? I've seen you on the talk shows." Turning to her husband, who sat behind her in an overstuffed pale-gray easy chair, she asked, "Who is this, Hector? He's that Jewish comedian, isn't he?"

"That's Jack Sternberg," her husband responded, his face twisted into an impatient scowl. "Everybody knows who he is."

Josh's heart sank.

"No, I'm not Jack Sternberg," he said in a deeply sad voice as he slunk away to the opposite corner of the room.

Shit, I've already been forgotten. I might as well be dead, too, for all they care. Victor is actually lucky to be dead — he no longer has to put up with all this bullshit and constant disappointment.

Josh's cell phone rang, sharply interrupting his thoughts. He didn't bother to answer it. He didn't feel like talking to anybody. Besides, the call couldn't be that important. Greg might be calling, and he would miss out on another crappy gig he didn't really want. Holly might be calling, but if Josh answered the phone, he would probably say something stupid and she would never want anything to do with him ever again. It could be Paul calling to tell Josh that his screenplay had been sold to Monumental Studios — nah, that wasn't going to happen. Then again, somebody might be calling to tell him that he'd won a billion bucks in a lottery —

Josh tried to force himself to chuckle at his private joke. But he couldn't. All he could think about was Victor. Josh couldn't believe he was gone. He had just spoken to Victor a couple of weeks ago, and he seemed fine. Maybe his voice sounded a bit ragged, but Josh thought that all the touring just tired him out.

Josh looked at Victor's body again, trying hard to remember the colorful character who made him laugh. He wished he could give the eulogy. Instead of all of the usual sentimental claptrap, Josh would tell people about the real, crazy, gloriously nutty Victor Hernandez:

"Friends, we are gathered here today to celebrate the life of an extraordinary spirit. Of all of the comedians I knew, Victor had the wildest sense of humor, along with an even wilder lack of inhibition. Once, when Victor and I were working together at a club — I had been the headliner on that tour, even though Victor ended up getting the bigger laughs from audiences — the club's owner refused to pay us our full fee, claiming that we had offended some of his customers with our racy material. To get revenge on him, Victor stuffed several rolls of toilet paper into one of the club's toilets so that it would overflow and spill its putrid contents all over the bathroom floor. Of course, Victor did

his business in the toilet beforehand, just to make sure it would be as stinky as possible. I also heard rumors that on another occasion, Victor — a real dog lover who often traveled with his pooches — locked another stingy club owner in his office with Victor's massive German shepherd. The terrified man, cornered by the large, snarling dog, finally agreed to pay Victor his entire fee if he removed the scary beast from the room.

"That was the real Victor, the Victor that I remember — and the Victor that I miss."

Nobody wants to hear a eulogy like that. Too honest. Oh, well.

Josh fished his phone out of his front jacket pocket and scanned it for messages. One call from Greg. Groaning, he punched in Greg's number. From the corner of his eye, he could see the disapproving glances of fellow mourners.

"So, you finally decided to call back. Hey, don't you answer your own phone anymore?"

"I happen to be busy right now. One of my friends just died, and I'm not in the mood to take on another shitty gig."

"Listen, Mr. Big Shot, since when is an appearance on a popular TV talk show a shitty gig? Anyhow, you have an offer to appear on *The Ally Barrett Show* tomorrow night."

"Tomorrow night? Isn't that short notice?"

"It is, but your friend Victor Hernandez was booked for that episode, and they need someone to fill in for him. Are you interested? Yes or no?"

Josh paused. *Ally Barrett ... isn't she that young black comedian?* Josh loved edgy comics like Ally, but right now, he just didn't have the stomach to appear on a TV show like hers, where anything could happen and usually did. But he needed the money.

"Oh, okay, tell them I'll do the show."

"Don't do me any favors. I'll email you the details," he added before abruptly hanging up.

Josh stared at his phone for a full minute, trying to gather his thoughts. What the hell had he gotten himself into now?

Victor's presence continued to haunt Josh long after he went to bed. That night, Josh dreamed he was standing in a lush, green field, surrounded by gray tombstones and dozens of mourners dressed in black, a light, warm drizzle raining down on them from a cloudy, gloomy sky. Victor was standing in front of Josh, a striking visual contrast to the mourners in his bright red sweater and blue jeans, an oddly unhappy smile on his face.

"Don't worry, Josh," Victor told him, "I'm not really dead."

Josh heard a loud creaking sound. Wheeling around, he saw an open casket being lowered, slowly and cautiously, into a hole in the ground. In the background, Josh could just barely hear a man talking about "a big, fat loser."

Curious, Josh peered into the casket — only to find himself inside it, dead.

"Shit," Josh said, to no one in particular. "I'm still fat."

No one laughed at Josh's joke. In fact, no one seemed to even hear him.

"I said, 'I'm still fat.' Didn't you hear me?"

Josh felt someone tap him on his left shoulder. It was Victor.

"I'm the only person who can see you or hear you. Better get used to it."

Better get used to what? I'm still alive ... aren't I?

"Didn't you used to date Josh Steinberg?"

The voice belonged to a ruggedly handsome young man standing behind Victor. On his arm was Holly Brannigan, ravishingly lovely in a low-cut black dress that clung seductively to her slim curves.

"I did," she said, looking up at the man, her eyes full of adoration. "But I broke up with him. He turned out to be too needy and neurotic, and I guess the novelty of dating a comedian wore off."

"How dare you say that! How dare you even think that! You bitch!"

Holly didn't respond. Instead, she continued to stare at the handsome young man.

"Did you hear me?" Josh shouted again, walking up close to Holly's face. "You're a real *bitch*, Holly. I hate you. I wish I'd never met you."

Just then, Josh woke up, bathed in cold sweat. He turned on the bedside lamp and glanced at the clock. It was 4:32 a.m. He was too rattled to sleep. He might as well try to do some writing.

***

Early the next morning, Paul Cohen received an email from Josh Steinberg with the subject line "New scene for screenplay."

Confused, Paul clicked on the email, which told him where to insert the new material in the screenplay, and opened the attached file. *This is a scene in a comedy? What was Josh thinking when he wrote this?*

"Howard Greenberg dreams that he's attending his own funeral. All of the mourners, including Hannah O'Leary, Howard's love interest, bad-mouth Howard, calling him an asshole, a prick, a monster, a disgusting human being. At the end of the scene, the mourners take turns spitting on Howard's corpse, visible in an open casket, and then Hannah walks to the edge of the graveyard, where she has sex with a dark-haired and muscular young man."

Paul was stunned. He couldn't understand why Josh thought the scene would fit into the movie — and it was the last thing he needed. He was having a hard enough time selling the screenplay without throwing this weird stuff into it.

Paul picked up his phone and called Josh. And called him. And emailed and texted him. After two fruitless hours, Paul gave up and emailed Holly.

Holly was sitting at her desk in her office, buried in paperwork, when she received Paul's email around noon. When she spied the message — with its "Very urgent!" subject line — she opened it right away.

She had been trying for days to reach Josh, without any luck. *I hope Josh is all right,* she thought, as Paul's email appeared on her computer screen:

Josh sent me a new scene for his screenplay. Have you seen it? It's one of the most disturbing things I've ever read. Could you please take a look at it and ask Josh to call me ASAP? New scene attached.

Heart beating wildly, Holly opened the file. What she read made her feel sick to her stomach.

How could you, Josh? Why on earth would you write something like this?

Once again, Holly picked up the phone to call Josh. And once again, she was met with nothing but silence.

***

Josh was too nervous to speak to Holly or Paul or anyone else. Victor's sudden death — and the unsettling dream that followed it — left him too flustered to prepare smart new material for his appearance on *The Ally Barrett Show* that night. And Ally Barrett's reputation for withering, sarcastic humor made him dread his upcoming interview with her.

To Josh's relief, however, his first few minutes on the show passed quickly and uneventfully as the two comedians traded quips and small talk. Ally was her usual sharp and abrasive self, but Josh — dressed in his navy blue wool suit of armor — was up to the challenge, defusing her verbal grenades with his own easygoing wit. Then, without warning, Ally's voice became sober.

"Tell me, Josh, what was Victor Hernandez really like?"

Josh opened his mouth to respond, but for the first time in his life, he couldn't think of anything to say.

"What was Victor like? You heard the question, didn't you?"

Josh stared dumbly at Ally, his mind spinning.

"Victor was …"

Josh couldn't finish the sentence. Instead, he broke down and started to cry. On television. Before millions of people.

Just then, Josh heard his cell phone ringing in his jacket pocket. He had forgotten to turn that stupid thing off!

"Josh, your phone is ringing."

Josh ignored the phone. It kept ringing.

"Josh, you better answer your phone."

Josh pulled the phone out of his pocket.

"Josh!" cried Holly. "I've been so worried about you. I read the scene, and I thought you might have become depressed about Victor."

Ally sighed. "Who the hell is it?"

The audience laughed.

"I'm fine, dear," Josh said to Holly.

"That scene scared the shit out of me, especially the part about the girlfriend. You don't really think I'm like her, do you, Josh? Or am I just reading too much into things?"

"Holly, don't worry, I'm fine. Let's talk about this some other time."

Ally glared at Josh. "Josh, you're on TV."

"Josh, I really care about you. Please tell me that the new scene had nothing to do with me or our relationship."

"Josh, you're not on a soap opera!" Ally yelled. "Turn off the phone."

"Holly, I can't talk right now. That scene has nothing to do with you or with us — "

Ally rolled her eyes and shook her head. The studio audience roared with laughter.

"Oh, my God!" Holly gasped as she heard the wall of laughter. "Are you in the middle of your act?"

"It's worse than that. I'm on *The Ally Barrett Show*. On live television." The audience laughed again. "Don't worry, honey. Everything's fine. The scene was a mistake. I'll talk to you later," he added before turning off the phone.

"What the hell was that about?"

"Oh, it was just a call about my latest movie project."

"Movie project? I thought you were washed up."

Josh smiled at Ally. "Jealous?" he asked as the audience again broke into laughter.

Ally gave Josh a hard, cold stare. "Someone actually hired you for a movie? They would have to be — "

Josh rose to his feet and put his right hand up to silence Ally. "I'm sorry, but I'm far too busy to bother with this garbage," he told her as he strolled off the set.

***

Unfortunately, Josh's career woes didn't end the moment he walked off Ally Barrett's TV show. Josh had heard nothing from Monumental Studios about the fate of his screenplay for over two weeks; even worse, the paparazzi, after Josh's disastrous appearance on *The Ally Barrett Show*, began to feast on the decaying remains of his career. Josh, his always shaky self-confidence creeping lower by the day, found himself being picked apart by bloggers, gossip columnists, and even so-called respectable entertainment journalists on television.

"How does he keep getting work?"

"There's a good reason why Steinberg has never made a decent movie."

"He's fifty-four and has never been married. Obviously, he's in the closet."

"Steinberg was never attractive. Fat body, hair in the wrong places, the nose of a clown."

I am a clown. After all, my job is to make people laugh. But people were no longer laughing *with* the clown; they were laughing *at* him. And Josh knew it.

Who the hell are these assholes, anyway? Why don't they just mind their own business and leave me alone?

"How dare they pick on you like this?" Holly shouted on the phone one evening after Josh complained about the onslaught of vicious comments. "You don't deserve to be bullied like this. You have to do something!"

"I can't do anything about it."

Besides, Josh believed that a lot of those comments were true. As far as he was concerned, he really was ugly. And he couldn't believe that Holly found him attractive. Why was she sticking with him? He wished he knew.

His confidence at an all-time low, Josh, now off the road, spent the next ten days locked up in his small house in Los Angeles, refusing to respond to calls, emails, or texts. He couldn't turn off the pain. No matter how hard he tried to relax, his thoughts kept beating him up with harsh memories. Promising career opportunities that suddenly dried up. Betrayals from people he thought were his friends. Hurtful comments from former girlfriends. No wonder he couldn't sleep.

And somehow Josh became glued to his stupid computer screen, wasting hours and hours of his life. Hours and hours spent jumping from site to site, looking for support, advice, insight, anything, from other men like himself. But there were no other men like Josh ... and he didn't really know what he was looking for. He had never felt so alone in his entire life.

One overcast morning, Josh couldn't take it any longer. He rolled out of bed, combed his hair, and forced himself to stare at his face in the bathroom mirror — a stare that was long, cold, and hard.

I just have to do it. No matter how difficult it is. No matter how much it hurts.

Gathering up as much courage as he could muster, Josh switched on his phone and punched in the number of a local plastic surgeon.

"How much do you charge for a face-lift, a rhinoplasty, and liposuction?" he asked in his voicemail message. "And how soon could you do them? What about next Tuesday?"

Chapter Thirteen

A few days later, Josh, dressed in a stiff navy wool blazer, tan cotton pants, and a white cotton shirt with a slightly too-tight collar, found himself sitting in the crowded waiting room of Beverly Hills plastic surgeon Dr. Andrew Chan, booked for a consultation. The room, lavishly furnished with a long glass-topped coffee table, chairs covered in dark green leather, and lush oil paintings of mountains and forests, had a cold, uncomfortable feel. Anxiety filled the air; patients and would-be patients buried their faces in dog-eared magazines or stared, glassy-eyed, at a small, nearly mute TV screen on one wall as it flashed an endless series of urgent headlines from CNN.

My career hasn't been doing so well lately. I wonder if I have any fans left?

Josh pulled his new smart phone from his jacket pocket and typed his name in the search engine.

"21,763 results for Josh Steinberg."

Josh chuckled to himself. *Not bad, not bad at all, especially for an old guy like me.* He stopped chuckling when he glanced at the search results.

"Old, fat, and forgotten."

"What happened to Josh Steinberg's career?"

"Who is Josh Steinberg?"

Josh scowled. With the air of an imperious emperor, he wiped the offending sites off the screen by typing in a new search: "Josh Steinberg successful."

A headline popped up at the top of the screen: "Become Part of the Josh Steinberg Success Story! Enter here."

The Josh Steinberg Success Story? What Josh Steinberg Success Story?

Josh clicked on the link. A video appeared featuring a muscular young man driving a bright yellow sports car. At the top right corner of the screen, a small red banner promised, "Video starts after ad."

Josh tried to skip past the obnoxious ad. *The hell with this.* No luck. Twenty-four long seconds later, the ad dissolved ... and Paul Cohen, looking as rumpled as ever in a bright green shirt and beige pants, popped up on the screen.

"Hi, everyone! I'm Paul Cohen. My family has been making hit movies in Hollywood for almost a century, and collectively, we've won twelve Oscars — that's twelve Oscars — for writing, producing, and directing a slew of classic movies."

Josh turned up the sound a notch.

"And *you*," Paul pointed to the camera, "you, too, can become part of the Cohen family's proud legacy just by making a financial contribution to our latest project. I'm producing a film written by and starring one of the biggest, most legendary comedians of our time, the great Josh Steinberg, star of *Guys Like Us* and dozens of classic movies."

Classic movies? What classic movies?

"This is a rewarding and unique investment opportunity. For only $5,000, you'll get an autographed picture of Josh Steinberg ... a limited edition picture. If you invest $20,000, you'll get two free tickets to any club appearance, in any city, with Josh Steinberg. For $50,000, you'll get your own onscreen credit at the end of the film. Imagine that!"

Big deal. You'll get an onscreen credit for a movie nobody will ever see.

"... just click on the link at the end of this video. It's easy." Paul paused. "And for our top, gold-level investors, at the $100,000 and over level, we have a real treat: a private cocktail reception with the great man himself!"

The camera cut away from Paul and zoomed in on a photograph of Josh's face.

Josh's current face, with its receding hairline, deep wrinkles, and sagging double chin. The face of the man who would be performing in clubs, starring in the movie ... and meeting deep-pocketed investors at the cocktail reception.

Josh stared at his own image for a few seconds, then put down his phone.

He couldn't go through with it. Those investors would be paying for the *real* Josh Steinberg, that old guy in the photograph, not some *schmuck* with a smooth face and a hair transplant.

"Mr. Steinberg?"

Josh glanced up at the receptionist at the desk, a young blonde woman with a face covered in a thick coat of makeup.

"Dr. Chan will see you now," she said with a smile. "You can go right in. Room three down the hall."

Staring at her dumbly, Josh rose from the chair, muttered something unintelligible, and strolled out of the office.

Paul's video kept playing in Josh's mind, over and over again, for hours after he had left Dr. Chan's office. Each time it played, Josh's feelings toward Paul Cohen became more bitter.

Josh changed into his pajamas. *That dirty little bastard.* Why hadn't Paul told him he was crowdfunding? Why did Paul make all of these extravagant promises to investors without speaking to him first? Hastily, he grabbed his phone and pulled up Paul's number. His voicemail picked up.

"Listen, Cohen," Josh began, "that stupid video of yours is a real piece of garbage. You should have had the decency to speak to me before you — " He was suddenly cut off by an ear-shattering screech.

"Josh?" came the now-live voice of Paul Cohen. "Are you okay?"

"That — that video is total crap! Twenty grand to see me in a club? Cocktails with me for a hundred grand? You must be kidding. I rarely drink. Where did you get these dumb ideas from?"

"From Holly. Those were her ideas, Josh."

"Oh, so Holly the Not-So-Smart Brain dreamed them up?"

"Well … yes. Holly thought that Monumental Studios would be more willing to buy your screenplay if we raised some of the money to produce the film." He paused. "But why are you — and my uncle — so pissed off at the video?"

"Your *uncle* is pissed off?"

"Well, yeah. 'Cause I'm using the Cohen name to raise money for a movie. You know, the Cohens are big shots around Hollywood. We're not supposed to beg for money from the public."

"But your uncle isn't willing to invest in my film, so who cares what he thinks?" He paused for a second, then added, "What if this fundraising scheme doesn't work, Paul? Then what do we do? What if — "

"Josh, that video has already worked. We've raised over $300,000, and it's been online for only four days. Four days!"

Over $300,000! Maybe Josh wasn't as unpopular as he thought.

"Where did you get that money? Who gave it to you?"

"Lots of people. Film school contacts of mine, friends of Holly's, fans of Josh Steinberg."

"Any takers for the cocktail reception?"

Paul laughed. "No, not yet. Anyhow, I think Holly had a brilliant idea, Josh. It's working, isn't it? I can see why you call her Holly the Brain."

Yeah, sure, Josh thought, after he turned off the phone a few minutes later. Why hadn't Holly run these brilliant ideas past him before she started making wild promises to investors? Sometimes he wondered if she cared about him at all.

***

Holly *did* care about Josh, and as several days flew by without any contact from him, she began to worry desperately about his welfare. Unable to reach him, Holly searched online, scanning as many celebrity gossip sites and viewing as many clips of Josh's stand-up comedy routines as she could, trying to find some clue, any clue, that would explain why he was upset and unwilling to speak to her.

Finally, after two hours of fruitless searching on her computer, Holly found a new video that had been posted on a comedy club's website only two days before. What she found made her cringe.

"So glad to be here tonight," Josh said as he shuffled around a dusty, poorly lit stage. He smiled angrily at the audience; his big brown eyes were tired and bloodshot, his face craggier and more deeply lined than ever before.

"Let me tell you about my girlfriend."

Holly turned up the volume, her heart pounding hard and fast.

"A lot of the ladies aren't attracted to us big guys, but I met this woman on the road who seemed to be into me. She started chasing me, asking me out for a date, and even lured me into her bed. Now," he paused, moving in for the kill, "I know women can't resist men with pot bellies and multiple chins …" The audience laughed. "Still, since this woman was pretty hot-looking — I mean, before she met me, she had been dating a young guy — I kept wondering, 'Why does she want me so badly? What does she see in me?'" He paused. "I think I know what was making her so horny."

Holly's heart pounded faster. *Oh, God, please don't. Please don't say it.*

With a bitter smile, Josh reached into the pocket of his jacket and pulled out his wallet. *"This!"*

Holly recoiled from the screen as if she had been struck. *Did he really say what I think he just said? And did he say it about me? Of course it was about me ... but why? What did I say to make him feel like this? What did I do? I tried my best to help him.* Tears sprang to her eyes.

Just then, the phone rang. Holly let the call go to voicemail, but when she saw that it was from Paul, she couldn't resist listening to the message.

"Holly, great news!" exclaimed Paul. "We've raised almost two million from the website, and Monumental Studios is serious about buying Josh's screenplay. And we — you, Josh, and I — have an interview with some of their top people in New York next Tuesday. I'll email you the details tomorrow."

"I don't care about Josh and his screenplay!" Holly yelled at the phone.

"... and I hope you'll be there," the recording continued. *Don't worry. I won't be.*

But she couldn't let Paul down. *He's really stuck his neck out for us,* Holly reminded herself as she checked into her hotel in New York. Paul had let them use the Cohen name, and he had even ticked off his uncle — and who knew what his prick of an uncle might do to him. Besides, Paul knew nothing about negotiating contracts, and Josh was useless when it came to business.

Holly didn't need to worry about Josh messing up the contract negotiations. He didn't bother to attend the meeting.

 Greg attended the meeting in Josh's place. "He's tied up," Greg told Holly. As they sat in a drab waiting room of beige walls and beige carpeting, Holly found herself forgetting about her companions. All she could think about was Josh.

His rant on the video really disturbed her. His appearance bothered her more than his words; his words were angry, but his eyes were full of fear. She was starting to worry about him; she could sense he was in trouble. She knew that was why he wasn't here today.

"Holly." She felt someone tap her sharply on the left shoulder. "The receptionist just called us," Greg told her in a stern voice. "The meeting is about to start."

The meeting passed in a blur. It was presided over by a quartet of conservative people in their early thirties, dressed identically in dark blue suits: three smug men and a cool, imposing woman. All four of them were tall and distantly polite but not friendly, and they spoke in an unfamiliar lingo about "demographic targets," "name recognition," and "hot trends." Both Greg and Holly scribbled notes furiously, smiling and nodding during the appropriate breaks in the conversation. Paul was sullen and silent throughout, constantly shifting in his chair.

After about half an hour, the quartet stood up, shook hands, then waved the three visitors out of the room, promising to run Josh's screenplay past some focus groups.

"We'll be in touch," said the woman with a smile.

"Thanks for coming," added one of the men as he shut the door behind them.

"What do you think?" Paul whispered to Greg a little too eagerly. "Went pretty well, didn't it?"

Greg shrugged.

Holly seemed to forget about the meeting as soon as it ended. Within minutes, she had turned on her phone, determined to reach Josh once and for all. But she still couldn't.

That evening, she couldn't stop thinking about Josh. *Stop worrying! You're just being silly. He's fine. Just turn on the TV, watch something — anything — and relax.*

But the moment Holly turned on her TV, her worst fears were confirmed.

Comedian Steinberg hospitalized for carbon monoxide poisoning, ran a banner headline on CNN.

***

Josh, distraught over his aging face and lackluster career — and heartsick over Holly — had woken up early that morning, paralyzed by painful thoughts, unable to move. When he had finally forced himself to climb out of bed, all he wanted to do was to end the constant hurt eating away at him from inside.

I have to stop the pain. I can't stand it anymore. I can't take another second of this. It's time to end it. Get it over with as quickly and painlessly as possible.

Having read somewhere about the suicide of another celebrity by carbon monoxide poisoning, Josh had wheeled his large, gritty barbeque off the backyard patio indoors. Within minutes, thick smoke had enveloped the kitchen as the heavy smell of burning charcoal filled the room.

He had lain down on the kitchen floor … and waited for it to happen. Almost immediately, he'd felt ill, coughing as the dirty smoke filled his lungs.

I don't want to die! What do I do now? How do I save myself?

He'd struggled to rise to his feet to turn off the barbeque but hadn't been able to. Slowly and feebly, Josh had crawled to the kitchen table and grabbed his phone. Half-conscious and filled with fear, he'd called for an ambulance before abruptly blacking out.

Several hours later, Josh opened his eyes to find himself in a hospital bed.

"Where am I?" he asked in a weak voice. "Why am I here?"

A slim woman with short gray hair, dressed in a white uniform, glanced at Josh from the other side of the room, where she had been talking to another patient.

"Mr. ... Steinberg?" she said, peering at the clipboard in her hands, as she rushed over to Josh's bed. "It looks like you've been poisoned by carbon monoxide. We're doing all we can to help you."

"Oh," Josh replied, his voice faint. The woman then disappeared and the room became dark.

The next time Josh opened his eyes, there was another woman beside his bed: Holly.

And, to Josh's great surprise, she was crying. Hard.

Sinking down into a chair beside the bed, Holly took Josh's hand and gazed intently into his eyes, her face full of concern.

"Why did you do this, Josh? It had something to do with me, didn't it?"

"No ... what are you talking about?"

Holly swallowed hard, struggling to force the words out. "That video ... where you talked about dating a woman who was only interested in your money ... oh, Josh, what did I do or say to make you feel like that?"

"You didn't have anything to do with that video — "

"Yes, I did! Only a very angry and depressed man would say something like that. You were angry at me for some reason." Holly paused to wipe the tears from her eyes. "What made you think I don't care about you?"

Josh started to cry. "Believe me, honey, you didn't say or do anything. Honest. I've been depressed on and off for most of my life." He paused. "I know you care about me, dear."

"Then why did you stop talking to me? And why did you try to kill yourself?"

Josh didn't respond. Instead, he stared blankly at the opposite wall.

"Answer me, Josh!"

Josh kept staring at the wall, silent.

"You really need to see a shrink."

Josh snapped to attention. "I've already been to three of them. Big waste of time and money. The last one tried to put me on anti-depressants. Last thing I need is a pill to destroy my sex drive." He wiped tears from his eyes with the sheet. "I guess what I really need is someone to be there for me."

"I thought I was that person."

"You are, honey. Look, you don't understand ... you're a wonderful woman, but I have serious trust issues. It's hard for me to believe that you — or any woman, really — could care about me. I feel so alone and hopeless ..." He started to cry again.

Holly hugged Josh warmly. "I do care, Josh. Why don't you trust me? Please trust me."

"I'll try." Josh squeezed Holly's hand.

"And you'll try again to get some professional help? There must be someone out there who can help you."

Josh nodded. "Okay, I'll try to find some help. As soon as I get out of this place."

"And Josh?"

"Yes?"

"If you have ... issues with me, if you're mad at me about something, you need to talk to me about it. Don't just bitch about me onstage when you're performing your act."

"I never bitched about ..." Josh began, then paused as Holly glared at him. "Okay, honey, I'll talk to you first. But don't worry, Holly, I'm not mad at you." He added in a soft voice, "I love you, Holly."

Did he just say what I think he said? Calm down, Holly! He probably didn't mean it.

The look in Josh's eyes told her otherwise.

"I love you too, Josh," Holly smiled and kissed him gently on the cheek.

Chapter Fourteen

"I don't feel like getting out of bed. What's the point?"

In the half-dark, half-light bedroom, shaded by thick, pale gray linen curtains, Holly glanced at the digital clock beside the bed. It was 10:00 a.m.

"Come on, honey. I'll make you a nice big breakfast. Isn't that worth getting up for?"

Josh grunted and rolled over in bed.

Holly sighed. She had moved temporarily into Josh's modest house, located on a leafy street in Los Angeles, when he was discharged from the hospital three days before. Some days were better than others. Even though Josh's physical strength gradually improved, his emotional strength was another matter, as he battled the depression, cynicism, and fear constantly eating away at him. On some days — such as today — Josh was so paralyzed by anxiety that Holly spent hours trying to coax him out of bed.

Hungry and half-tired from a restless night of fractured sleep — Josh woke her up several times to dump his worries about his not-so-stable career on her — Holly threw on her fluffy white robe and pulled on a pair of slippers, then padded downstairs to the sunny living room. Flopping down onto the pale gray leather couch, she dug into her handbag for her phone, pulled it out, and punched in Diana's number.

"It looks like I'll be stuck here for a while. Josh isn't doing too well right now, and he really needs my help. You understand, don't you?"

Diana sighed. "Holly, why do you put up with this guy's drama? I think you ought to give up on him and come home."

"I can't. Anyhow, I promise I'll make this up to you. You can take a nice long vacation when I get back — "

"I don't need a vacation."

"And I'll try to drum up some new business while I'm out here."

"Don't bother. Just come home. Now."

"I can't. I can't leave Josh alone. He's lonely and depressed and vulnerable and can't take care of himself. Besides, I promised to help him, and he's depending on me."

Holly kept her word to Josh. Over the next three days, she did everything she could for him: she fed him, helped him find a new therapist, and, most important of all, she gave him a much-needed shoulder to cry on. Josh soon found himself opening up to Holly more and more, digging out the deepest and most painful thoughts and memories from his psyche. Painful thoughts and memories he never shared with anyone else.

"All my life, I've felt like a total failure," he told Holly one afternoon as they sat sipping tea on the back patio, shaded from the hot midday sun by a large awning. "Ever since I can remember. My dad, a big-shot judge, preferred my brother, Ira, over me. As far as he was concerned, I wasn't half as smart or as good-looking as Ira ..." His voice trailed off.

"But you became a successful comedian. Wasn't your dad impressed by that?"

Josh shook his head. "My dad doesn't respect comedians. He doesn't think of comedy as real work."

"But it's a tough and competitive business. You have to be smart to make it as a comedian." Josh shook his head again. "I don't understand why your dad would feel that way. I mean, there's a whole great tradition of Jewish comedy and Jewish comedians — "

Josh snorted. "According to my dad, there's no such thing. When I told him I was thinking of becoming a comedian, he actually said that Jewish comedians use comedy to denigrate themselves so that Gentiles will accept them."

"You don't believe that, do you?"

"Of course not. Successful Jewish comedians don't denigrate themselves for anyone. They're starring in popular sitcoms, headlining big-budget movies ..." Josh paused, and a pained look crossed his face. "Well, *some* Jewish comedians do. But my dad was right about one thing: Ira *is* better looking. Not fat and ugly like me."

Holly sighed. "You're not ugly. Not even close."

"How can you say that? Look how fat I am. No fat guy looks good!"

"That's not true. You're very attractive. I mean it. And you must stop putting yourself down like that."

"I'm not putting myself down; I'm only being honest." He paused again. "You're beautiful."

Holly groaned. "You really think so? I've never felt attractive to men."

"But why wouldn't you? You've had boyfriends. You've even been married."

To Josh's surprise, Holly's eyes suddenly welled up with tears.

"Yeah, married and divorced."

He gently wrapped one arm around her shoulder and drew her close to him. "What happened to your marriage? Did he — your ex — did he hurt you, dear?"

Holly nodded, wiping her eyes roughly with the back of her hand.

"Did he cheat on you? Hit you?"

"He only hit me with his words," Holly responded, choking back the tears, "but it really hurt. He — Doug — picked on me because I had no self-esteem, and he knew I didn't have the heart to stand up for myself. He called me a dirty bitch when I did nothing to him, swore at me, broke my personal things …" She started to cry.

"Oh, Holly," Josh said tenderly, hugging her tightly, "I wish I'd known about this. I would never have said all those stupid things about you in my act."

Holly blew her nose and shook her head. "You didn't mean to hurt me in your act. Doug actually wanted to hurt me. It's not the same thing."

"I still feel bad about it."

"Don't."

"How did you get away from him?"

"I finally found the guts to stand up for myself. I told Doug that he was a bully and that he had to stop picking on me. But that only made matters worse. He flew into a rage and threatened to hurt Kyle — who was only a toddler — and me. I couldn't stand it any longer, and I was scared shitless for both of us. So, the next day, when Doug was at work, I moved out with Kyle."

"Did he try to follow you? Threaten you?"

"No, thank God. I thought he would, but he didn't. He just disappeared." She paused. "But even after that monster was out of our lives, I still didn't feel good about myself. In fact, I felt even more unattractive to men than before."

"You shouldn't feel that way. You're a beautiful woman." He kissed her softly on the cheek. "And thanks for opening up. It means a lot to me."

Holly smiled at him. "I'm glad, Josh. And I hope you know you're not alone, that other people also feel bad about their looks. Just please promise me you won't tell anyone about my ex-husband. Especially not in your stand-up act."

"Don't worry about that. Your secret is safe with me. I promise to keep it out of my act."

When Josh and Holly weren't engaging in long, intimate talks — and whenever Holly could coax Josh to get out of bed — they spent their days enjoying each other's company. They cooked delicious and elaborate meals together, took long, romantic strolls along the beach, and made love — in Josh's bed, on the living room couch, on the thick, shaggy rug in the basement — always hot, wild, and deeply satisfying.

***

One warm and sunny afternoon, Holly tried to lure Josh out to the pool in the backyard. But it wasn't easy, especially when Josh saw Holly walking around the bedroom in a bright orange bikini that showed off her slim curves and taut body.

"I can't fit into my swim trunks. I'll just put on a t-shirt and shorts and watch you swim."

"Try on your swimsuit. I'll bet it still fits. Besides, wouldn't it be nice to cool off with a swim?"

Josh shook his head. "I told you, it doesn't fit. Maybe I'll try it on again when I lose weight." He sighed. "You look so perfect in that bikini."

"Come on, honey, put on the suit. You look fine."

"But I'll gross you out. My belly hangs out over the suit."

"That won't bother me. There's just more of you to love."

Josh sighed again. "Okay, I'll try it on. Meanwhile, you go ahead."

As Holly made her way out the back door of the house, the warm spring sun partly shaded by gray clouds, she spied a small, trim, elderly woman standing on the front porch. Thinking she was a fan, Holly shouted, "Mr. Steinberg is too sick to see anybody!"

"Even his own mom?"

Oh, no, it's Josh's mom! What'll I say to her ... how should I introduce myself?

Trying to look as calm as possible, Holly ran to the front porch.

The woman smiled at her.

Holly forced herself to smile back. "I'm — "

"I'll bet you're Holly!"

How did she know who I was? I must be pretty important to Josh if he's been talking to his mother about me.

"Yes, I'm Holly."

"I'm Miriam."

"Oh," Holly said, extending her hand, "nice to meet you, Mrs. Steinberg."

"Not Steinberg, Goldstein," the woman said, taking Holly's hand. "I divorced Josh's father ages ago, so I use my birth name. But I don't like any of that Mrs. stuff. It's for boring old fogeys. Just call me Miriam."

"Okay. I'm sure Josh will be happy to see you." She led Miriam to the deck by the pool. Josh, who was dressed in a pair of loose swim trunks, was lounging in a chair, absorbed in a car racing magazine. He glanced up at his mother and Holly, a startled expression on his face.

"Mom, what are you doing here? Did you come all the way here by yourself?"

"I did. Josh, what the hell were you doing in the hospital? Were you trying to kill yourself or something?"

"Please, ma, not today."

Turning to Holly, she asked, "Is he seeing a shrink? He clearly needs help."

"I made an appointment for him with one this morning."

Miriam smiled. "Good girl," she said, then hugged Holly. "This is a smart and classy lady," she told Josh. "Hang on to this one."

Just then, Josh's phone rang. Beckoning his mother and Holly to be quiet, he snatched it up from the table beside him.

"Great news, Josh," Paul said. "Monumental Studios has decided to buy your screenplay *and* they want me to produce it."

"Oh." *My whole life is in tatters. Who cares about a screenplay?*

"Oh? Is that all you can say? Aren't you excited?"

"Sure, I'm excited. But there's a catch, isn't there? There always is."

"A catch?" Paul paused. "Well ... the studio gets to pick the director; you and I have no say." He paused again.

There's something he's not telling me. I just know it.

"Anything else? Am I ... can I ... be in this movie?"

"You're in the movie, but ... you're not the star. You have a part, but it's kinda small."

Josh's heart sank. "Well, then, who is the star?"

"Jason Williams."

"Jason Williams?" Out of the corner of his eye, Josh noticed Holly and Miriam watching him intently, their faces both worried and excited. "He's not Jewish! And I could play that part perfectly."

"Josh, I know. You would be perfect for the lead, I agree. I'm sorry. What can I say?"

"You can say, 'No deal,' and sell my screenplay to another studio. Tell 'em to buzz off."

"Look, Josh, you're not feeling well. You're not in any shape to make a decision. We haven't signed anything yet. Just think about it for a few days. Okay?"

It's not okay. It totally sucks!

"Josh? Is that okay?"

"Just do what you want!" Josh yelled, then abruptly turned off his phone.

Chapter Fifteen

What the hell am I doing here? Maybe I should just disappear.

Josh shivered in the cool morning drizzle of a late June rain, trying to silence the angry voices inside his head. Across the narrow side street, tucked away in a corner of Manhattan, a crew of burly young men aimed powerful lights on a nondescript pub covered in dirty yellow bricks. On the sidewalk in front, a dozen extras of various ages, shapes, and sizes strolled aimlessly, their voices a low hum. A couple of blocks away, the intersection was blocked off with a row of neon orange cones; nearby, a wooden sign propped up at the side of the road announced: *Monumental Studios Prods. It Only Hurts When I Laugh. Dir: M. Labelle.*

Against his will, Josh had sold his beloved screenplay to Monumental Studios.

"Nobody else will look at it, Josh," Paul told him. "Most people in Hollywood have forgotten that you even exist. I'd sell it to them if I were you."

But you're not me. You have no clue how much that screenplay means to me.

"Just take their money and run," Holly told Josh when he turned to her for support. "Screw them."

"But this movie is my dream, my only real chance to make a comeback. And my screenplay is so *personal*. I wrote the lead part for myself. I don't want anyone else to play it."

Holly sighed. "I know Josh, but — "

"*You* were the one who told me to write it," he said, pointing an accusatory finger at Holly. "And I did. If I sell out now, I'll just be another old, fat, washed-up nobody." He paused, then added, "No woman wants to end up with a guy like that."

"Josh, I know you're disappointed, but I don't care whether or not you're a celebrity. I love *you*, Josh Steinberg the *man*, not Josh Steinberg the celebrity. In fact, I would love you even if you never told another joke."

So Josh sold his screenplay. But now he wished he hadn't.

And he also wished he hadn't accepted the unfunny and far too small role he had been offered in the movie: Lou McClain, the unsympathetic boss of the lead character. Most of Lou's dialogue consisted of terse, unexpressive lines: "Uh-huh," "Sure," "Are you crazy?" and "We'll see about that." To make matters worse, Josh, as Lou, was forced to wear uncomfortable, cheap business clothing for the entire shoot, the type of clothing he would never wear in real life: ill-fitting suits; shirts with too-tight collars; drab knit ties.

Josh knew why he had ended up with such a meaningless role: the director, Mike Labelle, had made it clear from the moment they met that he hadn't really wanted Josh to be in the movie at all.

"You're very lucky to get this job," Mike told Josh when he complained about the size of his part.

Josh's eyes glazed over. *Lucky? To get such a dinky role in my own screenplay?*

That was five weeks ago. Five long, uncomfortable weeks of bitter, festering resentments. Josh glared at the pudgy young director, who sat on the steps of the pub sipping a coffee and chatting with one of the camera operators.

Mike Labelle — unlike Josh — wasn't exactly known for comedy. In fact, he'd never directed a comedy. Most of his movies were violent, testosterone-fueled action flicks featuring oversized sweaty, muscular men and their even more muscular guns. But Monumental Studios didn't care; as far as they were concerned, Mike Labelle was a comedy director because of his friendship with the star, Jason Williams.

Josh stared at the tall, dark-haired young star as he emerged from his trailer, smiling and waving at the crew. *I simply can't stand Jason! I just can't.* He knew that Jason's looks got him the leading role in this movie. And even though Jason was the hottest young comic in Hollywood right now — his movies made buckets of money — he wasn't funny. He was famous for his idiotic voice and facial contortions, not for his ability to make people laugh.

As far as Josh was concerned, Jason was the wrong choice to play his lead character, the thoughtful, sensitive, gentle — and *Jewish* — computer geek, Howard Greenberg, now known by the less Jewish name of Hank Andrews. And he also felt that Irina Wallace was the wrong choice for the female lead, Hannah O'Leary. Even though Irina was a stunningly beautiful young woman — tall, dark, and lanky — she hardly fit his vision for the character, a warm, sweet, feisty — and small — woman. A woman like Holly.

Josh pulled out his phone and scanned it for messages. Still nothing.

He couldn't do anything about these poor casting decisions. He had no clout in Hollywood, thanks to his own less than impressive movie credits, a long list of bitter disappointments and dashed dreams: *The Donut Man, Always in Trouble, Loveable Losers, Big Bad Bart Rides Again.*

I guess it's my fault. Every time I got an offer to star in one of those duds, I told myself, "Maybe this turkey will lead to something better. My big breakthrough could be just around the corner."

Josh's big breakthrough never came. No matter how hard he tried — with acting lessons, a strict diet, workouts with a professional trainer — Josh could never manage to snag a leading role in something better, always losing out to taller, slimmer, and far better looking actors. All of the directors of those well-written, well-produced, big-budget movies seemed to see Josh as just another *schmucky* comic. They never gave him a chance.

At least those trashy movies, bad as they were, paid the bills ... for a while. But after a few of them failed to turn a profit, Josh's movie offers dried up, and he began "starring" in TV commercials. Then, when offers for commercials also dried up, Josh found himself "starring" in seedier and seedier TV infomercials.

Out of the corner of his eye, Josh saw one of the extras, a delicately pretty young woman with long, shiny black hair and olive skin, dressed in a white sweater and a white miniskirt, walk over to Jason, giggling. Jason hugged the woman, then he pasted a grotesque, exaggerated smile on his face as she snapped several pictures of him on her phone.

I suppose this job isn't the worst one I've ever had; it's better than "performing" in a TV infomercial. But just being on this pressure cooker of a set made Josh sick to his stomach. And he was lonely. Thanks to Labelle, almost none of the crew or cast members would speak to him.

Josh glanced across the street. Mike and Jason were huddled together, laughing.

He couldn't take this any longer. He just had to hear a friendly voice.

Josh pulled up Holly's number on his phone and called her.

***

Holly was in no mood to talk to Josh. Just that morning, she had helped two clients — a happy, prosperous couple in their fifties — plan a special event, an elaborate, sit-down dinner at an upscale Italian restaurant in Toronto, to mark their twenty-fifth wedding anniversary.

Doug and I were married on the same day as this couple, Holly thought, as she jotted down the pertinent details: five-course meal with dessert, bouquets of red long-stemmed roses on the tables, a band to play oldies after dinner. *One wedding day, two marriages, one divorce.* She entered the calculations for the food bill on a spreadsheet. *I feel like a total failure. Maybe everyone can't be good at marriage. I sure wasn't. I'm not even good at dating; just look at the rocky relationship I have with Josh.*

He keeps telling me he loves me. And, deep down, I believe him. Okay, Josh does perform those funny-but-mean jokes in his act, but he doesn't intend to hurt me. I have to stop taking his words so personally. On the other hand, he'll be surrounded by gorgeous young actresses on the movie set. I do trust him ... but I hope he doesn't forget I exist.

Depressed and anxious and, for the moment, consumed by the work of planning a happy celebration for other people, Holly barely heard her phone ring.

She couldn't be bothered to answer it. If the call was important, whoever it was would call back or leave a message.

***

Josh didn't feel like leaving a message. Frustrated by his unsuccessful attempt to connect with Holly, Josh began to tuck his phone back into his pants pocket when it started to ring. He pulled it out.

"Holly?" he asked.

"It's me," Greg said in his usual cool voice.

Greg was the last person on earth that Josh wanted to talk to. He kept booking the crappiest gigs, like the one at a country-and-western-themed bar in Ohio full of drunks who barely laughed at Josh's best lines.

"I got a call from a club owner."

I found out from another comic on the club circuit that you've been dating Jill. Okay, we broke up a long time ago — and I no longer have feelings for her — but you started seeing her behind my back, you sneaky bastard.

"Said your act was dirty. Especially the sex jokes."

"Sex is a normal and healthy part of life. Besides, anyone running a comedy club shouldn't be so easily offended."

"The owner of the club wasn't offended; a customer was offended and complained about you."

"So, one customer complained. Big deal."

"That's one customer too many. Besides, it's bad for business. Just tone down the sexual stuff."

"Why should I? There's nothing dirty about sex. You yourself have sex, don't you?"

Sure, you do. Admit it.

"Listen, smartass, do you want to keep working in this business or not?"

"Not at those kinds of crappy gigs."

"Beggars can't be choosers. You're not exactly in great demand anymore."

"You're full of crap, Fanelli!"

Out of the corner of his eye, Josh saw Mike staring at him. A cold, unfriendly, *mean* stare.

"Hey, Mr. Big Shot Comic! Your almighty presence is requested on the set."

Josh squirmed at the poisonous tone of Mike's voice. *Okay, asshole. Whatever.* Reluctantly, he trudged across the street, as the sun struggled to shine behind a heavily clouded sky. Mike and Jason, his tormentors, were laughing and pointing at a script that was covered in bright red marks.

Josh's script.

As Josh approached the two men, they abruptly stopped laughing and glared at him.

"Oh, look who's here," Jason said, as he flashed a nasty smile at Josh. Today, his perfectly toned body was clad in a bright yellow jacket and tight blue jeans that had been strategically faded and torn in all the right places. His brilliant blue eyes were shaded by sunglasses, and his thick dark brown hair was tousled.

"What do you guys want? I'm not due on the set for another hour."

"We're having a bit of trouble with the script," Jason said. "It's not funny."

"Jason's part isn't funny," Mike said. "It's also not big enough. You'll have to make some changes." He tossed the injured script at Josh. Before Josh could catch it, it landed at his feet, face down, in the mud.

The nerve of these bloody pricks. "How the hell would you bastards know what's funny? The script is about a Jewish guy, and you guys aren't Jewish. What makes you think you're experts on Jewish humor?"

"You're full of crap, Steinberg!" Jason shot back. "For your information, one of my ancestors happens to be Jewish."

"What, a distant ancestor five hundred years ago? That hardly counts, Williams. You really don't understand my script. Do you want me to explain it to you?"

"Explain what? Any moron could write a better script than this piece of crap."

Before Josh could respond, he felt a hand tugging roughly on his right shoulder.

"I think," Mike said, as he yanked Josh to one side, "that Steinberg and I need to have a serious talk. Alone. Right now."

Josh's heart sank. Jason shot another nasty smile at Josh, then ambled toward his trailer.

Once Jason was out of earshot, Mike got right down to business.

"Look, Steinberg, you can't talk to the star that way. He — not you — is the only reason that this movie is getting made. If you talk to him like that again — and if you don't fix this crappy script good and fast — I won't hesitate to get rid of you. Do you understand?"

"Are you threatening me, Labelle?"

"Do you understand me, Steinberg? Do you *understand me*?"

Josh muttered something unintelligible, snatched up his script from the mud, and, defeated, slowly made his way back across the street to his trailer. As soon as he was inside, Josh tossed the pages into a trash can, picked up his phone, and called Holly.

"Hello, Josh," Holly said in a cheery voice.

"Holly the Brain."

"Is something wrong?"

"Is something wrong?" Josh said, mimicking her voice. "Holly, these assholes are killing what's left of my career. They've ordered me to chop down my already miniscule part and build up Williams's. I should sue you for misguided advice."

"Very funny, but I'm really busy right now. We'll have to talk about this later."

"Don't hang up on me, Holly. We have to talk about this *now*. I can't take these assholes any longer."

"Calm, down. You're still the screenwriter, am I correct?"

"Uh-huh. So what?"

"So, you control what goes into that screenplay, don't you?"

"But I don't. They're ordering me to make changes. I have to make Williams's part bigger and my part smaller."

"So make Williams's part bigger and your part smaller. Make 'em happy."

"But how would that make *me* happy? How would that help *me*?" he demanded, sweat forming on his brow.

"Use your imagination. It's not the size of the part, it's the *quality* of the part."

Josh turned off his phone and retrieved the crumpled pages from the trash can. *Hmm, the quality. Yes, the quality.*

Spreading the pages out on a small table, he switched on his laptop and, with the razor-sharp precision of a skilled surgeon, electronically cut out most of his lines, as dictated by the red marks on the paper. He then grafted a few witty remarks here, some sarcastic retorts there, onto Williams's part — reluctantly and with great difficulty.

Once Williams starts mouthing these lines, he'll try his best to drain every last ounce of humor out of them.

He then turned his attention to his own now humiliatingly shrunken role. Reading over his scanty, meaningless lines, Josh's usually fertile mind suddenly went blank.

What the hell was he going to do with this? Maybe he should just write himself out entirely. Or just take off from this place, not come back, and let these stupid bastards sort out their own mess.

But Josh really couldn't leave. Like it or not, he was chained to this ill-fated movie by bills, debts, and the need to salvage his already precarious professional reputation. He had to keep reading the lines. Keep trying. No matter what.

Josh forced himself to read over his lines again and again.

How was he going to fix the script? He couldn't make Williams funnier … and he resented having to write unfunny lines for himself. But what choice did he have? He was surrounded by small-minded, mean-spirited people who were all too eager to see him fail. To hell with this.

Once again, Josh picked up his phone and called Holly. This time, he was greeted by her voicemail.

"Holly," Josh told the recording, "listen to me very carefully. I'm going to ask Paul to shut down production for a week so I can try to fix this screenplay. I need your help. If you can, please join me in New York. As soon as possible."

Josh paused, then added in a softer voice, "Please come, honey. No matter how busy you are. Please don't abandon me now."

Chapter Sixteen

Two days later, on a warm and humid June evening, Holly boarded a plane for New York.

"I've got the perfect plan for cheering you up," she told Josh when he picked her up at the airport. "Tomorrow night, we're going out to a great restaurant for a nice, comforting kosher dinner. The food you love best: matzoh ball soup, roast chicken, potato latkes — "

"You don't have to go to any trouble," Josh said as the cab driver steered his vehicle onto a packed highway.

"I don't mind. Anyhow, everything's already done. I've made a reservation online. I even invited your dad and stepmom. Your mom said she was too busy to come."

Josh sighed. "Why did you invite them?"

"I thought you'd be pleased. You seemed so stressed out on that movie set. I wanted to do something special."

"But you know I've always had trouble getting along with my dad. Why did you invite him — them?"

"Because he's your *dad*. He's family." Holly paused, then continued in a sober voice, "Don't you want me to meet your family? Are you embarrassed by me or something?"

"Don't be silly. Of course I want you to meet them. But this isn't the best time. Besides, you haven't bothered to introduce me to your own family."

"I promise I'll introduce you to them as soon as your movie shoot wraps up. Relax, Josh. We're going to have a great time tomorrow night."

***

But both Josh and Holly knew that they wouldn't, from the moment that retired judge Harold Steinberg, a tall, gray-haired man in his mid-eighties, greeted them with a scowl and refused to shake Holly's hand. His forty-something trophy wife, Candy, the latest of Harold's four wives, a tall, curvy blonde with a pretty but hard face, muttered a stiff greeting, accompanied by a wan, half-hearted smile.

The tense atmosphere lasted through the entire dinner. Seated across from Josh and Holly in the cozy, dimly lit restaurant at a long polished oak table, Harold barely spoke to his hosts all evening.

"What exactly makes paunchy guys like me irresistible to hot women?" Josh ventured in an attempt to break the uneasy silence as he picked up a Mandelbrot cookie. "Well, for one thing — "

"Knock it off, Josh," Harold said. "You've been cracking these stupid jokes all evening. You're not exactly the world's most talented comedian."

"How would you know? You've never seen my act in a club. You've never even seen me in a movie or on a TV show."

"Look," Harold said, putting down his cutlery and leaning across the table, his voice edged with impatience, "it's obvious. If you really were talented, you'd be a household name. You'd be living in a mansion, flying around the world in a personal jet …"

"Josh doesn't need all that garbage to be successful," Holly said. "He's starred in a popular TV show, made lots of movies, is still in demand on the comedy club circuit after decades of working in a very tough and competitive business. Okay, so maybe he isn't rich, but he's been able to make a comfortable living doing something he loves. He's not exactly starving, is he?"

"Who the hell cares what some *shiksa* thinks of my son?" Harold grunted, looking away from both Josh and Holly.

A ... shiksa? Did he actually call me that? Holly glanced at Josh, an anxious expression on her face.

Josh frowned. "Dad, leave her alone. Please."

"Why should I leave her alone? You saw how rude she was to me."

"Holly didn't mean to be rude. She was just trying to defend me. Besides, she went to a lot of trouble to make you guys feel welcome; she even made reservations for us at a kosher restaurant."

"So what? She was still rude to me."

"I'm sorry," Holly said, blinking back tears. "I was only trying to support Josh." She paused. "And I tried to find a good kosher restaurant. The chicken you ordered came from a kosher butcher — "

"It probably didn't!" Harold shouted, pounding the table so hard with his fist that the cutlery jumped into the air. "Anyhow, you're hardly an expert. You're just a *shiksa*. What the hell are you doing with my son, anyway?"

Holly rose to her feet, glaring down at Harold.

"For your information, Harold — I mean, Judge Steinberg — I tried my very best to find an authentic kosher restaurant! And this *shiksa* happens to love your son a great deal."

"You love him?" Harold waved his hand dismissively. "Sure you do ... for now. But you're not serious about Josh. No woman has ever been serious about Josh."

"You're wrong. I'm very serious about Josh. I'm even thinking of meeting with a rabbi to discuss converting to Judaism."

Josh shot a startled, slightly sharp look at Holly. "You want to convert? Why, Holly? You never mentioned this to me before."

Harold shook his head. "Big waste of the rabbi's time. She wasn't born into the faith. She'll never be a real Jew."

"It's not a waste of time. Leave her alone!" Josh shouted at his father. "Don't listen to him, honey," he added, turning to Holly.

It was too late. Holly had already stormed out of the restaurant.

***

Half an hour later, Josh found himself knocking on the deadbolted door of his hotel room. Harold and Candy, unnerved by Holly's sudden disappearance, had abruptly left the restaurant, ignoring Josh's awkward attempts at polite small talk.

"Honey," Josh said, as he twisted the doorknob, "please let me in."

Josh's words were greeted by muffled sobs.

She wasn't going to open this door. He just knew it. But she was being unfair — he had no control over his pig-headed father and his idiotic wife.

"Holly, I really appreciate your attempt to host a dinner for my family. Okay, so maybe everything didn't go perfectly, but you tried your best." He paused. "And please, don't let my dad get to you. He's mean to almost everybody. He always picked on me, even when I was a kid. My mom couldn't get along with him either; she divorced him when I was a teenager because he tried to control her whole life."

Josh twisted the doorknob again. Still locked. He sighed, a resigned sigh of defeat. This was going to be a lot harder than he thought.

"Look ... okay, you deserve the truth." Josh paused, then drew a deep breath. "My dad was mean to you — and to me — tonight because he's ... jealous of us. He's not getting much action at home from that bitchy Candy."

The hotel room was suddenly filled with the sound of lusty laughter, followed by the clear, distinctive *click* of a deadbolt being released.

Josh opened the door. The room was filled with a shadowy darkness, the type of half-darkness that only appears in the early evening before the sun fades away. Holly was standing at the window, her puffy red eyes at odds with the laughter pouring out of her throat. But as soon as Holly spied Josh, her laughter quickly dissolved into tears.

"Holly," Josh said in a soft voice, taking her into his big, strong arms, "what's wrong? Why are you so upset, dear?"

Holly blew her nose. "You must think I'm an idiot."

"Don't be silly, honey. Why would I think that?"

"Because you got angry at me when I told you about my plans to convert. Aren't you serious about our future together?"

Josh sighed. "Of course I am. Honey, I wasn't angry at you, just surprised. And I'm deeply touched. Out of all the women I have dated, you are the only one who offered to convert for me." He leaned forward and kissed her lightly on the cheek. "Now I really know for sure that you care about me. But you don't have to do it, dear."

"I want to, Josh," Holly said, her eyes softened by tears. "I want to share your life with you."

"But you don't have to do this — "

Just then, Josh's phone rang in his pants pocket. He pulled it out.

"Steinberg?" came the rough voice of Mike Labelle. Josh groaned. "I hope you've been working on that screenplay. We have important deadlines to meet."

Josh muttered an incoherent answer.

"Would it trouble you, Mr. Comic Genius, to email me a few pages tonight?"

Josh had just started to work on the revisions. He didn't have anything to send to Mike.

"I'd like to go over my new material first. I'll try to send you something tomorrow."

"You haven't done any work, have you, Steinberg? That's why you can't send me anything tonight."

Bloody prick! "Look, Mike, I'll send you some material as soon as I can," he responded, then snapped off the phone.

***

Ten days later, a very different Josh Steinberg sat in a small, dark screening room with Mike Labelle, Jason Williams, and several other members of the cast and crew to view that day's rushes ... and the results of Josh's revised screenplay.

I can't wait to see this, Josh thought as Irina Wallace, the actress cast in the leading female role, entered the room and sat next to him. He wasn't impressed with Irina's acting in the movie. As far as he was concerned, her cold and unexpressive personality wasn't right for the character he had created, a warm, bubbly, down-to-earth woman — a woman like Holly. But today, for the first time in ages, he felt so full of energy and spirit and pride, he was almost happy to see Irina.

The ice queen glared at Josh and began texting on her phone.

I don't care. Go on, ignore me. Nobody can frazzle me today.

The rushes didn't disappoint Josh. In fact, he couldn't stop laughing, especially at himself. Most of the other people in the room also laughed — uproariously — at Josh ... but fell strangely silent whenever Jason Williams spoke one of Josh's witty lines, now weighed down by his awkward, leaden delivery. If anything, Williams's now-bloated role, puffed up to match his equally bloated ego, made him even less funny than before, and Josh found himself wincing as the star mangled his carefully crafted turns of phrase.

"Josh, that was brilliant!" said Gus, one of the camera operators, as the lights flooded on. "Keep up the good work."

"Yeah, great work, Josh," Irina smiled as she stretched out her long, slim legs. "Big improvement."

"Thanks, Irina. You were pretty good yourself." Out of the corner of his eye, he spied the director and star, huddled together at the opposite end of the room. They weren't smiling.

"How dare you disobey me, Steinberg!" Mike shouted at Josh a few minutes later when the two of them were sitting alone in a small, dusty office. "I told you to make Jason's part bigger and funnier. I even wrote the changes on the script."

"I did *not* disobey you, Mike. I did make Jason's part a lot bigger and gave him some of the best lines in the picture. I made my own part smaller — "

"You didn't."

"I *did* make my part smaller. I made all of the changes you asked for. If you want, I can show you exactly what changes I made."

Mike shook his head. "You might have made your part smaller, but you also made it funnier. You're stealing all of Jason's scenes."

Josh sighed. "Look, Mike, I tried my best to make Jason's part funnier. It's not my fault if his comic timing sucks."

"*You* look. As I told you before, Jason is the star of this picture. It's your job as the screenwriter to make him look good, not the other way around. Believe me, you're not exactly a box office name. Nobody wants to pay good money to see an old fatso like you star in a movie."

***

Nobody wants to pay good money to see an old fatso. Josh couldn't get the words out of his head, his heart. Back at home in Los Angeles, two days after his brief, nasty meeting with Mike, he kept playing them over and over again in his head, trying to tire them out, rob them of their power to hurt, to shock, to cripple his spirit. But they stuck deep in his psyche, and he just couldn't pull them out.

Josh surveyed his face and body in his bathroom mirror, trying in vain to suck in his protruding belly. He couldn't get rid of that belly, no matter what he did. And he felt so vulnerable and alone. Even though he was a big guy, he was actually defenseless, a big, homely man being bullied by smaller, meaner, and prettier people. And there was absolutely no one in the universe who could help him. Josh knew that Paul had been trying his best to help him; he even met with the studio's executives to try, somehow, to rein in Labelle and Williams, to get them off Josh's back, maybe even replace them. Paul's efforts came to nothing.

Josh never heard back from Paul after he met with Monumental's executives. Paul was too disheartened to speak to him. But Josh knew what had happened. And now, he stood before the mirror alone and lost and confused, as hard reality stared back at him and dared him, taunted him, into taking action, any action.

Warm, salty tears rolled down Josh's cheeks. *Why did I let myself get like this? It's my fault that I got so fat, so bald, so wrinkled. Shit, I can't take it anymore.*

His eyes clouded by tears, Josh reached for his phone and punched in Dr. Chan's number.

"I don't need a consultation!" he yelled at the young woman's voice at the other end of the line. "I know exactly what I want done, and I want it done *fast.* How quickly can you schedule a face-lift, some liposuction, and a hair transplant?"

Chapter Seventeen

Josh didn't bother to keep his appointment with Dr. Chan. Instead, he booked one for the same afternoon with a psychologist, Dr. Craig Riley.

I just have to fix myself inside, Josh thought as he entered the calm, hushed waiting room, its vanilla walls, ivory linen curtains, upholstered beige chairs, and soft, sand-colored carpeting a vision of comforting blandness. *I simply can't live like this anymore. Besides, I promised my mom and Holly that I would start seeing a shrink ... and I cancelled the appointment that Holly booked for me. I have to stop putting it off.*

But after his first session with Riley, Josh felt more hopeless, lost, and deeply sad than ever before.

"You know, Josh," Riley said after Josh recited the latest round of humiliations he suffered at the hands of the studio, "you're not coping very well."

Who the hell could cope with these assholes? Could you?

"The thing is," Riley continued, chewing nervously on a pen, "you really don't have to struggle like this."

I don't? What am I supposed to do, tell them to screw off? That'll teach them a lesson, all right — I'll get fired from the movie, then blacklisted from clubs and movie studios, and then my car will get repossessed.

"And the great thing is that your problem isn't hard to treat. Try this."

He wrote Josh a prescription for an anti-depressant.

Josh filled the prescription as soon as he left the doctor's office. When he got home, he rushed to the kitchen, filled a large glass with tap water, and popped a pill into his mouth.

What the hell am I doing? I could be poisoning myself, for all I know!

Josh spat out the bitter green pill and rinsed it down the sink. He grabbed the bottle from the counter, pried open the top, and then walked into the bathroom and flushed all of the remaining pills down the toilet.

"Stop it, Josh!" Miriam shouted as she watched him flush away the pills. Increasingly alarmed by his deepening bouts of depression, she had shown up at his house, unannounced, the previous morning. "You really need to take those pills. If you don't take them, you'll end up destroying yourself."

"Ma, those pills will destroy my sex drive. And if that happens, for sure I'll end up destroying myself."

"But Dr. Riley prescribed them."

"Dr. Riley is a world-class idiot. Going to him is a big waste of time and money. He's done nothing at all to help me; all he's done is drain what's left of my bank account."

Miriam sighed. "He's only trying to help you. You should listen to him."

"Listen to him? He doesn't listen to *me*! And I paid him good money to listen to me."

That was the problem. No one was listening to Josh.

Certainly not Monumental Studios. Enthralled by the growing popularity of Jason Williams, the studio allowed the star and the director to keep chopping away at Josh's already small role, bit by bit by bit. And especially not Mike Labelle.

"Oh, look! The Great Comedian has decided to grace us with his presence this morning," Mike said as Josh arrived on the set, an abandoned soft drink factory on the outskirts of Pittsburgh, two hours late one cloudy morning in mid-July.

"Mike," Josh responded, trying hard to ignore the glaring eyes of the other actors and crew, "it's not my fault I'm late. My car broke down this morning."

Indeed, it had. Just a few miles south of the set, Josh's old car had overheated, forcing him to pull over to the side of a busy highway. Forty-five long minutes later, a large tow truck pulled up behind Josh's car. The young man operating it, an enthusiastic Josh Steinberg fan, drove Josh to the filming location, peppering his passenger with a long string of questions about his career.

"Do you know how much money you wasted by making everyone wait around for you, Steinberg?"

"Yes, I know. But I did everything I could to get here. I even called you — "

"A professional actor with a good attitude would have made sure that he had reliable transportation to a job. Excuses, excuses, excuses."

There's no point in trying to argue with him. Besides, I have no power to fight back, Josh told himself.

But he did.

The following evening, Josh drove his car, newly strengthened by thousands of dollars' worth of repairs, to a bar on a side street in downtown Pittsburgh for a stand-up gig. The bar, an insignificant-looking hole-in-the-wall, was a small, seedy room full of plastic dark-brown faux-wood tables and chairs, dated chestnut brown wood paneling on the walls, and faded gray-green carpeting speckled with food stains and cigarette burns; the air was stale with the smell of old drunks. It was exactly the type of dive that Josh usually hated. But not tonight.

This bar might be a bit shabby, Josh thought as he walked onto the stage, *but tonight it will become* my *place, the one and only place on earth I can really speak my mind.*

Josh surveyed the sea of excited faces in the audience, feeling his power. He was dressed powerfully, too, in a finely tailored black shirt and black pants.

Josh smiled warmly at the audience. "You probably wonder why I'm in town. I'm here to make a movie with a famous director named Mike Labelle." He paused. "I never realized what a gifted comedy director Mike is. Just look at all the legendary comedies he's directed: *Ten Gun Massacre*, *Murder, Inc.*, and *Destroy the Earth!*

The audience roared with laughter.

"My co-star in this movie is a real handsome guy, Jason Williams. Looking at him, it's hard to buy into Darwin's theory that people were descended from apes thousands of years ago. I mean, it's only been a couple of generations in Jason's family."

The audience laughed louder and harder and longer.

"And, interestingly enough, the hero of the movie was supposed to be a Jewish guy," Josh said. "The hero is played by Jason." Josh paused, moving in for the kill. "I auditioned for the part, but the director told me I wasn't Jewish enough."

The audience laughed again. Josh beamed, savoring the warm reception. They really got him! What a nice change after spending his day with a couple of idiots who were too stupid to appreciate his talent.

Out of the corner of his eye, Josh spied a young woman seated at a table near the stage, holding up a phone. It looked like she was taking some photos of him. It was nice to know he still had some loyal fans.

But Josh's "loyal fan" got him into deep trouble when he returned to the movie shoot at the abandoned soft drink factory three days later.

"Who the hell do you think you are, Steinberg?" yelled Mike as Josh, radiating confidence, strode onto the set that morning.

"Good morning to you, too, Mike. What a nice greeting."

Scowling, Mike shook his head.

What the hell is going on? Why does he always have to be so pissed off at me? Glancing around, Josh saw dozens of pairs of eyes, belonging to actors, crew members, and extras, critically scrutinizing his face for any signs of weakness.

"Mike, look, I wasn't late today — "

"That's not the problem. *I'm* the person in charge of this movie. I don't think you understand that."

What is he talking about? What brought all this crap on? Josh surveyed the faces surrounding him for clues, only to be met with nothing but blank stares.

"What are you talking about?" Sweat formed on his brow. "Why are you so mad at me?"

"You know what I'm talking about."

"No, I don't."

"You questioned my credentials. In public, of all places."

"I did?"

"God, you're stupid," Mike said, raising the volume of his voice. "You had the nerve to make fun of my directing credentials in some comedy club."

Holy shit! He had forgotten about that woman in the club with her cell phone. She must have posted a clip of his act online. How else would Mike know what Josh had said about him in his act?

"I was only joking," Josh said, meekly lowering his eyes.

"*You* are the joke, Steinberg. *I'm* the one with the reputable and successful career. *I'm* the one who's still in demand these days. And *I'm* the boss on this set. You, on the other hand, are none of those things. You're nothing but an old, cheap, washed-up comic who's lucky to have any job." He paused. "Have I made myself clear?"

Josh stared at Mike for several seconds. Then, without saying a word, he turned around and walked slowly back to his trailer, his eyes downcast, his spirit crushed.

***

While Mike was yelling at Josh Steinberg, a roomful of small children was screaming at Holly Brannigan.

How can such tiny people make so much noise? Holly wondered as the colony of three dozen four- and five-year-olds swarmed around her, knocking over trays of chocolate chip cookies and depositing trails of crumbs all over the thick brown carpet. Holly and the children were celebrating the fourth birthday of shy, dark-haired Amanda, the daughter of two well-heeled lawyers, at Make Your Own Bear. Amanda's parents hired Holly to throw a make-your-own-teddy-bear party for their daughter at the small, brightly lit shop.

Holly's thoughts were interrupted by an eruption of loud crying from a small boy at the opposite end of the room, his wails piercing her eardrums and making her head throb.

I can't take this anymore, Holly shuddered, closing her eyes and covering her ears with both hands, desperate to shut out the relentless, painful barrage of noise. Spying a dark and empty room at the end of the hall, she dashed toward it as fast as she could, tripping over a half-finished, headless teddy bear along the way. Holly picked up the discarded plush carcass, rushed into the room, switched on the light, and shut the door.

Sighing, she sat down on an uncomfortable plastic chair. Almost absentmindedly, she pulled out her phone from the front pocket of her denim blazer and scanned its screen for messages.

Three new voicemails from Josh. Holly played the first one.

"Holly, I can't take these people anymore," Josh said in the first voicemail, his voice wretched with anguish. "I'm ready to quit right now."

I wonder what happened. What did someone say or do to make Josh so upset? Was it that stupid director Labelle, or someone else?

Hands shaking, Holly played Josh's second message.

"I'm a real loser. I don't know why you're sticking with me."

You are not a loser! The people who are treating you like garbage are the real losers.

She paused, almost afraid to play the third message. *But I have to. Josh might be in trouble, for all I know.*

Holly played the third message.

"Holly," Josh said, his voice even more mournful than before, "I feel so *alone*. I can't take this crap anymore! I don't know what to do."

Josh really needed her. She had to get in touch with him — now! Holly immediately called Josh. And texted him. No response, not even a voicemail message.

Holly turned off the phone. *I have to do something, but what?* She couldn't reach Josh … but somehow, some way, she just had to let him know that she cared about him, that he wasn't alone.

She heard a resounding *thud*. Flinging open the door, she rushed out of the room, clutching the teddy bear torso in one hand, just in time to see a pair of small hands push dozens of teddy bear parts onto the carpet: glass eyes, plush heads of various sizes, miniature articles of clothing. Dumbfounded, Holly watched as they slid off a table and spread out over the carpet, then she glanced at the teddy bear torso in her hand.

She knelt down to pick up the pieces from the floor. *So many possibilities … so many personalities … for* my *bear.*

***

The next day, while taking a mid-afternoon nap on a large, saggy bed in a musty motel room just outside of Pittsburgh, Josh was awakened by an abrupt knock at the door.

He hoped it wasn't some jerk from the movie studio. Peering out the window, which was shaded by filmy pale green curtains, he spied a courier carrying a large box with pink shipping papers attached to the top of it.

"Are you Josh Steinberg?" the man asked when Josh opened the door.

Josh nodded.

"Package for you."

Josh quickly signed the papers and took the box. Tearing it open, he found a small yellow Post-it note inside: *To my real teddy bear. Love, Holly.* Hidden under a layer of white tissue paper, Josh found a large, golden plush teddy bear with big brown eyes, dressed in a white polo shirt and beige chinos, a tiny gray plastic microphone attached to one paw. On the bear's head was a tiny black velvet kippah, the traditional head covering worn by Hebrew men.

Where on earth did Holly get this? She must have had the bear made just for me. He examined the teddy bear again. *As a matter of fact, this teddy bear is me.*

Josh called Holly, only to get her voicemail.

No, I won't be leaving a message. There's a much better way to thank her.

The following morning, bleary-eyed and weary from long hours of work, Holly arrived at her office, sat down at her desk, and promptly turned on her computer. She scanned her email for new messages.

A brand-new message from Josh! I hope he's okay, she thought as she clicked on the email.

Greetings, Holly the Brain, began Josh's email. *Please click on the link in this message. It's essential viewing.*

Holly clicked on the link. A video clip with Josh — dressed exactly like the teddy bear she sent him — popped up on the screen. Josh stood on the stage of a club with a guitar slung around his neck. In one hand he held something large, golden, and familiar.

"This," Josh said, holding up the fuzzy object in front of him, "is what a certain lady thinks of me."

It's the teddy bear I sent to Josh, she gasped, turning up the volume.

Josh seated the teddy bear on a folding chair behind him. Smiling warmly at the audience, he started to strum the guitar.

"I'm nothing but a teddy bear," he sang, "just a Jewish teddy bear …"

Just then, Diana burst into Holly's office, scowling.

"Turn that thing down, Holly. I'm trying to finish a rush job."

Holly responded with peals of laughter.

"… but I don't care," Josh sang, strumming the guitar, "'cause I have Holly, Holly, who's kinda small-y …"

"How can you possibly laugh at that?" Diana demanded, shaking her head. "He's making fun of you again."

"… some little girls never outgrow their big teddy bears," Josh sang.

The audience laughed and applauded robustly.

But nobody laughed harder at Josh's act than Holly.

"He's not really laughing at me," she reassured Diana as the video drew to a close. "He's serenading me."

"Hardly."

"Diana," Holly began as she closed Josh's email, "I laughed at Josh's act because it was funny. And I don't care anymore if Josh makes fun of me, because I know how he really feels about me."

"You're just trying to make yourself feel better."

Holly didn't respond. *Josh seemed a bit anxious in that video clip*, she thought. *He was just a little too frantic and eager to please. For all I know, he might still be obsessed with Victor's death. He sounded really depressed in those voicemails.*

"Holly, did you hear what I just said?"

"Yes." She glanced out the window, trying hard to gather her thoughts. "I'm leaving on a business trip tonight. Just for a few days. You can look after things while I'm gone. Okay?"

"Do you really need to keep chasing after this buffoon?" Diana asked, then sighed, "I guess I have no choice."

Holly looked away from the window and smiled at Diana. "Thanks, Diana. I really appreciate it."

Diana shrugged then turned and walked out of the room.

Holly scanned her calendar for the meetings she would need to reschedule.

She hoped that Josh was okay. It looked like he really needed her now. But what could she possibly do to help him?

Chapter Eighteen

The early morning sun, slightly weak for late July, cast a harsh glare on the tall, narrow red brick box, pockmarked with broken windows and ugly black iron balconies. The old, forbidding structure seemed more like a prison than an apartment building, created more to confine the urban poor than to provide the comforts of home.

The actors and crew had gathered in front of the building, located in one of the poorest neighborhoods in New York, to shoot that day's scenes. Their surroundings, so harsh and gloomy, cast a deep pall. That is until Josh Steinberg, dressed in a stiff gray polyester suit and a navy-and-white striped tie, strode onto the set, a warm smile on his face.

"Wow!" Josh exclaimed with fake enthusiasm as he surveyed the seedy building. "What a great location!" A few people tittered mildly. "I'm sure Jason is thrilled to be back in the old 'hood," he added in a bright, robust voice.

"Maybe he never left!" one of the camera operators, a slight, red-haired young man with a red beard, shouted back.

Several crew members, actors, and extras laughed heartily. But not Jason. Dressed in a form-fitting green t-shirt and blue jeans, his hair carefully mussed, the young actor walked up to Josh and tapped him roughly on the shoulder.

"What the hell was that supposed to mean, Steinberg?"

Josh wheeled around, an expression of mock surprise on his face. "What was what supposed to mean?"

"You know what I'm talking about. That crack you just made about my origins."

"I didn't say anything about your origins," Josh said, rolling his eyes. "I was only joking."

"Joking? At my expense?"

"Look, it was just a joke. God, you take yourself way too seriously."

"You're the joke, Steinberg. You better take that stupid comment back or I'll have you thrown off this movie in no time."

Josh shrugged. *I don't give a shit about what he thinks of me.* Forcing himself to smile at Jason, he said, "Okay, Jason, I take it back. Whatever." And with that, Josh turned and strolled calmly down the street to his trailer.

I better hide out until the prick calms down. It's too hard for me to handle all this crap so early in the morning. I need some time to think.

Two of the extras, a young man and a middle-aged woman, were standing on the sidewalk, talking and laughing animatedly. As Josh passed them, they instantly fell silent, staring at him with a mixture of annoyance and curiosity.

Josh knew that he needed to look over his lines, but he didn't really want to. As far as he was concerned, his lines were all-too-visible reminders of his insignificant, unfunny role in this movie. The movie Josh created for *himself, his* special vision, now shrunk down by petty minds inflated by oversized egos. He just had to force himself to get through this shoot. Just get through it, take the money, and ignore all of the bullshit.

Just as Josh grabbed the door handle of the trailer, he heard footsteps, loud and clumsy. Turning around, he spied a woman with shoulder-length pale blonde hair dressed in a black t-shirt and thigh-length denim shorts, her face covered by a pair of sunglasses with large round black frames, her feet clad in a pair of high-heeled black sandals.

It was one of the extras. Josh had noticed her when he came on the set this morning. Something about her just seemed to be off. Josh wondered if Labelle liked to hire weird, sleazy street people. Or maybe she was Labelle's girlfriend ... or even a prostitute he picked up last night. Wouldn't surprise him.

Josh glared at her. The woman, teetering dangerously in her high-heeled sandals, stared back at him, smiling nervously.

"Whoever you are, I'm in no mood to sign autographs this morning. And it's very rude of you to invade my privacy."

"Since when have I, of all people, ever invaded your privacy?" the woman responded in a familiar voice. Hastily, she peeled off the blonde wig and dark sunglasses and tossed them onto the grass, then kicked off the sandals.

"Holly! What are you doing here?"

Holly smiled. Without saying another word, she grabbed Josh's hand and led him into the trailer, then shut the door.

"I was worried about you," she said as soon as they entered the trailer. "You seemed so edgy, so desperate, the other day."

"I did?" Josh asked, as he sat down on a hard gray metal chair.

"Don't you remember those voicemails you left on my phone?" she said, seating herself across from Josh. "Something about you not being able to 'take these people' anymore?"

"I shouldn't have bothered you."

"That's okay, I want you to bother me. Anyhow, I thought it was a good idea to get a job as an extra on your movie so I could check on you. From what I saw out there today, it looks like you really are getting bullied."

Josh sighed and took Holly's hands in his. "Don't worry about me, dear. I can handle these assholes." He paused. "You're very sweet. No other woman would have ever done something like this for me." He glanced at his watch. "I have to learn my lines for my next scene. Why don't we plan to have dinner together tonight?"

"I didn't come all the way out here just to have dinner with you." She winked slyly at him.

"I really do have to work on my lines. I can't spend time with you right now."

Rising to her feet, she pulled the tattered black t-shirt over her head and flung it into Josh's face.

He tried hard not to drool over her sexy black lace corset. "I'm busy right now. We can do this later — "

Holly peeled off the tight denim shorts, revealing a black satin garter belt holding up a pair of seamed black stockings, and kicked them vigorously across the room. Pulling Josh to his feet, she slowly took off his clothes, stripping him down to his white cotton undershirt and boxer shorts.

"There, isn't that better? So much more comfortable."

"Not now," Josh protested, growing hard.

"Shut up, Steinberg, and kiss me. Now."

With that, Holly flung her arms around Josh, pulling him close to her, and kissed him long, hard, and deep.

Josh glanced at his watch again. "Holly, we can't do this now."

Holly pushed Josh firmly back onto the chair, then plopped down onto his lap, wrapping her legs around his body. "Make me stop."

"Naughty girl." Josh kissed her lustily on the mouth. "Dirty temptress. Lowly wench. Strumpet!"

Josh quickly pried Holly's legs away from his body and rose to his feet. Scooping her up into his arms, he carried her to the other end of the trailer and gently laid her down on a small couch. In an instant, he had pulled down his boxer shorts and climbed on top of her.

"Mmmm," Holly moaned with pleasure as he entered her.

"Mmmm yourself, you naughty little thing."

Holly laughed lightly. Josh thrust deeper and deeper, the heavy weight of his body making the couch shake vigorously.

"You wanted this, didn't you? This is a lot more fun than memorizing some dull lines, isn't it?"

Josh grunted his agreement, continuing to thrust, making the couch shake harder.

"Steinberg! What the hell are you doing in there?" a man shouted from outside the trailer.

Startled, Josh pulled out of Holly and glanced out the postage-stamp-sized window above the couch, which was half-covered by faded curtains. The angry face of Mike Labelle stared back at him.

"Answer me!" Mike pounded so hard on the window that Josh thought the glass would shatter. "I'm not paying you to sleep with whores."

"What's going on?" Holly asked, sitting up, a dazed expression on her face.

Shaking uncontrollably, Josh pulled on his shirt, boxer shorts, and trousers, then grabbed Holly's t-shirt and shorts and flung them at her.

"Put these on *now*. Holy shit, we're in big trouble. Why doesn't the prick just mind his own business?"

"Steinberg!" Mike yelled again, rapping harder on the small window. "If you don't come out of there right now —"

Panting and wild-eyed, Josh thrust the trailer door open and stepped outside.

"Hi, Mike," Josh said, attempting to mask his fear with a smile. "Just trying to relax a bit before the next scene."

Mike glared at Josh, his face reddened by the rough wind. "Who the hell is she?" he demanded, pointing a finger at the flustered Holly, now dressed in her t-shirt and shorts. "Some dirty whore you picked up off the street?"

Dirty whore? I was on your set this morning, you bastard. Don't you remember me?

"Mr. Labelle," Holly began, "nobody 'picked me up off the street.' I was hired as an extra for this movie."

"Whoever you are, you're no longer employed here," he told Holly. "Get lost." Turning to Josh, he added, "You have real nerve. Bringing this tramp into your trailer and sleeping with her on my time. I should get rid of you, too."

Josh sighed. In the distance, he could see the crew members, actors, and extras huddled together, listening intently to their conversation. *No, I should have you fired for endlessly bullying and harassing me, you stupid asshole. But I don't have the power to do anything.*

Holly stepped out of the trailer, picked up the wig, sunglasses, and sandals from the grass, and handed them to Mike, a calm expression on her face.

"Mr. Labelle, I only took a job as an extra on your set because you've been treating Josh like crap; he was upset and needed someone to talk to."

"Don't you dare speak to me that way. Get off my set!"

"You're the one who should get off this set. You have the right to disagree with Josh, but you have no right whatsoever to keep picking on him. No one deserves to be treated that way."

"Holly," Josh interrupted her, "don't worry about me. I'm fine. And mind your own business!" he yelled at the group of actors, crew members, and extras who had inched closer to Josh's trailer, their faces a sea of mean stares and malicious smiles.

Mike glanced at the small, motley group, then back at Josh. "Are you going to make her leave, or do I have to call in a security guard to get rid of her?"

"Don't bother. I can get rid of myself," Holly told Mike. "But let me make something clear: *no human being deserves to be treated like crap!* Remember that." Before Mike had a chance to respond, Holly turned around and walked down the street, a jaunty spring punctuating every step, and hailed a cab.

Mike stared, dumb with surprise, as Holly got into the cab and drove away.

Josh, buttoning up his now-sweaty shirt, pasted a fake smile on his face.

"Not seeing much action, Mike?" he asked the director in a teasing voice, as the people around them filled the air with peals of laughter.

Chapter Nineteen

I still can't believe I got through it, Josh sighed. He was sitting by the pool, sipping his morning coffee as he watched two squirrels chase each other around the backyard, the early November sun casting shadows on the water. It had been more than three months since that horrible movie shoot ended, but he kept having nightmares about it. He just had to look on the bright side. No more long hours of retakes. No more endless butchering of his script. And no more bullshit from the studio or those two idiots, Labelle and Williams. It was finally all over.

It wasn't really all over, of course. Monumental Studios had scheduled a press conference after the shoot at a hotel in Los Angeles. The producer, the director, and all of the stars had agreed to show up to promote the movie.

But not Josh Steinberg.

The hell with them. Josh tore up the invitation, engraved on fine white linen paper, which had landed in his mailbox the previous afternoon. Maybe he should hold his own press conference instead. Tell the whole world what these assholes were really like, tell everybody how they stole his ideas and then jerked him around. But it wasn't worth the hassle; they would probably sue him, and he just couldn't take any more garbage from them.

Josh's phone rang on the small white metal table beside him. He picked it up.

"Josh, I've got a lucrative gig for you at The Gag Shop Comedy Club in Toledo," Greg said. "Do you want it?"

You're offering me a "lucrative" gig? Since when?

"Is the pay really decent? And when is it?"

"Believe it or not, the pay's generous. And it's next Saturday night."

The night of the press conference! The perfect excuse to miss it.

"Sure, I'll take it."

"Are you sure? A big-shot comic like you settling for a gig in a Toledo club?"

Lay on the sarcasm. Just bring me the gigs. I don't care. For once in my life, I've found a woman who can really make me happy.

***

The following Saturday night, onstage at The Gag Shop, with his beloved in the audience, Josh — in his own indirect way — found himself expressing his deeper feelings for Holly.

"Being a big guy, I used to only date big women — the tall, statuesque ladies," Josh began, a wide, self-conscious grin slowly spreading across his face. He paused, then gestured to Holly, who was seated at a table at the front of the room. "Then I met this little lady." He paused again, moving in for the kill. "What can I say? The smaller the woman, the bigger the firecracker."

The audience — including Holly — roared with laughter.

Thank God Holly laughed. I'm glad she trusts me.

"And she's nutty about us Jewish guys. I guess she found out that we're hung a certain way."

"You sure are, Steinberg."

Startled, Josh glanced around the room for the heckler, only to see Holly beaming up at him.

"Excuse me?!" Josh shouted at Holly in a mock-angry voice. "Did you just heckle me?"

"Heckle you?" Holly said, trying hard not to laugh.

"Quit playing stupid games, Brannigan. Come up here if you have something to say to me."

"Come up … where? On the stage?"

"Yes, of course."

"I can't. I don't belong up there. I'm not a comedian."

"Then you should have kept your big mouth shut."

The audience roared with laughter again.

"Are you going to come up here, Brannigan? Or do I have to drag you up here myself?"

Head hung in mock shame, Holly reluctantly climbed up onto the stage.

Josh grinned. "Now, Holly, please tell me one thing: Did you just say what I thought you said?"

"Josh," Holly responded in a loud whisper, "cut it out."

"Did you just say what I thought you said?" Josh repeated in a loud voice. When Holly failed to respond, he said in an even louder voice, "Did you just agree with me when I talked about Jewish men being … *you know*?"

Holly sighed. "Josh, please let it go."

"So, you want me to ignore what you just said?" Josh asked, staring intently at Holly. Out of the corner of his eye, Josh spied a small elderly woman in a pale pink shirtdress staring at him from a table in the corner, a hostile expression on her face. *There's at least one of those in every club. If they're so easily offended, why don't they stay home where they belong?*

"Josh," Holly said, a nervous expression clouding her face, "stop it, please."

"Why should I ignore what you just said? Are you … ashamed?" When Holly failed to respond, he added in a loud voice, "Answer me."

The audience giggled.

Shit, Holly thought, *what can I say now? How the hell can I get out of this?*

"I-I'm sorry. I have nothing against Jewish men — "

"Holly the Brain, this is a *comedy* act. You can do better than that."

"But I'm not a comedian. I'm just a normal person."

The audience laughed again.

"Okay, Holly," Josh said when the laughter died down, "so you're not a comedian, you're just a comedian's stooge."

A few audience members guffawed. The elderly woman glared at Josh. She turned to the slim, sandy-haired young man seated beside her and whispered something into his ear.

"Do you find Jewish men unmanly or something?" Josh asked Holly, a note of vulnerability creeping into his voice. "What do you really think of me, anyway?"

Holly drew a deep breath. "Josh," she began, searching carefully for the right words, "you're a great guy, a real, loveable ... *schlemiel.*"

The audience laughed uproariously.

Holly felt her face getting hot. *What did I just say?* she asked herself. Josh looked at her with a sad expression on his face and shook his head. "I meant ... I just called you a loveable guy. Didn't I?"

"Holly," Josh began, wagging a finger at her, "get your Yiddish words straight. A *schlemiel* is *not* loveable. *Oy vah!*"

More laughter.

"Anyhow," Josh continued, his face and voice now solemn, "I guess what I really want to know is how a beautiful lady like yourself could possibly be attracted to a big, fat guy like me."

Holly smiled at Josh and gently squeezed his hand. "Well ... big men are vulnerable ... and soft ... and the combination of big, soft, and vulnerable is very sexy." She paused. "Big guys like you are cuddly teddy bears. Some girls never lose their love of teddy bears, even when they grow up. Especially when they grow up." She winked coyly at Josh.

Josh rolled his eyes. "Something stuck in your eye, Brannigan?"

The audience laughed.

Without waiting for a reply, Josh yelled, "Go in the ladies' room to wash it out! And get off the stage. You're stealing my act."

Grinning, Holly climbed off the stage, accompanied by the sound of raucous laughter, applause, and loud whistling.

Thank God that ordeal is finally over, she told herself. *How did he manage to trick me into joining his act?*

"Good night, everyone!" Josh said, waving at the audience. "And thanks for coming and for putting up with this craziness tonight." As he climbed off the stage, he saw Holly walking toward him, accompanied by the angry-looking elderly woman and the lanky young man. It didn't look good.

Holly smiled. "Josh, I'd like to introduce you to my family. I decided to bring them along to keep me company on the trip. I hope you don't mind."

Of course I mind! You should have warned me that you planned on bringing your mom here tonight. My act wasn't exactly fit for elderly ears.

"Mom," Holly said, turning to the elderly woman, "this is Josh Steinberg. Josh, this is my mom."

"I'm Margaret Brannigan," the elderly woman said, extending her hand.

Josh shook Margaret's hand, an uneasy smile pasted on his face. "I guess Holly's dad couldn't make it tonight?"

"He died fifteen years ago," Holly said, a pained expression in her eyes.

"Oh," Josh mumbled. "Sorry to hear that."

"And this," Holly said, turning to the young man, who was dressed in a black t-shirt emblazoned with a rock band logo in neon yellow and faded blue jeans, "is my son, Kyle. He's a university student."

"Hi, Kyle," Josh said, extending his hand. "Let's all sit down and have a drink," he added, pointing to a table in a dark corner. The spacious room, packed with young couples, was tastefully decorated, with dark green walls, red and gold Tiffany-style lamps, solid hardwood floors, sleek glass-topped tables, and high-backed cushioned wicker chairs.

It's definitely a step up from the places I've been playing, Josh thought, as the four of them made their way to the table. It looked like Greg had been selling Josh as the "star" of an upcoming "major movie." Or maybe, just maybe, Josh's online shenanigans with Holly boosted his ticket sales. Maybe he should make a fool of himself online more often.

"So, Margaret — Mrs. Brannigan," Josh began as soon as they were seated, "did you have fun tonight? Did you like my act?"

"It was very nice, Josh," Margaret said, smiling.

"Glad you liked it."

"But I have to tell you ... well, it was kind of dirty."

Dirty to you. Nobody else in the audience seemed to think my act was dirty.

"You enjoyed Josh's show, didn't you, Kyle?" Holly asked.

"It was great," Kyle said in a flat and unenthusiastic voice.

Great? Is that all you can say? Wasn't I funny?

"Was it what you expected?" Josh asked.

"What I ... expected?" Kyle asked, squirming in the chair. "To be honest, I wasn't expecting anything. I never heard of you before."

Never heard of me? Are you kidding? I'm the Jewish Comedy King — everyone has heard of me.

"I thought Josh did an excellent job tonight!" Holly said, smiling a little too eagerly at Josh. She sighed. "I guess Josh's sense of humor isn't for everybody."

"Yeah, I guess I'm an acquired taste." Josh glanced around the room, his eyes darting nervously from table to table. "Looks like the waitress forgot to take our order."

"Forget the drinks," Holly told Josh. "Let's get out of here and go someplace better to eat. There's a good pizza restaurant near here — "

"Holly," Margaret said, "Kyle and I are tired. We're driving home early tomorrow, and we need to get to bed."

"But Mom, the pizza place is just across the street."

"We really can't go," Kyle said. "Some other time."

"I'm sorry, Josh," Holly said, rising from her chair. "Looks like I have to drive them back to their motel. We'll all get together for dinner soon. I promise."

Sure you will. I can hardly wait.

"Oh, that's okay," Josh said, trying to disguise his hurt with a breezy wave of his hand. "Hope you have a good trip home," he said to Margaret and Kyle.

They didn't respond.

"I'm sorry, Josh," Holly said, hugging him. "You really were funny tonight." She paused. "You're not hurt, are you?"

I am, but so what? I seem to get hurt in comedy clubs all the time. Maybe I really should give up on the comedy business.

"No." Josh smiled at Holly. "You're not hurt either, are you? I was pretty rough on you up there."

"Of course not. I just need to brush up on my Yiddish." She kissed Josh lightly on the mouth. "*Mazel tov*, baby!"

"Yeah. *Mazel tov.*" Josh got up from the table, as he watched the three of them walk away. "Whatever."

"Josh!"

Josh turned to face Arnie, the manager of The Gag Shop, a beefy, muscular man with strawberry blond hair and a ruddy complexion.

"You nailed it tonight, Josh," Arnie smiled. "And your girlfriend, she was great, too."

I just live for praise like that. Thank God someone in this club wasn't offended by my act.

"Thanks, Arnie."

"Is she part of your act?"

"Not if I can help it."

"Buy you a beer? You must be thirsty from all that talking."

Before Josh could respond, he heard his phone ringing in his jacket pocket. He pulled it out.

"Steinberg!" snarled Mike. "What the hell are you doing?"

"Mike, I — "

"You were supposed to show up at the press conference tonight. Why weren't you there?"

"Something important came up."

"The hell it did. You were too busy to show up at the press conference but not too busy to pick up a gig in Toledo."

"I booked the gig months ago."

"Sure you did. Anyhow, there's a sneak preview of your brilliant movie on Monday night. Some very powerful critics and reporters will be there. *You* better be there."

"But I can't. I have to — "

"Steinberg, did you hear me? I said you *have* to be there. You don't have a choice. If you don't show up on Monday night, I'll personally make sure that you're blacklisted by every movie studio, TV network, and comedy club in the country."

Okay, asshole. "Where is it?" he asked, then quickly jotted down the name of the theater on the back of a napkin.

Resigned, Josh hung up. Only two days until the preview. There was no time to do anything. He had to rush back to Los Angeles, take his tux to the dry cleaners, find a date …

Josh started to pull up Holly's number, but then changed his mind.

He couldn't take Holly — she had an important meeting with a big client in a couple of days. There was no one else he could ask out, but he had to take a date to the preview. But who?

Chapter Twenty

The following morning, Josh flew back to Los Angeles with only one thing on his mind: finding a date for the preview of his movie. And he only had a day to do it.

That evening, he decided to tackle the problem by paying a visit to The Laugh Quest, a local comedy club, to see its current headliner, Jill Boudreau. The small room was decorated like a cabin, with log walls, dark brown wood planks on the floors, and brown wood picnic tables. A smattering of moose heads, mounted on the walls, stared glassy-eyed at the customers.

"Here she is!" exclaimed a short, thin young man, dressed in a red-and-black plaid shirt, from the stage. "Please welcome ... Jill Boudreau!"

Jill stepped onto the stage, a wobbly smile pasted on her face, accompanied by light applause. Her long, glossy blonde hair had been chopped to a more manageable shoulder length; her abbreviated, form-fitting dresses had been abandoned for a black, stretchy tunic and simple black leggings. She wore minimal makeup — just a little blush on her cheeks and bright red lipstick — and deep, tired-looking bags had formed under her blue eyes.

Jill's act wasn't much better than her appearance.

"As you can see," she began, gently rubbing a conspicuous baby bump, "I got myself knocked up."

A faint guffaw from the back of the room. Josh winced.

"Ah, the joys of pregnancy. The sudden weight gain, the sleepless nights."

The joys of pregnancy? You've got to be kidding.

"The best part of pregnancy has to be the morning sickness. You eat breakfast, then throw it up. It's nature's way of controlling your weight."

Maybe it is, but it's not funny.

Jill clutched her abdomen and made an exaggerated retching sound. A couple of people laughed.

All she's doing is exploiting her condition. How unimaginative can you get?

Finally, it was over.

"Thank you," Jill said to the audience, as they applauded hesitantly. She hastily climbed off the stage and made her way to Josh's table.

"Great work, Jill!" Josh smiled as she sat down across from him.

"Josh! What a nice surprise." Her voice was tired, haggard, and sad.

"Just thought I'd check out your act."

"How bad was I?" she asked, lowering her voice. "You can tell me the truth."

Josh smiled gently. "You were great, kid." He paused. "But you don't seem very happy. Are you okay?"

Jill frowned. "I wish I were okay. My boyfriend is making my life hell. Somehow, he found out about my stand-up career. He's been pressuring me to give it up; he's also been complaining about bad publicity concerning my pregnancy. I guess he thinks it'll jeopardize his business deals. The truth, though, is that he heard some rumors about a romance between Greg and me and became jealous. Last month, with no warning, he turned up at a comedy club that I was working at in New York, proposing marriage and promising to take care of me and the baby for the rest of our lives. Of course, that was only on condition that I give up my stand-up comedy career for good."

"Is that what you plan to do?"

"Yes, well, sort of. I don't love Jacques, not really, but he *should* provide financial support for his own child." She sighed. "Anyhow, I have a plan. I'll marry him, divorce him after the baby is born, take whatever settlement I can get, then return to the States with the kid and relaunch my stand-up career." She took a sip from her bottle of mineral water. "Beat the bastard at his own game."

"Oh." He paused. "But what about Greg? How does he feel about your plan? You're still dating him, aren't you?"

"Greg?" Jill sighed again. "I don't know where he is. When I told him about my plan — and I did tell him that I wasn't serious about Jacques — he disappeared. I can't find him." She paused. "Do you know where he is? Could you please tell him to call me?"

"I'll try my best, honey. I'm sorry to hear you've been having such a hard time."

"What about you, Josh? You've been doing pretty well, haven't you, with that movie ..."

"It's really the movie from hell. I wish I'd never had anything to do with it," he said, then proceeded to recount the long list of indignities he had suffered at the hands of the director and star.

"You don't deserve to be treated like that," Jill said, shaking her head. "I wish I could do something to help you out."

"Actually," Josh began, a nervous smile playing around his lips, "you can do something for me. I need someone to go with me to a preview of my movie tomorrow night."

"You want me to go? In this condition?"

"Look, Boudreau, you owe me big-time. I got you started in this business, coached your act, helped you find your first bookings."

"Plus, I stood you up at the altar."

Josh winced.

"Okay, Josh, if you don't mind my delicate condition, I'll go." Josh sighed with relief. "But don't be surprised if I throw up in front of the theater."

"Some comics will do anything for publicity."

Thank God this problem was out of the way. Now, all he had to do was to get through this preview. Maybe it wouldn't be as bad as he thought. He just wished Holly could be with him tomorrow night. In fact, he'd better call her soon to let her know what was going on.

***

Holly didn't answer her phone when Josh called her a couple of hours later.

I don't have the time to speak to anyone right now, she thought, as she steered her vehicle around cars, minivans, and hulking trucks on the crowded highway.

"Thank God this trip is finally over," Margaret said, glancing out of the front seat passenger window at the blue sky and the glowing sun, as a gentle autumn breeze swept decayed leaves onto the road. "I've never been so bored in my entire life."

"What do you mean?" Holly asked, as a brown minivan abruptly cut in front of her car. "Why were you so bored?"

"That club. That horrible, horrible club. Crowded, noisy, ugly decor."

Don't start on me, Holly silently protested. *It's been a long, hard day, and I simply don't have the energy to fight back.*

"I thought it was a nice place," she declared, maneuvering her car into a less-crowded lane. "You liked the club, didn't you, Kyle?"

"It was okay," Kyle responded, half-asleep in the backseat.

"At least Josh was funny," Holly said.

"No, he wasn't," Margaret said, kicking off her shoes and rubbing her feet. "His whole act was dirty and *not* funny. Honestly, I don't know what you see in him."

"I've never heard of him," Kyle said. "Has he made any movies?"

"He's made lots of movies. He's even starred in a hit TV sitcom."

"He did?"

"Look it up online." Turning to her mother, she added, "His act wasn't dirty. Most comedians' acts are like that nowadays."

"I don't care what you say. His act was dirty, and he wasn't funny, period. And he's so … ugly. So fat. You're still an attractive woman. Why settle for a fat loser like him?"

"Because he's attractive to *me*. And he's kind, smart, sensitive …"

"He wasn't very kind when he made fun of you last night."

"That was just an act."

"Sure, it was. Anyway, what happened to that Ed guy you dated? He was nice."

"No, he wasn't," Holly responded, her eyes livid. "That 'nice' Ed guy was the biggest jerk. For your information, I happen to love Josh. And — whether or not you like it, I'm sticking with Josh — and I plan to convert to his religion."

Margaret shot an incredulous look at Holly. "Convert? To what?"

"To Judaism. I'm going to become a Jew."

Margaret's jaw almost dropped to the floor.

I'll start working toward that conversion tomorrow, Holly told herself. She had scheduled a meeting with a rabbi and his wife to make arrangements for his mother's ninetieth birthday dinner the following month.

***

Rabbi Dan Friedman entered Holly's sun-dappled office promptly at 9:30 the following morning. He looked just like her idea of a rabbi, with his curly brown hair spiked with gray, his dark brown beard, hazel eyes, and warm smile.

"My wife couldn't make it today — she has a bit of a cold," he said. "But she told me to go ahead and make all the arrangements for the party."

He went over what they wanted for the birthday party. Pink and lavender carnations on the tables. A live band to play old songs. A buffet for appetizers and table service for a sit-down dinner. Kosher food, of course — matzoh ball soup, gefilte fish, roasted salmon, and cheese blintzes for dessert.

"I guess that's about it," Rabbi Friedman said as Holly printed out the invoice and handed it to him.

No, it's not. Ask him, Holly. Don't chicken out now.

"Oh, uh, Rabbi?" Rabbi Friedman looked up from his watch. Holly cleared her throat. "Do you — do you know of anyone — who does conversions?"

"Conversions?"

"Yes ... to Judaism."

"You know someone who wants to convert?"

"Yes. I do."

"Oh."

It didn't sound promising. What if he turned her down?

The rabbi looked at Holly intently, his face solemn. "Why, may I ask, do you want to convert?"

"Because ... because I've fallen in love with a Jewish man and I want to share his life." She paused. "Do you perform conversions?"

"I do," the rabbi said, stroking his beard, "but only for certain candidates."

"What do I have to do to qualify? Take a course — ?"

"Look, I think you should forget about conversion. It's a lot more serious than you realize."

Holly sighed. "I know it's a serious commitment. I'm more than willing to make it."

Rabbi Friedman shook his head. "You can live a fulfilled life without becoming Jewish."

"But why won't you at least give me a chance to convert? I'm a decent human being."

"I'm sure you are. It's quite possible to be a responsible, moral person without converting."

"But I still want to convert. Maybe I can talk to another rabbi."

"You don't have to talk to another rabbi," Rabbi Friedman responded, his voice a mixture of amusement and annoyance. "I'll email you a list of recommended books. If you're as serious about this as you claim, read all of them from cover to cover. Then you can talk to me about converting." He smiled. "Most people don't bother with reading the books. Once my mother's party is over, I'll probably never hear from you again."

That's what you think, Rabbi.

***

"The rabbi gave me a really hard time," Holly told Diana the following morning as they sat in their office, sipping coffee. "Why would he do that?"

"I don't know what to say. Are you really serious about converting?"

"Of course I am. I'm very serious about joining the religion."

Diana sighed. "How does Josh feel about you converting?"

"I'm not sure. He's never made a formal commitment of any kind to me — he's never even talked about marriage. I don't know if he ever will. Maybe I'm wasting my time with Josh."

Holly's phone rang in her handbag, but lost in conversation with Diana, she didn't notice it.

Pick up the phone, Josh thought, as it rang, unanswered. *Pick up the damn phone, Holly, and speak to me.*

After six long rings, Josh, sitting alone in a brightly lit diner in Los Angeles, devouring a greasy brunch of fried eggs and sausage, gave up and turned off his phone. He couldn't keep calling her. The preview was tonight, and he had to start getting ready for it. Somehow he just knew it wouldn't go well.

***

Josh's problems started the moment that he and Jill arrived at the theater.

"Move out of the way!" a heavy-set young man with a goatee yelled at Josh as he and Jill approached the theater. "I need to get a shot of the stars."

"Do you know who I am?" Josh asked in an imperious voice.

"I don't care who you are, fatso!" the man shouted. "Just move."

"Why the hell should I move for you?" Josh's face grew hot. He felt someone tug at the sleeve of his jacket.

"Just do what he wants," Jill said in a loud whisper. "Don't make a scene. Please."

Frowning, Josh stepped aside. Jill didn't move at all. Smiling radiantly, she struck a dramatic pose, extending one bare leg through the slit of her red evening gown as several photographers pointed their cameras at her.

Josh watched the photographers fighting among themselves to capture her image. *Why are they taking her picture? She has nothing to do with this film. Oh, God, I wish I could run away right now.*

Out of the corner of his eye, Josh spied a familiar sight: the camera crew of the popular TV show *Entertainment Alert.*

That's all I need. They probably caught everything on camera. Tonight wasn't going well for him, and it wasn't going to get any better. He just knew it.

The next few minutes passed in a blur for Josh. As soon as the photographers turned away, he and Jill were ushered into a theater by attendants.

Josh's heart started to pound as he entered the cramped, darkened room and blindly made his way to the middle row, surrounded by dozens of whispered conversations.

How will I survive this? he wondered as he lowered his plump frame onto the upholstered seat. Labelle and Williams had taken *his* movie, *his* special dream, *his* vision, and totally destroyed it. It was almost as if they were torturing Josh by forcing him to watch this garbage.

The lights went down.

I feel sick to my stomach.

The opening credits rolled. Jason Williams appeared, sitting alone on a bench in a leafy park, his face contorted in an exaggerated frown, dressed in a drab brown shirt and tight, too-short gray pants.

"I have no luck with women," he said to the camera. "They never give regular guys like me a chance."

I can't take this, Josh thought. *I won't take it. I won't.*

Josh reached into his jacket pocket and pulled out his weapons. He inserted a small white foam plug into each ear, then pulled a heavy black velvet mask over his eyes.

***

The evening wasn't going well for Holly, either. Even though she was thousands of miles away from Josh, he was constantly on her mind. She had noticed his number on her call display, and she had called and texted him dozens of times that afternoon, with no response.

"I hope Josh is okay," Holly told Diana as they finished eating dinner at Holly's townhouse. "He gets down so easily."

"Holly, quit worrying. I'm sure he's fine. You just saw him a few days ago."

"I did, but things didn't go well. My mom hated Josh's act, and she didn't want to have dinner with him afterwards. He might be upset."

"You're worrying about nothing. I'm sure he's okay."

"No, I'm not worrying about nothing. Josh gets depressed easily. He's probably depressed about the movie. I can sense that something's bothering him. I just know it."

Diana sighed.

"You'll end up stressing yourself out by worrying so much," Kyle said. "Why don't you do something fun to get your mind off him? Maybe watch TV."

"Oh, all right," Holly moaned as she switched on the remote and sank down on the couch. *Maybe this show will relax me*, she thought, as she settled in to watch *Entertainment Alert*.

After a brief rundown of current movie releases, the show turned its attention to the "sneak" — and not so secret — preview of Josh's new film, *It Only Hurts When I Laugh*. And there, together in front of the theater, smiling artificially for the paparazzi, her in a clingy red gown and him in a black tuxedo, were Jill Boudreau and Josh Steinberg.

Calm down, Holly told herself, squirming a little and turning up the volume, *it doesn't mean anything. Josh did call me a few times — he was probably trying to give me a warning. And he knew I was tied up with a big client this week. Plus, she looks pregnant. I guess she has a serious boyfriend.*

"Oh, look," Kyle said, as he entered the room and plopped down on the couch beside Holly. "Your boyfriend knocked somebody up."

"Very funny. That baby belongs to another man."

"How do you know?" asked Diana as she placed a tray of peanut butter cookies on the coffee table before sitting down on an easy chair.

"Don't be silly, you two," Holly sighed. "Josh isn't like that. His relationship with that model is strictly business. He even told me so himself."

"But Mom, do you really trust him?" Kyle asked. "Doesn't it bother you that he's parading her around in public?"

"Look, it doesn't bother me at all. I trust him — totally."

And she did. The only thing Holly was worried about was Josh's welfare. Maybe she shouldn't worry so much, though. It looked like he was doing okay.

But Josh wasn't doing well at all. Under his cheerful and confident smile, he was starting to crumble.

Chapter Twenty-One

"Why was this awful thing even made? It's so bad, it's indescribable. This is what happens when a bunch of unfunny people try to make a comedy." The camera then cut away from the speaker, a plump, middle-aged man with thin, graying hair and thick glasses, to a brief clip of Jason Williams and Irina Wallace sitting at a table in an old, dingy diner, with Williams gazing deeply into Wallace's eyes.

"I'm the real hunk, baby," he told her in a flat, wooden monotone. "I'm your dream man."

"Believe it or not, that's the high point of this movie," film critic Roger Harper scoffed as the camera cut back to the television studio. "Director Mike Labelle just doesn't have a feel for comedy. He should just stick to those action flicks with exploding cars and special effects."

Paul sighed as he flicked off the large-screen, high-definition television in the sparsely decorated living room of his small apartment. *Why did I ever get involved with this? The first movie I produce turns out to be a disaster. It'll ruin my career before it even gets started, and it'll degrade the Cohen name in Hollywood.*

He snatched up his phone and rang Josh's number.

"Hi ... Josh," Paul began when Josh picked up the phone. "Guess what? Roger Harper showed up at the preview and trashed our movie on his show."

"So what else is new?" Josh responded with a heavy sigh. He was lying half-naked on a bed in a motel room in San Diego, a calming oasis of blandness with its ivory cotton curtains, beige walls, and worn dark-brown carpet, a musty, stale smell filling the air.

"Well, you and I are, unfortunately, involved in a movie that's going to flop, big-time, even though we had no control over it." Paul paused and took a deep breath. "I think the two of us need to visit a lawyer and get our names taken off this turkey before it gets released."

Paul's suggestion was met with stony silence.

"Josh? What do you think? Should we take our names off this movie?"

"Will it cost me anything? Lawyers aren't exactly cheap."

"It'll probably cost us a fortune, but our reputations are at stake. These assholes are trying to make us unemployable."

"I'm already unemployable," Josh laughed bitterly. "But you don't deserve to be. I'll think about it and get back to you." He sighed again. "I'm sorry I did this to you, kid."

"It's not your fault. And don't worry about me — I'm sure I'll be okay. The Cohens have survived bigger turkeys than this one."

"I hope so. Oh, uh, Paul?"

"Yeah?"

"Did I appear in the clip on Harper's show? Did he even mention me in his review?"

"N-n-no. He didn't mention you at all. But, hey, isn't it great that you're not associated with this piece of trash?" he added in a bright voice.

"Oh, it's wonderful. Nice to know that the world has forgotten that I even exist."

With a resigned sigh, Josh turned off the phone. Maybe Paul was just exaggerating. So what if one stupid critic didn't like the movie? Maybe someone else liked it. Josh turned on his laptop and typed his name and the movie's title in the search engine.

Find something good! he silently commanded the computer. *Prove Paul wrong. Please!*

Almost instantly, a long list of sites appeared on the screen. Eagerly, Josh scanned the search results … and groaned.

"Film Weakened by Crappy Script, Claims Movie's Director" blared the headline of one site in bold red letters.

His right hand trembling, Josh clicked on the link. A few seconds later, reporter Susannah Peters, young, slender, and petite, her hot-pink sequined dress contrasting dramatically with her waist-length blonde hair, popped up in a video. She was standing in front of the theater where the preview of *It Only Hurts When I Laugh* was screened.

Clutching a microphone in one hand, an awkward smile pasted on her heavily made-up face, Susannah said, "Welcome, everyone, to *Entertainment Alert*. I'm your host, Susannah Peters, here at the preview of Jason Williams's hot new release, *It Only Hurts When I Laugh*."

Hot new release? What "hot new release" are you talking about? Did you actually see this movie before reporting on it?

"And here," Susannah smiled, turning to Mike Labelle as he walked into the camera's range, "is the director of *It Only Hurts When I Laugh*, Mr. Mike Labelle."

Josh groaned. He wondered why Susannah hadn't interviewed him, the real creator of this movie, instead of Mike. If she had, Josh would have told her the truth: the awful movie she had just watched was not *Josh's* movie.

Mike, attired in an uncomfortable-looking tan cotton suit and light blue shirt with no tie, muttered an unintelligible greeting. He did not smile back at Susannah.

"Mike," Susannah said, her voice suddenly grave, "some of the critics at tonight's preview, well, they haven't had many positive things to say about your movie. How do you feel about that?"

"How do I feel about that?" Mike said, his face and voice growing tense. "All I can say is that Jason and Irina and I, we all tried our best with this material. But you can only do so much when you're saddled with an inexperienced producer and a crappy script."

"A crappy script!" Josh shouted at the screen. "My script was perfect — you and your stupid star turned it into a piece of crap."

"Do you also feel this way about the movie?" asked Susannah, turning to Jason Williams, who had appeared behind Mike, dressed in an impeccably tailored black suit and white shirt, its collar opened just enough to provide a glimpse of his broad chest.

"I sure do. Our producer and scriptwriter didn't have any idea what they were doing. Josh Steinberg should stick to stand-up comedy … or whatever the hell he does."

"Or whatever the hell he does," Josh said, mimicking Jason's words in an angry voice. "What do *you* know about comedy, you unfunny prick?" He snapped off the computer with a flourish. *You bloody jerks. How dare you screw with Paul and me, then turn around and blame us. This whole mess was your fault — we could only do so much with a couple of idiots like you guys.*

Without missing a beat, Josh snatched up his phone and called Paul.

"Paul," Josh said as Paul's voicemail picked up, "not only will we be taking our names off this movie, we'll also be suing these pricks for defamation of character. Call me or email me as soon as you can."

Josh tossed his phone onto the bed and stared at the blank screen of his computer. He wasn't really surprised that this film sucked. It just hurt to hear it from somebody else. But why was he being blamed for this fiasco? The director managed to strip away all traces of Josh, his ideas, his quirks, his personality — even his Jewishness. It hadn't been Josh's idea to change the lead character's name from Howard Greenberg to Hank Andrews.

But as far as Josh was concerned, all of the hostility directed at this movie was really hostility directed at him. Lately, he had been finding far too many websites attacking him for just about everything. Complete strangers, people he had never met and probably never would meet, hurled insults at him, calling him fat, ugly, and old. The worst insult came from someone who accused him of being *unfunny*. That really hurt. Josh was used to getting insults about his appearance, but he had always been proud of his ability to make people laugh. Now even that was being taken away from him.

Josh knew that his career had been going downhill for a long time, and he couldn't keep denying it. Maybe he'd lost his touch. Maybe — just maybe — he wasn't funny anymore.

***

Three days later, the disastrous preview was the last thing on Josh's mind.

He winced as sharp slivers of morning sunlight filtered through the filmy blue curtains of his cramped motel room in New Hampshire. *I've barely slept for days. How much longer can this go on?*

The nightmares had started four nights before, the night Josh took Jill to the preview. Every night since then, they played in Josh's head, an endless loop of heartache projected on the screen of his memory. And each and every night, it was the same old thing; only the names and the faces kept changing.

Why do I keep having these nightmares? Josh stared at his bloodshot eyes in the bathroom mirror. *I thought I was over these women a long time ago.*

The women haunting Josh's dreams were the three most powerful women in his past: the three former fiancées who dumped him on the way to the altar.

Leonora Thompson — the second woman Josh had been engaged to — was the first of his exes to reappear. Josh met Leonora, a tall, stunningly beautiful actress with long, glossy brown hair, in his mid-twenties when she guest-starred on *Guys Like Us*. The two of them dated for almost three years and were engaged for only six weeks when Leonora disappeared from Josh's life without saying goodbye.

Josh hadn't seen, or spoken to, Leonora for three decades when she mysteriously resurfaced in the dream, clad in a tight black satin bustier, a black garter belt, and seamed black stockings, her feet clad in sky-high red stilettos.

"Josh, do you remember me?"

"Of course I do, Leonora. You look the same." Indeed, she did. Leonora was as slim and unwrinkled as she had been the last time Josh saw her thirty years ago.

"You don't. Just look at you: fat, balding, lined, saggy face."

"Look, Leonora, I'm middle-aged. Thirty years older. I'm supposed to look this way."

Leonora didn't respond. She stared at Josh, an impatient expression on her face.

"Why did you leave me? Why did you just disappear from my life?"

Leonora gave Josh a withering look. "Do you have to ask?"

And then Josh woke up.

I thought I'd forgotten about her ages ago. Well, at least that horrible dream is over.

Josh's horrible dream about Leonora was over, but the following night's dream was even worse. He was sitting in a brightly lit diner, scanning a long, plastic-coated menu, when he heard a familiar woman's voice.

"Do you ever look up from that thing?"

Josh dropped the menu on the table. Seated across from him was a young woman with a pretty face, shoulder-length dark hair, and large brown eyes, dressed in a deep purple shirtdress.

"Amy ... Levy?" Josh asked, squinting.

Amy was the first woman Josh had been engaged to. The two of them met in university and dated for two years. Unlike Leonora, Amy formally broke off her engagement to Josh. In a diner. In fact, in the very same diner they were in right now.

Amy smiled. "You remember me."

"You haven't changed at all. I also remember this place. We were here on our last date together."

Amy smiled and nodded.

"But ... I don't remember why you dumped me."

"You don't?"

"Did I do something wrong? Did I say something stupid?"

"Of course not. You told me you were going to try to make it as a stand-up comic. I told you that you were wasting your life. I couldn't see a future for us together."

"But Amy, I did make it as a stand-up comic. You were wrong. Aren't you sorry now that you didn't give me a chance?"

"You wasted your life."

"But I didn't. Haven't you seen me in movies and clubs and on TV? I made it, Amy. You were wrong about me."

"What movies and TV shows, Josh? What clubs?"

Josh woke up, bathed in sweat.

God, why on earth am I having these awful nightmares? Why would I still care about what that stupid Amy thinks?

The reign of nighttime terror wasn't quite over. The following night, Josh was confronted by his most recent ex, Jill Boudreau.

"Josh, what are you doing here?" Jill asked him. Dressed in a floor-length white chiffon bridal gown with a slim skirt and long lace sleeves, a delicate veil perched on her head, Jill looked a couple of years younger — and her baby bump had mysteriously vanished.

Josh glanced around. They were sitting on a wooden bench in what appeared to be an old, decaying train station — alone.

Josh smiled. "The question is what are *you* doing here? None of this is real. It's only a dream. You're supposed to be pregnant right now."

"I am? By who? You?"

"What's that supposed to mean? You think I'm beneath you or something? Why did you really dump me?"

"Come on, you know."

"No, I don't. Tell me."

"Surely you didn't think I was serious about you, did you?"

"What kind of a question is that?"

"You couldn't really have thought I was serious about you."

Josh woke up and flicked on the bedside lamp.

Another one. Shit! I can't stand this any longer.

Josh started to call Holly.

No, I better leave her alone. Holly will think I'm crazy if I tell her about my nightmares. Anyhow, I don't want to upset her.

But Holly herself upset Josh. One night later, she appeared in a dream, dressed in a black shirt and a knee-length leopard-print pencil skirt — the same outfit she wore the very first night they met. They were seated at a table in the same club in Toronto, the Yahoo Comedy Club.

"Holly," Josh said, taking her hands in his from across the table, "I'm so glad to see you. I've been having the worst nightmares. My three ex-fiancées have been showing up in them, saying mean things about me."

"Oh?" Holly arched an eyebrow.

"Yes. But Holly, I didn't want to see them again. I don't care about them anymore. I only care about you."

"Uh-huh. Sure, Josh."

"'Sure, Josh'? What do you mean? You believe me, don't you, Holly? Don't you trust me?"

Holly gave Josh a hard look. "I trust you ... but you don't get it, do you?"

"Get it? Get what?"

Holly sighed. "Don't you know why you've been having these nightmares?"

"They're only dreams."

"No, they're not. They're *messages.* Face it, Josh. You're jinxed."

"Jinxed? Me?"

She nodded. "Haven't you figured it out yet? You're jinxed. No one will ever marry you. *No one.*"

The room went dark. Josh opened his eyes to see the green display on the bedside digital clock. 5:11 a.m.

That's it. I'm scared to ask Holly to marry me because I think I'm jinxed.

Josh had been burned too many times. But he had to get past this. He knew that Holly loved him, and he knew that she was different from the women in his past. It was time to take action.

That afternoon, the November sun shaded by clouds, Josh found himself in a large jewelry store stuffed with dozens of holiday shoppers, their eyes glued to the sparkling rings, earrings, necklaces, bracelets, and other treasures gleaming in the glass display cases.

"I'm looking for something a bit unusual," Josh told the solemn young man behind the counter. "Do you have a ring with a diamond and another stone? Such as a peridot?"

"A ... peridot?"

"Yeah. It's her birthstone."

"Well," the man began, unlocking the display case, "I have a ring with just a peridot." He reached into the case, pried a delicate gold ring with a single yellow-green peridot from its white velvet cushion, and placed it on the counter.

"It's perfect!" Josh exclaimed, mesmerized by the stone's brilliance. "I'll take it."

"Josh!"

Josh wheeled around. Steve Hunt, a popular stand-up comedian in his sixties, grinned at him. "Looks like you're in the market for an engagement ring. Again. Don't know when to quit, huh?"

"Quitters never win."

"Is it anybody I know?"

"Why, are you afraid it's someone you slept with?"

"I've bedded so many women, I wouldn't recognize her name. I'll bet it's that woman you made fun of in your act."

"Think what you want." Josh handed over his credit card to the clerk. "Why would you ask? You want some advice from me on buying your, what is it, tenth or twentieth engagement ring?"

"Ah, no. Unlike some people, I know when to quit. No, I'm looking for a necklace for my girlfriend. She's only twenty-two, but she already has expensive tastes. It has to be diamonds."

The clerk handed a receipt to Josh, along with the ring in a small gold box.

"Better hang onto that receipt. You never know when you might need it."

"What the hell is that supposed to mean?"

"Look, I was only trying to help," Steve responded in a mock-hurt voice. "Sometimes these things don't work out, and you might have to return that ring."

"I won't have to," Josh said, brushing past Steve as he headed for the door. "And I certainly won't be wasting my money on expensive baubles for some bimbo half my age."

"She's actually one-third my age," Steve said with a smirk. "We make the perfect couple."

Obnoxious loser. You've had at least five or six divorces. You're the last person on earth who should be doling out advice on marriage.

But Josh couldn't get Steve's words out of his mind. *Maybe I should keep that receipt,* he mused that night after a local club gig as he sat down in the lounge at the back to call Holly. *On the other hand, Steve has always been full of himself. Just ignore him. Call her, Josh.*

Josh punched in Holly's number. He had been calling and texting her for days, without success.

I guess she's been busy with her work. I hope she's okay, though. Please pick up your phone, Holly! I need to hear your voice.

"Holly?" He finally got through. "Are you okay?"

"Well, well, if it isn't the Great Lover," Holly began in a playful voice. "Saw the woman you knocked up on TV."

"You saw the preview?"

"Yeah. When is the little one due?"

"Very funny, Brannigan. Believe it or not, I wanted to take *you* to the preview, but I knew you were tied up. I even called and texted you several times." He paused. "Are you mad at me, dear? Are you hurt?"

"Of course not. I figured it all out. I'm Holly the Brain, remember?"

"Yeah." *Ask her, Josh. Don't put it off any longer.*

"Sorry I didn't get back to you sooner, but I've been tied up with bookings for my clients' holiday parties." She paused. "Is everything okay, Josh?"

"Yeah, everything's fine. Holly, I've got a gig at the Laugh Riot in Montreal this Saturday night. I think you told me you had some business in Montreal next week."

"I do. You want me to meet you at the club?"

"Of course. The show starts at nine."

"Okay, I'll be there. See you then."

Josh turned off his phone. It was time to prepare for the hardest performance he would ever give. It was time to propose. He couldn't put it off any longer.

Chapter Twenty-Two

Josh's plans for a romantic evening started to fall apart the moment he entered the Laugh Riot. He had reserved a front-row table for Holly, complete with a dozen long-stemmed red roses and a bucket of fine champagne. But when he arrived at the club, that table was occupied by three paunchy, middle-aged men in dull gray suits and ties, their presence magnified by the scent of their powerful colognes.

"Can you please move them?" Josh asked the club's manager, Marcel. "I reserved that table for my girlfriend."

"Sorry," Marcel said in a thick Québécois accent, "but I didn't receive your request in time. I can't move those men; they're very important customers."

And I'm not? Josh fumed to himself. *Those "important customers" of yours came here to see me!*

"Well, where are the roses I ordered? Where's the champagne?"

"What roses and champagne? Don't know anything about them," Marcel responded in a cold voice.

Josh sighed. Okay, so there had been a couple of minor glitches tonight. He just had to get on that stage and do his act, walk over to wherever she was sitting, and pull out the ring. He quickly examined his reflection in a mirror behind the long, polished mahogany bar. Crisp black shirt, perfectly pressed black wool pants. At least he looked decent tonight.

Thirty minutes later, Josh stepped onto the stage of the dark, spacious club.

"Good evening," he began, his eyes frantically sweeping the room.

The place was jam-packed. He couldn't see Holly. Where was she? He hoped she made it.

Then he saw her. She was sitting alone at a table in a back corner, wearing what looked like a black lace dress, smiling up at him.

At least she was here. He shouldn't worry about the flowers or champagne. He just had to toss out some jokes and pull out the ring.

Josh patted the left front pocket of his pants. It was empty. So was the right pocket. He had left the ring in his hotel room.

The audience stared at Josh, their impatience mounting. Josh opened his mouth to speak … then his mind went blank.

"Face it, Josh. You're a loser," Amy said, her voice cold and unemotional.

Shut up. Leave me alone.

"Did you really think this time would be any different?" asked Leonora. "It's not, and you know it. You didn't forget to bring that ring. You left it behind on purpose."

No, I didn't. You're wrong.

"You're jinxed!" Jill said. "You're doomed, Steinberg. No one will ever marry you."

Leave me alone, you bitches.

Josh stared at the audience, trembling. They were getting pissed off. He had to throw out the first joke.

Again, Josh opened his mouth to speak. Nothing.

Holy crap, I've forgotten all the special jokes I wrote for tonight's show. I'm going to bomb, big-time. In front of Holly.

"Hey, Josh," Steve shouted, a mean grin on his face. "Forget all those fancy schmancy jokes you wrote. Look, if you're scared of marriage, just make fun of it. Works every time for me."

Josh cleared his throat and forced himself to smile at the audience.

"Single guys like me often dream of having a beautiful, caring wife. Well ... so do most married men."

Mild titters from the audience.

"Glad you liked that one. Okay. So, how do you turn a fox into a pig? That's easy. You marry it."

Mild laughter. Very mild. He wasn't exactly killing them, but at least they were laughing. He had to keep going.

Josh smiled weakly. "Now, please don't think I have anything against marriage. As far as I'm concerned, marriage is grand ... and divorce is at least a hundred grand."

Robust laughter.

Josh sighed, the tension draining out of his body. He had to keep going. He couldn't stop now.

"Marriages are a lot like fat people." Josh paused and rubbed his rotund belly for emphasis. "Most of them don't work out."

Faint laughter, accompanied by some long, painful groans.

Josh peered at the back corner of the room. Holly was staring at him, a shocked expression on her face. Why wasn't she laughing at him? She wasn't hurt again ... was she?

"Holly," Josh began, after the audience had settled down, "what's the matter? Why aren't you laughing at me?"

"Why should I?!" she shouted, rising to her feet. "You suck tonight."

"Come on, Hol, don't tell me you're hurt by my jokes. You should be able to trust me by now."

"Trust you? How can I? You've been stringing me along for the past year."

"What are you talking about?"

"You know what I'm talking about. You pretended to be serious about me, but you have no intention of making any type of commitment. You have some very serious problems with marriage — "

"Holly, those were only *jokes* about marriage."

"Bullshit!" she yelled, her eyes livid with anger. "Those weren't jokes; those were messages. To me. You brought me here tonight to tell me, in a very cowardly way, not to expect marriage — or any kind of commitment — from you. Thanks for enlightening me, Steinberg."

"That's not true!" Josh stepped off the stage and ran toward Holly. "You took my comments way too personally. I thought you knew better by now."

"Coward! Liar!" Holly snatched up her black satin clutch from the table and headed toward the door of the club.

"Holly, this is silly."

She kept walking.

"Holly, come back. Calm down."

She rushed out of the room, slamming the door behind her. The audience stared at Josh.

Why did she have to get so angry at me? I was only joking.

"Some people have no sense of humor," Josh said, as he walked back to the stage.

"Better hang onto that receipt," Steve said, smirking. *"Try to get your money back. Do it tomorrow."*

Shut up, asshole!

"I was only trying to help. I gave you good advice," Steve said, still smirking.

No, you didn't, you jerk! I love Holly, and I never wanted to hurt her. What the hell is the matter with me?

***

Josh couldn't stop thinking about Holly. He spent weeks trying to contact her, but all of his phone calls, emails, and texts went unanswered.

"Holly, I'm sorry about the way I treated you."

"I need to know if you're okay. Call me and let me know."

"You have every right to be mad at me. And you can call me and tell me off if you want to ... but please call me. Please!"

Holly never responded to any of Josh's messages.

I guess Holly has every right to be mad at me, Josh told himself one evening after several fruitless attempts to contact her. *But maybe not. I only poked fun at marriage. She should know better by now than to take my words at face value.*

He scanned his phone once more for messages, then shut it off.

Maybe she would get in touch with him sooner or later. And maybe once this movie was released, it would do okay. He was sure Paul could deal with this. He was Hollywood royalty, after all.

***

But Paul couldn't. In early December, he found himself in a meeting — alone — with the very same Monumental executives that he, Holly, and Greg had met with several months earlier.

"What the hell are we going to do about this?" The voice, coming from a man named Peter, who was dressed impeccably in an expensive gray wool suit and yellow paisley silk tie, was cool but angry. The room, an office in an anonymous-looking cement tower in downtown Los Angeles, was spacious, bright, and airy, full of high-backed brown leather chairs, shelves of hardcover books, and an Oriental carpet in rich shades of chestnut, burgundy, and gold.

Peter turned to the other three suited executives in the room. "We can't afford to waste money on promoting this trash. We're not getting any return from it."

Paul, seated in front of Peter's desk, shifted uncomfortably in his chair. "I understand where you're coming from," he said, his voice quivering, "but I had no control over the film. Mike Labelle ruled the film with an iron fist. He wouldn't listen to me or to anyone else."

Paul's comments were politely ignored.

"Why should we lose our shirts?" said Chris, one of the other men, as he paced around the room, nervous and restless. "We trusted you guys, gave you a chance, then you turned around and screwed us."

"But *you* picked the director. You wouldn't allow me to have any say."

"The studio picked the director," Peter said, glaring at Paul, "not us. You should have supervised him."

I can't talk to these people, Paul sighed. *As far as I'm concerned, they live on another planet.*

"Maybe there's some way to fix this movie," said Jessica, the lone female executive in the room. "Maybe do some retakes." She turned to Paul. "Can you do some retakes, replace some of the scenes that don't work?"

"Retakes? Sure, I'll do them, but only if I get to pick a new director."

"It'll cost too much money to hire another director," Chris said as he stared out the window, a vacant expression on his face. "And you've already gone way over budget. Guess you'll just have to work with the director you already have."

But I can't. I simply can't stomach Mike, and even if I could, there's no way he can fix this movie. The stupid bastard is clueless.

"I'll see what I can do."

"You'd better do something fast," Peter said. "You have until January fifteenth to come up with a solution. If you don't meet that deadline," he added in a menacing tone, "you'll be hearing from our lawyers. You don't want that, do you?"

"Of course not," Paul said, struggling to swallow his anger. "I'll get back to you by then."

That evening, Paul lay awake in bed, staring at the gray shadows dancing on the ceiling, his stomach increasingly uneasy. *How can I fix this? I have no idea. God, I'm screwed!*

***

The movie was the last thing on Josh's mind that December. As the weeks passed and his unanswered messages to Holly piled up, Josh found himself facing the prospect of spending Hanukkah alone.

"Maybe I'll just stay on the road," he told his mom when he called her from a noisy pizza restaurant after a club gig in Cincinnati. "Pick up a few lucrative gigs, maybe even a high-paying one on New Year's Eve."

"Joshua," Miriam responded, "you shouldn't spend Hanukkah working at those clubs. You belong at home with family. Besides, you're certainly in no condition to be alone right now."

Josh knew his mom was right. He would probably get depressed if he spent Hanukkah alone. Anyhow, there was something pathetic about a single comic entertaining other people during the holidays.

So Josh — tired and lonely and angry and hurt and worn down from constant disappointment — reluctantly canceled two weeks' worth of jobs to drive, through a blinding snowstorm, to his mother's home in upstate New York.

When he arrived, he wished he hadn't made the trip.

"Josh," Miriam said as she threw open the front door. "You managed to get here in one piece, I see." Behind her, on a small table in the hallway, a tall silver menorah glowed with three lit candles. Josh could smell the rich aromas of

Hanukkah: roasted paprika chicken, crispy potato latkes, sweet Mandelbrot cookies.

"Uncle Josh."

A slim young man dressed in a gray sweatshirt and faded blue jeans dashed into the hall. As soon as Josh removed his snow-covered coat and boots, his nephew pulled him down the hall toward the family room.

"Where are you taking me?"

"I have a surprise for you," Joel said, his voice racing with excitement.

Josh's older brother, Ira, a wiry, well-heeled lawyer dressed in a navy cashmere crewneck sweater and gray wool pants, and his wife, Nancy, a plump, fifty-something chartered accountant wearing a bright pink turtleneck and black wool pants, barely acknowledged Josh and Joel as they entered the room.

Don't bother to greet me, Mr. Rich Attorney. After all, I'm nothing but a lowly comedian, struggling to pick up crappy gigs for peanuts. And thanks for out dressing me. Josh was painfully aware of his cheap dark-green crewneck sweater, now threadbare, and worn gray corduroy pants.

"You're in for a real treat," Joel told Josh as he settled into a soft dark-brown leather recliner.

"Joel," Nancy said, "not now. Please."

"What is it, Joel? What do you want to show me?"

Without missing a beat, Joel launched into one of the worst stand-up comedy routines Josh had ever sat through.

"Well," Joel grinned, turning to Josh at the end of his ten-minute act, "what do you think? Was I any good?"

"It was great." *You stink.*

"Thanks, Uncle Josh. After the holidays are over, I'm moving to Los Angeles to become a stand-up comedian. Just like my cool uncle."

Josh shot a horrified look at Joel. "But Joel, what about veterinary school? You were doing so well there."

Joel shrugged. "I'm going to quit school. I'd rather be a comic."

"How does your girlfriend feel about that?"

"We're not together anymore. She didn't support my dream."

"But do you really think this is a good idea?" Josh looked anxiously at Ira. "It's not easy to make a living as a comic."

"Listen to your uncle," Ira said. "Go back to school. You don't want to become washed up and alone like Uncle Josh."

Josh sprang up from the chair. "And I don't want to become a smug old fart like *you*. I knew it was a mistake to come here."

Josh bolted down the hall to the guest room and slammed the door. Miriam rushed after him.

"Josh," she said in a firm voice as she entered the room and closed the door, "why are you so upset at Ira?"

"He acted like a jerk. I refuse to let him insult me like that."

"Ira didn't mean — "

"Yes, he meant it. He's always looked down on me. But I can't take his crap anymore. I have enough crap of my own to deal with right now. I'm going home tonight."

"You took his words the wrong way. Anyhow, you can't go home — it's not safe to drive in that storm." She paused. "Exactly what crap do you have to deal with? Something's bothering you, Josh. I just know it."

Josh sighed. "It's nothing. I'm just frustrated about my career."

Miriam shook her head. "No, it's not your career. You've been unhappy about your career for years." She paused again. "It's Holly, isn't it?"

"Yeah." He drew a deep breath. "I planned to propose to Holly during my club gig in Montreal last month. I made arrangements for her to sit at a front table with roses and a bucket of champagne. I wrote some special jokes ... even bought an engagement ring. But everything went wrong."

"What happened? Did she turn you down?"

"No. She never even got the chance."

"Then what happened?"

"I'm jinxed, that's what."

"Jinxed?"

"Yeah. Everything that could go wrong did go wrong. A few nights before, I started having nightmares. My ex-fiancées tormented me, and Holly told me that no one would ever marry me."

"They're just dreams."

"No, they're not. When I was buying Holly's ring, I ran into another comic who told me to keep the receipt just in case I had to return it. That was a sign, Mom, an omen."

Miriam shook her head. "He was just teasing you."

"Oh? Then why was there no front table with champagne and flowers? Why did I leave the ring in the hotel room and forget my routine?"

"Because you were nervous and tired." In a softer voice, she added, "It was all just a silly misunderstanding. Holly loves you, Josh. I can tell."

"Sure she does. I've called and emailed her dozens of times, but she won't even speak to me."

"She'll come back to you, Josh, I know it. Just give her some time."

"Are you sure?"

"I'm sure. Unless you want to get into a car accident, you'd better forget about leaving tonight. Meanwhile, I'll try to talk some sense into Joel ... and that brother of yours." She smiled and patted Josh on the shoulder. "You're staying. Okay?"

"Okay," Josh smiled back. But he wasn't happy. Holly wasn't coming back. She probably didn't even give a shit about him.

***

Josh was wrong. Holly couldn't stop thinking about Josh ... or worrying about him. So worried that she found herself searching online for news about him.

How can people be so mean? Holly thought late one evening, gasping as she stared at the nasty comments directed at Josh on the computer screen in her office. Unhappy about spending the holidays without him, she decided to cope by burying herself in paperwork, coming into an empty office day after day. But the long hours of work couldn't blot out her pain and loneliness.

Josh must be pretty depressed right now. I should call him.

Holly picked up her phone but hung up after two rings. She couldn't speak to Josh. She just couldn't. He made it clear to her that he had no intention of ever making a serious commitment. But maybe she had taken his jokes way too personally. She just had to find out how he really felt about her. If she tracked down a new clip from his act, perhaps she could pick up some clues.

Holly typed "Josh Steinberg video" into the search engine, and immediately, a clip from *Standup Roundup*, a popular showcase on cable TV, posted only one week before, popped up on the screen.

She clicked on the link.

Josh appeared on a dusty stage, dressed in a scruffy black t-shirt and faded blue jeans, his eyes tired and bloodshot. In a worn-out voice, he rattled off a series of one-liners about a certain young egotistical male movie star and his lazy and incompetent pal, the director of mindless, violent action films. Holly laughed along with the audience.

"I guess you're wondering why I haven't been doing my regular *schtick*," Josh said when the laughter died down.

Is he talking about me? She turned the sound up.

"I used to talk a lot about a certain tiny woman who beat me up at a club." He paused. "I can't do that anymore. She's disappeared into thin air, and I can't make fun of her anymore."

"I haven't disappeared!" she shouted at the screen.

I must be important to him if he's still talking about me in his act. At least he hasn't forgotten about me. And I guess I enjoyed his insults more than I realized.

Chapter Twenty-Three

As soon as Hanukkah was over, Josh threw himself back into his work. On a bitterly cold and snowy morning in late December, he hopped into his car and drove away from the frigid ice and snow and somber gray skies of New York to the warm, sandy beaches, blue skies, and majestic palm trees of Miami.

The following week, while performing an evening show at the Coconut Comedy Club, a beachside venue full of brown wicker chairs, slow-moving ceiling fans, and dozens of shells of various sizes, shapes, and colors on the walls, Josh spotted a familiar face in the audience.

Who the hell is she? Josh wondered, squinting hard at the tall, slim, fiftyish woman dressed neatly in an orange polo shirt and navy Bermuda shorts. *I know I've seen her somewhere ... but where? I've just got to find out!*

Clutching the microphone, Josh climbed off the stage and made his way to her table. As Josh approached, the woman looked up at him, an annoyed expression on her face.

"Good evening. Hope you're enjoying yourself." Josh peered closely into the woman's face. "You look familiar. Have we met someplace before?"

"What kind of a pickup line is that?" the woman responded sharply.

The audience roared with laughter.

Oh, no. Another stupid heckler. Just what he needed.

"Look, lady, if you think that's a pickup line, you're in the wrong club." This time, the audience merely tittered. "Look, I know I've seen you somewhere before — "

The woman gave Josh an exasperated look. "I don't think so," she said in an icy voice.

Josh looked closely at the woman.

I know who this is! It's my ex-fiancée, Leonora.

But as he moved closer to Leonora, he noticed that she was holding hands with a short, muscular woman wearing glasses with thick black frames.

Leonora's gay! She probably dumped me for a woman!

Josh cleared his throat. "Well, well, if it isn't my old pal Leonora." He smiled at the other woman. "Looks like you switched sides."

Leonora glared at Josh. "What the hell are you talking about?"

"You know what I'm talking about ... babe."

The audience tittered.

"I don't."

"Come on, Leonora. We dated for what, three years? Don't you remember how hot I was in bed?"

Leonora shook her head. "Maybe we met years ago, but I never went out with you."

Maybe his memory wasn't quite what it used to be. But she *had been* his fiancée, and he couldn't exactly forget about someone he bought a ring for.

"Come on." A playful grin spread across his face. "How could you manage to forget about a hunk like me? Just look at this magnificent physique!" he added, pointing to his big, round belly.

The audience laughed. Leonora scowled.

"You're nuts. I never dated you."

"Oh? Then how did we become engaged? Don't tell me we weren't."

"I never dated you. I wouldn't be caught dead with someone who even looks like you."

"Bullshit. Liar."

"Look, asshole, you're out of touch with reality."

"What do you know about reality?"

"Quit harassing me!"

"I'm not harassing you."

"Yes, you are! And if you don't stop it, I'll go online tonight and tell the whole world what a big prick you really are."

"How would you know anything about pricks?" Josh asked, pointing to Leonora's companion. The audience roared with laughter. "If you think I'm such a big prick, then why did you spend good money to see my act tonight?" Josh asked when the laughter died down. "I'll tell you why. Because you're a *moron*!"

The audience responded with a mixture of lusty laughter and gasps.

Leonora rose from her chair and gestured to the woman beside her. "Come on, Jane, let's get out of here. This untalented jerk is a complete waste of our time." She turned around and stormed out of the room, Jane running after her.

I don't care what she thinks. I now know that my past doesn't matter. None of the women in my past matter. The one and only woman who matters now is Holly.

***

But five days later, cooped up one miserably cold, snowy evening in a small motel room in Michigan, Josh was forced to confront the hard truth.

Holly doesn't want anything to do with me. He stared at the long list of unanswered emails on his laptop. All the crap that had happened was his fault. He should have realized she'd get hurt by his stupid jokes about marriage.

A distant high-pitched whistling filled the room. Josh glanced out the window. The wind was whipping the branches of a tall evergreen tree into a frenzy, pushing them urgently against the glass. A thick blanket of snow covered the ground, glistening softly in the moonlight against an inky black sky.

Everything had been going so well, too. He should have screwed up the courage to propose to Holly, even though he had forgotten to bring the ring to the club.

Josh turned away from the window and scanned the list of emails.

No new messages, he thought as he shut off the cool, glaring eye of his laptop. But maybe there was something he could do to sort out this misunderstanding once and for all. Holly gave him her son's number a while ago. Maybe Josh could call him and ask him to talk to her, get her to call back.

Josh sank down on a faux brown leather chair, picked up his smart phone, and punched in the number of Kyle's cell.

Two rings. Three rings.

No response.

She would probably get mad at him if he talked to Kyle. He should call Greg instead and try to line up a gig.

"Greg, it's Josh. How's the agency biz going? How's Jill?"

"I don't know how Jill is!" the usually cool Greg yelled at Josh. "Frankly, I couldn't care less."

Couldn't care less? Doesn't sound good.

"But you must have some idea. Isn't she one of your clients?" In a gentler voice, he added, "Aren't you two still seeing each other?"

"No. Why would you ask a question like that?"

"Because ..." Josh sighed. "Look, Greg, Jill wants you to call her. She told me so herself."

"I told you, I have nothing to do with her."

You have nothing to do with her anymore because she broke your heart, just like she broke mine. Mr. Macho, you're still in love with her but too scared to admit it.

"Okay. I just wondered if you've lined up any new gigs —"

"By the way, Steinberg, I've gotten some complaints about your conduct at the Miami club. The owner said you picked a fight with a customer — "

"The customer picked a fight with me. All I did was defend myself."

"You were not at the club to defend yourself. You were there to work. If you don't smarten up and stop picking fights with customers, I'll drop you as a client."

"Go to hell!" Josh yelled, then hung up. *I can't take this garbage anymore.*

Josh felt a slight pain in the pit of his stomach. He glanced at his watch. It was almost seven already. His poor tummy was begging for fuel.

Josh pushed his bulky body off the chair and snatched his coat from the closet. Outside the window, the rough winter wind was whipping a newspaper across a nearby field, scattering its pages over the ground in dozens of directions.

He didn't feel like going out into the cold, but he had no choice. His stomach wasn't going to stop growling until he fed it.

Josh thrust open the door, and, stepping carefully onto the icy pavement, walked slowly across the parking lot to his car.

Thirty minutes later, a large, flat cardboard box tucked under one arm, two bright yellow plastic bags dangling from the other arm, Josh pried the half-frozen door of his room open. He set the bags down on a table, grabbed the TV remote, and sat on the edge of the bed, holding the cardboard box on his lap.

After changing the station to a hockey game, Josh opened the box. Immediately, the room was filled with the warm and cheesy scent of an extra-large pizza smothered in pepperoni, bacon, and anchovies.

Mmm, this smells so delicious. I could polish off the whole pie in one sitting. I adore food — it's my drug of choice, especially when I get upset.

Josh picked up the first piece of pizza and stuffed it into his mouth.

It definitely wasn't kosher. And it was definitely fattening. And this delicious, non-kosher, fattening pizza would probably give Josh a heart attack and kill him, right here in this motel room. But he didn't care anymore. Josh loved food; to him, it was way better than sex. All the pleasure without the hurt. It never let him down — unlike women.

As Josh finished eating the last scrap of pizza, the hockey game was interrupted by the abrupt appearance of a reedy teenage boy dressed in a white tank top and blue jeans, an idiotic grin on his face.

"Want to score without really trying? Just do what I did —"

Josh groaned and grabbed the remote to turn off the commercial. He jumped from station to station until an image, blurry and seedy, grabbed his attention.

Something about this looks familiar. He pulled a bag of potato chips out of one of the plastic bags on the table, picked up the remote, and turned up the volume.

The image was more than familiar — it was Josh himself, dressed in a tailored black shirt and black trousers, trying hard to look hip in an unhip setting: a TV studio decorated to resemble a family rec room, with light wood paneling on the walls, an off-white cotton damask couch with a matching ottoman, and a large glass-topped coffee table.

"Hi, everyone, I'm Josh Steinberg. A few years ago, I started to feel more and more run down. Just getting out of bed and getting through the day was a lot harder than it used to be. Then I discovered something truly amazing, something that changed my life forever." He picked up a plastic bottle full of aqua blue pills and dangled it in front of the camera.

Josh winced. He had forgotten about this stupid infomercial. He must have been hard up for money when he made it.

"Only $69.99 for a four-month supply. But that's not all. If you order in the next thirty minutes, we'll also throw in—"

Groaning, Josh snapped off the TV.

He took a swig from a large plastic bottle of cola. *That's all I'll be remembered for. A cheap, tacky infomercial. A desperate, washed-up comic begging for money, hawking something useless that he himself would never use.*

Josh grabbed a handful of chips and stuffed the salty, crispy treats into his mouth.

And he knew, he just knew, that he would die alone. And that no one would care now that he didn't have any fans left. Worst of all, he would die without knowing what it was like to be loved by a woman he truly cared about.

Concluding his greasy feast with a deep, earthy belch, Josh stretched out on the bed and quickly fell asleep, only to be woken up an hour later by the ringing of his phone in his pants pocket.

"Mr. Steinberg?" came a man's voice, unfamiliar and warm. "Have I called you at a bad time?"

"Not at all," Josh mumbled in a groggy voice, forcing his eyes wide open.

"That's good. I'm Dan Friedman. I'm the rabbi your friend Holly Brannigan approached about converting."

"Oh?" Holly must have given the rabbi his number. But why was he calling Josh about her while he was on the road? Josh was afraid to ask. "How can I help you, Rabbi?"

"I'm supposed to meet with Holly in a couple of weeks, and I have to ask her a few questions beforehand. But I'm having trouble tracking her down. I've called and emailed her for several days. My wife told me that she was going out with you — she keeps tabs on all the showbiz gossip — and I thought you could ask her to call me." He paused, then added sheepishly, "Holly's son gave me your number. I asked him to track down his mom, but he told me that he was also having trouble reaching her, so he suggested I call you. I hope you don't mind."

"Not at all, Rabbi."

Rabbi Friedman chuckled. "Your friend Holly is a real character. I turned down her request for conversion three times — it's my job to do that — but she's incredibly persistent. I also sent her a list of books and told her to read them — and she read *all* of them, cover to cover. Almost nobody reads all those books." He chuckled again. "Anyhow, Josh, could you please ask Holly to call me?"

"Don't worry, Rabbi. I'll tell her to call you as soon as I get off the phone."

Josh turned on his computer and sent an email to Holly: *Holly the Brain, Rabbi Friedman called me. He wants you to call him pronto ... that is, if you're still serious about joining the faith.*

Beaming, Josh hit Send, then shut down the computer.

So Holly still wants to join the faith. Maybe that means there's hope for us. And maybe that means I should put off pursuing Death by Food for another day.

He stuffed the now shrunken bag of potato chips into the garbage can.

Chapter Twenty-Four

The new year hadn't started out well for Paul. As Monumental's January fifteenth deadline loomed, he found himself unable to dream up that one magical idea that would transform Josh's troubled movie into a hit. Josh himself was no help.

"Please, Josh," Paul said when he called him the day after his meeting with the Monumental executives. "Just give me a rough idea of what I can do to salvage this movie."

"Why should I? Just take our names off this turkey."

"It's too late to do that. Besides, you worked so hard on the script."

"Screw the movie! Screw them! The director destroyed my script. As far as I'm concerned, it's no longer mine."

I guess I can't blame Josh, Paul thought as he lay awake in bed on the night of January thirteenth. Still no solution. He just couldn't come up with anything ... but maybe he didn't have to.

He rolled out of bed and turned on his computer.

Maybe somebody else has been in my shoes and solved a similar problem. I can do a quick search. Can't hurt.

Two dozen searches — and twenty minutes of work — turned up nothing useful for Paul.

Shit, I'm not getting anywhere. One more try ...

Paul typed in the phrase "Comeback comedy movie sucks."

Immediately a headline popped up on the screen: "Steinberg's Comedy Is Hopeless."

Paul clicked on the link.

Oh my God, Paul gasped, confronted with a screenful of angry comments posted on the crowdfunding site for the movie. And all the people Holly and Paul wheedled money from — dozens and dozens of small investors — were out for blood. Somehow they picked up on the rumor that the movie they invested in was going to bomb, and now they were scared, worried, and desperate.

The comments were painful for Paul to read.

Steinberg is nothing but a big, fat loser, one investor named Marcia complained. *Never found him funny. Now I know why.*

We've been robbed blind, folks, commented another investor named Nicky. *I don't think any of us will ever see a cent of our money again.*

It's not Josh's fault, chimed in a third investor going by the name of Pariah. *We should blame the idiots who talked us into throwing our money away on this ill-fated project, Brannigan and Cohen.*

"How dare you call us idiots!" Paul shouted at the computer screen. Below Pariah's comments, he noticed a box containing a link to a video with the words *This could have been brilliant* in bright pink letters above it.

Paul clicked on the link. Up popped Josh, dressed in a white dinner jacket, a white shirt, and black pants. Glaring at a pretty young brunette in a clingy, thigh-grazing white dress, he said, mimicking a woman's high-pitched voice, "I wouldn't sleep with a loser like you if you were the last man on earth," then stuck out his tongue at her.

Paul laughed so hard, tears ran down his face. He wondered who posted that outtake from the movie and how they got a hold of it. But that didn't really matter — he now had the solution he needed.

Paul snatched up his phone and punched in the number of Ken Wang, the movie's editor.

"Ken, you and I are under the gun. We've got to find all those brilliant scenes with Josh that were cut from the film and edit them back in."

"How does the director feel about this?" Ken asked in a sleepy voice. "Have you talked to him?" He paused. "It's 2:30 in the morning, Paul."

"Sorry, Ken, but our careers are on the line. And screw the director — this movie will bomb so badly that it'll end both our careers. Just promise to meet me tomorrow morning at the studio. Nine sharp."

"Are you sure this is a good idea? What if Labelle gets mad at us?"

"Don't worry about Labelle. Just meet me tomorrow morning. Okay?"

***

A couple of days later, Paul called Josh.

"Guess what, Josh?" Paul said, trying hard to hide his excitement. "The movie is going to be recut."

"So what?" Josh was in the middle of another greasy feast, this time at a deli near Monterey. To his disappointment, no one in the deli had recognized him.

"We need your help. You wrote the screenplay for this movie, and you're the only person who can fix it. Ken and I are restoring all of your scenes. This version of the movie will be a heck of a lot better, trust me."

"What about Labelle? He won't let you restore my scenes."

"He's not involved. Will you help us?"

"What kind of help are you talking about?"

"I need you to rewrite part of the screenplay. And reshoot a few scenes."

"Reshoot scenes? I'm not a director."

"Yes, I know, but you'll have to help me direct a few scenes. The studio won't give us the money to hire a new director, and we can't let Mike work on the revisions. He'd just screw up the whole movie again."

"I'd like to help you, but I'm in Monterey right now, and I have some gigs lined up." *I'm trying hard to forget that damn movie. I can't be bothered with fixing it.*

"Can you reschedule them? And can you get to LA by the end of the week? We really need your help. Besides, the success of this movie — and your own reputation — are at stake."

Josh sighed again. "I'll try my best, Paul."

"Thanks, Josh. Oh, one more thing: make sure you keep this a secret from Labelle and Williams."

"Of course," Josh said, a broad smile spreading across his face. "And thanks, kid, for hanging in with me. I know you've been put through a lot in the past few months."

An hour later, Josh hit the highway, weaving his car around vehicles on the crowded pavement, trying hard to focus on the road in front of him. But it was a losing battle: all he could think about was the movie.

So my vision for the movie might be brought to life after all. And, on top of that, I get to piss off the assholes who have been making my life hell. But first, I have to solve one small problem: How exactly should I end this movie? My original screenplay ended with the lovers staying together. In my second draft, they split up. How can I decide on the right ending? Should I call Paul and ask him? Toss a coin? Or ... should I call Holly the Brain?

Josh steered his car into the half-vacant parking lot of a small red-brick office building and called Holly's cell. He just had to ask her. Even though she had ignored his messages and calls for months ... and even though he was trying his best to forget about her. He couldn't even talk about her in his act anymore.

"This mailbox is full and not accepting any messages," an unfamiliar female voice said.

Josh sighed and punched in the number of Holly's home phone.

"... I'll get back to you as soon as I can."

Beep!

"Good evening, Holly the Brain." He couldn't stop his voice from trembling. "Joshua Steinberg here — you know, the Jewish Comedy King? Judging from your less than prompt responses to my earlier calls, you're either suffering from laryngitis or you simply hate my guts. Anyhow, I need your help with one crucial part of my screenplay: Should the lovers end up together or should they split up? Your prompt assistance would be greatly appreciated."

Josh's voicemail was picked up by Holly's ancient answering machine just as Holly flicked on the light in the front hall of her townhouse.

"Who the hell is this Joshua guy?" Eric said as he followed Holly through the front door. "He sounds like he's full of himself."

Holly gave Eric a long, cold stare. *Why the hell did I let you worm your way back into my life after you dumped me?* She wondered why she had been stupid enough to let Eric into her home when he showed up last Saturday morning claiming that he had made a mistake by breaking up with her, and pleading for one more chance.

"It's just business," she said in a crisp voice that implied that Josh's call was none of Eric's concern.

"Oh, okay. Anyhow, I have tickets to a Leafs game," Eric said, smiling nervously. "Tomorrow night. Pick you up at six?"

Holly didn't want to go to the game. She didn't trust Eric, and she didn't feel anything for him, not anymore. But she couldn't just spend the rest of her life crying over Josh.

"Sure, okay."

That evening, long after she sent Eric home, Holly played Josh's voicemail. And replayed it.

Why do I keep playing this stupid message? I guess I miss Josh's voice, but just hearing it again brings back all the hurt.

Holly played the voicemail one more time.

Why is he really calling me? She listened to the voicemail again, trying to decipher Josh's true feelings. Why would he care so much about her opinion? She wasn't a screenwriter or an expert on comedy. Maybe she should just delete the message.

But Holly couldn't. She kept staring at the blinking eye of the answering machine, the cold, hard light demanding an answer, any answer, to Josh's question. The truth was, she couldn't answer Josh's question. Part of her would adore it if the lovers got back together, but another part of her wondered whether that might be a mistake.

Two hours later, Holly heard the front doorbell ring. Shivering in the wintry darkness, she snapped on the bedside lamp, pulled on a robe, and stepped into a pair of slippers, then padded into the darkened hallway and unlocked the front door.

"Good evening, Holly."

Holly gasped. Josh stood on the front porch, smiling, dressed in a black tuxedo, starched white cotton shirt, and black bow tie, a white paper cone wrapped around a dozen blood-red roses in one hand.

"May I come in?" he asked gently, handing her the flowers.

Staring dumbly at Josh, she took the flowers and laid them, still wrapped in paper, on the small table near the door.

"May I … can I … come in?"

Holly kept staring at Josh, her heart pounding. "Why are you here? And why are you so dressed up?"

"I'm here for you, dear," Josh responded as he entered the townhouse. "I'm taking you to a red carpet movie premiere tonight."

"A premiere? In Toronto?"

"It's the Toronto premiere. Then, in a couple of weeks, we'll go to the New York premiere, then the — "

"Wait a minute!" Holly said, shaking her head. "This has to be some sort of demented joke."

"It's not a joke. I really am taking you to those premieres."

"But I can't go."

"Why not?"

"Because I don't belong on the red carpet. I'm not in show business ... and I'm not exactly a glamour-puss."

"Holly, you *do* belong on the red carpet — you belong with me! You're a smart, caring, classy woman."

Holly shook her head again. "No, Josh, I don't belong there, and I'm not going."

"That's fine!" Pulling a phone out of his jacket pocket, Josh punched in a number, then said, "I'd like an extra-large pizza, extra cheese, pepperoni, the works."

"Why are you ordering a pizza?!" Holly yelled, trying to snatch the phone out of Josh's hand.

"Look, I might as well order one. I'm not going to the movie premiere unless you go with me. If we're not going, then we might as well watch it on TV while we munch on a pizza."

"But Josh, you *have* to go. If you don't, you'll hurt your career."

"I don't care about my career." He kicked off his shoes and flopped down onto Holly's leather couch. "You're the only thing that matters to me now."

"I don't have anything special to wear."

"You look beautiful in anything, dear. Please go to the premiere with me. We belong together."

"How can I possibly say no? Okay, I'll throw something on. But what about that pizza?"

Josh shrugged. "Don't worry. I'll pay the driver and tell him to give the pizza to the homeless." He glanced at his watch. "Better hurry up. It's getting late."

"Sure." She rushed down the hallway to her bedroom.

Suddenly, the room went pitch black. The only thing Holly could see was the illuminated display on her bedside alarm clock. 4:53 a.m. Reaching over from the bed, she snapped on the bedside lamp.

It was just a dream. But it seemed so real. At least I now have the answer I was looking for.

***

Several hours later, Josh, now back home in Los Angeles, sat sipping a can of cola in his kitchen as he scanned his laptop for new emails. One message, with the subject line "Your call," caught his eye. He clicked on it.

THEY BELONG TOGETHER. Holly.

Three measly words after two months of calls and emails? Josh scoffed, disappointed by Holly's skimpy response. But at least it was something. After all, he hurt her feelings in that club in Montreal. He was actually grateful to get any answer from her.

Josh clicked on a file, flooding the screen with hundreds of words. He read the final scene of his screenplay again and again and again, playing out different endings in his head. But only one ending seemed to fit.

Holly's right. The lovers really do belong together, he mused, as he typed in the dialogue for the final scene. *That's the one and only way this movie can end.*

Josh printed out his changes, turned off the computer, and settled into an easy chair to read over his work. *Something about this new ending doesn't feel quite right, either. The lovers are together again, but ... they're not happy. But why aren't they happy? I wish I knew.*

Sighing, Josh wrapped a long rubber band around the pages of his manuscript, then he tossed the thick block of paper into a canvas bag on the table.

Chapter Twenty-Five

"What do you think this means?"

Holly pressed Play on her answering machine. Immediately, the small, dusty living room of her townhouse, gloomy with the weak, sunless late-January daylight streaming through the curtained windows, was flooded with the sound of Josh's powerful voice.

"... should the lovers end up together or should they split up? Your prompt assistance would be greatly appreciated."

"Well?" Holly asked, her voice brimming with excitement. This morning, she was dressed comfortably in a pair of faded, ragged blue jeans and the same navy sweater she had worn during her romantic dinner at home with Josh.

Diana sipped her coffee, the sober expression on her face as gray as her hoodie. "Did you ever get your money back from him?"

"My money back? What does money have to do with Josh's message?"

Why do you hate him? Why do you always have to assume the worst about him?

"It has everything to do with his message. This jerk only asked for your opinion because you invested your hard-earned money in his ill-fated project. He's just sucking up to you because he's afraid you'll sue him when his crappy movie loses money. And believe me, it *will* lose money!"

"I don't believe it. Josh isn't like that."

"I don't think he's like that either," Margaret said, helping herself to the tray of shortbread cookies on the worn oak coffee table, her black-and-white floral pullover and black pants dusted with crumbs. "Josh probably called Holly because he feels guilty."

"Guilty?" Holly asked. "Why would he feel guilty?"

"Because he's Jewish. You know, Jewish men always feel guilty about everything because they're neurotic. At least they are in Woody Allen movies."

"Mom, you watch too many movies." Turning to Diana, she asked, "Why do you think Josh is an asshole? Not long ago he helped us out by entertaining one of our clients for free at a business lunch after the magician we hired bailed out at the last minute. Don't you remember?"

"Of course I remember," Diana said, impatience creeping into her voice. "Yes, Holly, he helped us out. And I appreciate what he did for us. But none of that means that he's serious about you."

"Don't you think that message was Josh's way of telling me that he wants us to get back together? I mean, he did ask me whether the lovers in his movie belonged together. He based those characters on us!"

"Get real, Holly. He didn't tell you that he wanted to get back together with you, did he? Besides, if he can get a model like Jill Boudreau to go out with him, why would he bother with you?"

Holly stared at Diana blankly.

How can you say that? What right do you have to judge me like that? You're not exactly a supermodel yourself.

"He's no longer involved with Jill. He only took her to the preview because he knew that I couldn't go."

"Holly," Margaret said gently, "Diana only means well. She's just trying to save you from heartache in the future. Right?" She glanced at Diana.

Diana nodded. "Forget him. He's no great catch. Besides, you already have Eric. You'd be a lot happier if you settled down with a man like Eric who really wants you."

Does Eric really want me, or is he only chasing me because he doesn't have anybody else? Holly wondered. Anyway, it didn't matter. Holly didn't want Eric — she wanted Josh, and only Josh. If only she could understand Josh better, know what kind of man he really was.

Holly decided to find out. She took the following day off work, visited a nearby record store, and bought as many of Josh's old movies and TV shows on DVD as she could find.

Maybe if I study some of the scripts Josh wrote, I can get some clues. She popped the first DVD into the player before sinking down on the glove-soft leather couch in her living room. *Is Josh a good guy, a man capable of truly caring about a woman? Or is he just a player, a bed hopper, a jerk with an ego that's bigger than his heart?*

She hit Play and snatched up a notebook and pen from the coffee table, ready to jot down any insights and observations.

First, *The Donut Man*, a low-budget comedy movie scripted by Josh and filmed when he was still in his late twenties. During the movie's climax, Josh, playing a heavy-set baker named Craig Smith, catches a pair of crooks, two burly, rough-faced young men who robbed banks, by dumping a huge bag of flour on them from the ceiling. When the cops arrive at Craig's bakery in the next scene, they handcuff the crooks and haul them away, but they refuse to believe that "the fat guy" caught them. In the closing scene, the plump Craig is sitting on the floor of his bakery, awash in the flour that he had dumped on the crooks, stuffing donut after donut into his mouth.

"*This* is my reward!" Craig shouts at his assistant, Belinda, a young woman with short, feathery, pale blonde hair, and a round-cheeked, wholesomely pretty face. "Who needs a medal from the cops when you can have all the donuts you could possibly eat?"

"Food is a great source of comfort to Josh," Holly scribbled in her notebook. "Uses it to soothe himself when he gets upset."

Next, *Guys Like Us*, the sitcom that made Josh famous. In the episode Holly watched — also scripted by Josh — Josh's character, Nathan, and his two young, muscular roommates, Mario and Brent, join a health club to pick up women. Mario and Brent master the weight machines with aplomb, but the plump Nathan, dressed in an ugly aqua t-shirt with a cheesy white logo and droopy white gym shorts, can't do anything right. At one point, Nathan tries to pick up a pair of dumbbells, only to give up after three sweaty tries, falling down on the floor on his back.

"I think I should have joined a gourmet food club instead," Nathan says, struggling to stand up, as canned laughter fills the soundtrack.

Holly grabbed her notebook and pen from the coffee table. "Heavy men like Josh feel out of place in a world that idolizes muscled jocks," she wrote.

Six hours and several DVDs later, Holly reviewed her notes.

Lots and lots of insights about food, weight, and body image, she thought, flipping through the pages of her notebook. *But what about relationships? How does Josh feel about them, and about women?*

Sighing, she picked up the last DVD, *The Best of the Tom McKinnon Show*. A talk show. Josh couldn't hide behind a character here. She was bound to find what she was looking for.

"So, Josh," Tom McKinnon, a cocky, forty-something man with light brown hair and a loud voice, began, drumming his fingers nervously on the desk in front of him. "Tell us, is it true that you've just broken up with Jill Boudreau?"

Josh, attired in a rumpled sweatshirt and black jeans, his deeply lined face etched with pain, stared at the host for almost a minute. "Why do you want to know?" he finally asked. "Are you trying to pick her up?"

The audience howled with laughter.

Holly turned off the DVD player and closed the notebook. That wasn't quite what she had been looking for. She still didn't know how Josh felt about women — or about her. All she had learned was that Josh protected himself by hiding his vulnerability under wisecracks and punch lines. And judging from the way he dodged the host's question, he might still have feelings for Jill. Was he lying when he told her that he had been forced to take Jill to the preview of his movie? Did he love Jill … and did Jill love Josh? Or was Holly just being silly and insecure?

***

Holly didn't have to wait long for answers. The following Saturday evening, in an elegant dining room in a large hotel in downtown Toronto, Holly found herself face to face with Jill Boudreau.

It looks like one of my assistants hired her to perform her stand-up act, Holly thought as she entered the room. *Though she's an odd choice for a bachelorette party. Shit, I wish I'd worn something better than this dull white cotton shirt and old denim pencil skirt …*

Jill stepped onto the stage and grabbed the microphone, beaming down at the audience.

"This is what happens when the wedding night gets out of hand," Jill said, patting her now-enormous belly, which bulged under her stretchy and very short sleeveless red cotton knit dress. The bride-to-be, a tall, rail-thin black woman in her mid-twenties, dressed in a loose-fitting, ankle-length bright yellow cotton dress, her sweetly pretty face framed by short, curly raven hair, laughed lustily.

"Just think," Jill continued, "a few minutes of pleasure for nine months of pain ... and throwing up every morning."

Holly only half-listened to Jill's words. Instead, she found herself staring at Jill's belly.

She's huge. Looks like she's ready to deliver any time now.

"What's the matter? Haven't you seen a baby bump before?"

Holly looked up, startled. Jill was smiling at her, a smile that both teased and challenged.

Just whose baby is it?

"I've seen plenty of them," Holly said a little too defensively. "I've even had one of my own. It's just that—"

I should stop worrying. I have no reason not to trust Josh.

"Just what? You haven't seen a pregnant comic before? You don't think I belong here?"

"No, not at all. It's nothing. Forget about it."

"Forget about what?" Jill asked, now genuinely curious. "You didn't stare at my baby bump for nothing." She patted her belly again. "Come on, tell me and the Unborn One."

Holly sighed, trying to screw up her courage. "Is that ... Josh's?" she asked with some difficulty.

"Josh? Who's Josh?"

I should have kept my mouth shut.

Holly sighed again. "You know who. Josh Steinberg."

"Josh Steinberg?" Jill guffawed. "You gotta be kidding, lady. Old guys like Josh Steinberg can barely get it up, let alone — "

The audience roared with laughter.

How dare you say that about Josh!

"He's not that old," Holly said in a quiet voice when the laughter died down.

"No, I agree, he's not *that* old."

What does she mean by that?

"I guess you still have the hots for Josh?" Holly asked sheepishly, her eyes downcast.

"Who in their right mind could possibly have the hots for Josh Steinberg?" Jill laughed.

The audience laughed again ... except for Holly. "How could you say that?" Holly said, glowering at Jill. "Josh is a wonderful, kind, sensitive man. He's done so much to help you."

"I know all about Josh Steinberg," Jill responded. "He's lucky to find someone who feels that way about him," she added gently.

Holly smiled at Jill, both happy and relieved.

Jill smiled at Holly, then grimaced. "Oh, God, I think my water just broke." The audience laughed. "No," Jill cried, her voice wobbly, "my water really did break."

Holly rushed onstage. Without saying a word, she took Jill by the hand and led her off the stage. Fifteen minutes later, after battling heavy traffic, they arrived at St. Michael's Hospital. As Holly maneuvered her car into the packed parking lot, Jill flew into a rage.

"This wasn't supposed to happen! I'm five weeks early!" She grimaced again, her face contorted with pain. "I let that stupid Jacques Von Graff knock me up, and now I'll be tied to that controlling bastard for the rest of my life."

"Did you say Jacques Von Graff?" Holly asked. "The billionaire?"

"Yeah, that's him. He might be a billionaire, but he's no great catch."

The two women entered the emergency department and rushed to the registration desk. The drab, sterile room, its walls covered in beige paint, the carpet sporting muddy footprints, was packed with people: a frail elderly man in a wheelchair who could barely hold his head up; a short, muscular, red-headed teenage girl with her leg in a cast; an Asian couple trying to pacify their wailing baby.

"I'll take care of you right away," the nurse at the registration desk told Jill after Holly had filled out the required paperwork. "Come this way," she said to Jill, then led her down the hall toward the elevators.

"Jill!" Holly called out just as Jill and the nurse entered the elevator. "Do you want me to call anyone for you?"

"Call Greg Fanelli. Please ask him to contact me, Holly."

"Okay, I'll call him."

"Thanks, Holly!" Jill shouted as the elevator doors clanged shut.

Holly called Greg's number. "I'm tied up with another client at the moment," came Greg's crisp voice message, all business. "Please leave your name and number, and I'll try to get back to you as soon as I can."

"Greg, this is Holly Brannigan. We met a few months ago," Holly began, glancing around, hoping her voice was low enough not to be overheard by the hospital staff and patients. "Jill Boudreau asked me to call you. She's at St. Michael's Hospital in Toronto, having a baby." Holly paused, then added in an urgent voice, "Please call her, Greg. She's all alone, and she really needs you now."

Holly hung up and glanced at her watch. It was almost ten.

What a night, she thought as she hurried to the exit. *The girls at the party got far more entertainment than they bargained for, I took a woman in labor to the hospital ... and I made a big fool of myself over Josh Steinberg. Why didn't I just keep my big mouth shut? Josh will probably think I'm a real idiot once he finds out what happened.*

Three hours later, after stopping by Diana's house to go over the arrangements for a sales conference the following morning, Holly pulled her car into the driveway of her darkened and empty townhouse. From the front hallway she could see the light of her answering machine flickering furiously, a pale green beacon in the pitch-black room.

Holly flicked on the hall light, her heart pounding.

The hospital must have called. Thank God I got Jill there in time.

Holly rushed over to the answering machine and pressed Play.

"Good evening, Holly the Brain," came the warm voice of Josh Steinberg. "That was a very unselfish thing you did tonight. Mother and baby boy are doing quite well, thanks to you. And, by the way, you were right — the lovers in my movie really do belong together."

Yes, they do, Josh, Holly thought, a big smile spreading across her face. *Yes, they do.*

Chapter Twenty-Six

"I don't care about that stupid movie!" Josh yelled at Greg on his phone. Josh was polishing off the remains of an egg salad sandwich, washed down with a tall glass of cola, at a roadside diner in Ohio. Even though it was the middle of the day, the large, brightly lit room was almost empty, save for a middle-aged man and woman with two teenage boys, and an elderly man who sat at the table next to Josh, his face buried in a dog-eared sports magazine.

I'm too tired to deal with this bullshit. Just leave me alone, for God's sake.

"The premiere is tomorrow night in New York," Greg continued, seemingly deaf to Josh's angry outburst. "By the way, the whole thing has been recut."

"I know it's been recut — who do you think helped recut it? I've done way more than my fair share of work on this movie, and I'd like to forget about it and get on with my life. I won't be going tomorrow."

"Josh, you gotta go. There will be lots of media coverage and — "

"I don't care. I'm done with this piece of crap. I was finished with it four months ago." Josh wiped the crumbs off his chin with his shirt sleeve. "And Fanelli, I'm also done with the comedy business. You no longer have a job."

Greg sighed. "Josh, whether or not you're done with the comedy business, you have to be there tomorrow night. Paul's supported you from day one, and he's been working his ass off to rescue this movie. You can't screw him like this. Promise me you'll come."

"I appreciate Paul's help and support, but I can't change my plans at the last minute. I have an important gig booked for tomorrow night."

"No problem. I'll reschedule it for you."

"… and I don't have anyone to go with me. I can't go alone."

"What about that girlfriend of yours?"

"What girlfriend?"

"The one you used to make fun of in your act."

"Holly? She's not my girlfriend anymore. I can't take her to the premiere — she's not even speaking to me."

"I'll find a date for you. Just drive out to New York, and I'll take care of all the details. And stop sounding so glum. The event will be covered by *Entertainment Alert*. Nobody wants to watch a comedian cry on TV."

"Bully." Josh turned off the phone.

That's great. I have to waste a precious evening of my life in the company of some dull woman I have no interest in, watching a movie that's bound to dredge up a bunch of painful memories. Meanwhile, the woman I really want to be with will probably spend tomorrow evening with some hot young hunk.

***

Josh was only partly right. Holly did spend the following evening with a hunk, but he wasn't the man she really wanted to be with.

"Finally made it home, I see," Eric greeted her, a lazy smile on his face. Sprawled on the sofa in her living room, he clutched a frosty can of beer in one hand and a TV remote in the other.

"How the hell did you get in here? Did you break into my house?"

Eric glanced at Holly, a cold, mean smile spreading across his face. "What a warm and fuzzy greeting. I'm happy to see you, too. I dropped by to say hello, and your son invited me in and told me to make myself comfortable."

Kyle and Eric had always been buddies. When Holly was dating Eric, he'd taken Kyle to Blue Jays and Maple Leaf games and fan expos. And even though Eric dumped Holly over a year ago, he and Kyle still texted each other.

Holly peeled off her blazer and hung it up in the front hall closet. *Kyle has the right to stay friends with Eric, but he has no right to invite him into my home without my permission.* She glared at Eric. "I guess you and Kyle will be going out tonight?"

"Kyle's out with some friends. I thought it would be nice if we spent the evening together."

"Look, Eric," Holly said in a weary voice, "I've been working all day and I'm tired. Maybe some other time."

"You don't have to do anything," Eric said as he gulped down a mouthful of beer. "I can order a pizza and get it delivered."

"Don't bother," Holly replied, dumping her heavy briefcase on a nearby chair. "I'll just make us some sandwiches."

"And change out of those fancy clothes," he said, pointing at Holly's white ruffled blouse and slim black pants.

Holly ignored him and disappeared into the kitchen.

Eric took another swig of beer, then began jumping from station to station until an image captured his attention: the young face and slim but curvy body of Susannah Peters, the reporter on *Entertainment Alert*. She was standing on a red carpet in front of a movie theater, its entrance awash in powerful lights, with hordes of movie fans milling around the cordoned-off sidewalk behind her.

"This is an evening to remember!" grinned the petite Susannah, teetering precariously in a pair of silver evening sandals with sky-high heels, her short, tight, beaded silver dress revealing most of her thighs. Her waist-length pale blonde hair framed her pretty face. "Tonight, here in New York, a lucky audience will be treated to the premiere of Jason Williams's hot new release, *It Only Hurts When I Laugh*. And here he is!" Susannah squealed as Jason Williams emerged from a limo. "Jason Williams! Jason," she said, as she walked toward him, "there's a lot of positive buzz tonight about your new movie. How do you feel about it?"

Jason, dressed impeccably in a tuxedo, looked at her with a sour expression on his face, then, without saying a word, rushed out of camera range.

"Jason?" Susannah said in a slightly anxious voice, her eyes trailing him as he walked away. "Well," she continued, turning around and smiling brightly into the camera, "it looks like Jason is too excited to comment." She paused, scanning the crowd for a famous face, any famous face. She didn't have to look too hard or too long.

Josh, resplendent in a handsome black tuxedo, strode over toward Susannah sporting a wide, triumphant smile. Draped on Josh's arm was fashion model Bailey Diaz, a young beauty with long, glossy black hair. Her lanky figure was poured into a low-cut black evening gown that left little to the imagination.

Susannah smiled artificially at Josh and Bailey. "And here," she began, with forced excitement, "is another star of the film, comedy legend Josh Steinberg."

Just at that moment, Holly emerged from the kitchen carrying a tray of roast beef sandwiches. She almost dropped them on the carpet.

Why didn't he ask me to go instead? Neither Josh nor Paul even bothered to call me. Out loud, she snapped at Eric, "Turn that crap off. I can't stand him."

"Oh, sorry," Eric muttered. He grabbed the remote and changed the station to a hockey game.

Josh actually couldn't stomach Bailey. *She's been a real bitch all evening*, he thought, staring critically at her as a husky photographer with scraggly gray hair, his arms covered in tattoos, snapped photo after photo of her. When Josh had picked Bailey up at her hotel, she refused to even greet him; she just gave him a dirty look. Then, when he had tried to break the ice by starting a conversation, she barely said a word to him. She even accused him of getting too personal when he asked her about her career plans. Why did Greg have to fix him up with this stupid woman?

On the other hand ... Josh was overjoyed by the revitalized movie. Paul and Ken did an excellent job. Jason Williams was still the "star," but the movie now belonged to Josh and Josh alone. All of his funny scenes had been restored, *and* the audience at the second preview relished them. Best of all, the recut movie pissed off Williams and Labelle; both of them had refused to speak to reporters tonight.

"Our producer has done a really brilliant job," Josh said, snatching the microphone from Susannah's hand. "He has actually brought my vision for the movie to life. Go see it, everyone!" He beamed at the camera. "You'll love it." He paused for a moment, then added in a sober voice, "I especially want one very special lady to see this movie. I would never have been able to make it without her. I miss you, Holly." Josh's big brown eyes suddenly filled with tears as he handed the microphone back to Susannah and looked away from the camera.

"Oh," Susannah responded, clearly uncomfortable with this unexpected expression of honest emotion. Turning to the towering Bailey, she said, in a bright voice, "And what about you, Bailey? What's your reaction to the film?"

Bailey ignored Susannah's question. "Y'know," she began, gesturing toward Josh, who was staring at her with a cold, blank expression, "I can't believe I'm actually here tonight with a real comedy legend like Josh Steinberg."

"Really?" Susannah responded with fake interest. "Are you a big fan of his?"

"N-n-no," Bailey answered slowly. "It's just that he's been around for such a long time — he's so old. I thought he was dead by now."

"Dead?" Josh gasped, horrified. Before Bailey could utter another word, he grabbed Susannah's microphone again.

"You thought I was dead!" he shouted, turning on Bailey. "God, what the hell am I doing with a first-class idiot like you?" He pulled out his wallet and flung a wad of bills at Bailey. "Here, this should pay for your cab ride home."

With that, Josh abruptly turned around and ran down the street toward the parking lot, the cool late-April wind whipping his face, his heart pounding wildly in his chest.

Bailey and Susannah, still on camera, stared silently at Josh as he disappeared into the dark, velvety night.

Josh yanked open the door of his car. *I can't take this anymore. I miss you, Holly; I need you. I just have to see you again. I just have to!*

Within minutes, Josh had started speeding down the nearest highway, his car pointed toward Toronto, his mind racing.

What the hell had he just done? Josh just knew that he was going to get into trouble for taking off like this. And he also knew that Paul would never speak to him again, not that Josh blamed him. His already tattered reputation would be totally destroyed, and he would never be able to find work in Hollywood again. The comedy clubs wouldn't hire him again, either ... and he wouldn't even be able to get another part in an infomercial. Even worse, Josh knew that he was running after another woman who didn't really want him. He would probably find Holly in bed with another guy. Happened all the time to him.

***

Two hours later, his eyes clouding over with drowsiness, Josh drove into the parking lot of a fast-food restaurant at the side of the highway, a large, square building bursting with bright lights and the scent of warm, greasy food.

"One large coffee, milk and sugar, please!" he shouted into a crackly, staticky speaker, then steered his car to the pickup window.

A plump teenager with chin-length black hair and glasses poked her head out the window. "One large coffee to go?" She glanced at Josh briefly, her face expressionless, her eyes weary.

"Yes," he said, half-hiding his face in the deep shadows, as the girl reached behind a counter and handed him a white paper cup crowned with a brown lid.

Josh grabbed the hot coffee, steam flowing through the night air. *She doesn't know who I am. Thanks for making my evening.*

Josh drove to a corner of the dark parking lot, now almost empty except for a smattering of large trucks and their drivers. Sipping his coffee, he looked out at the still-busy highway filled with vehicles that whizzed by at lightning speed.

Josh's mood, already low, sagged even lower. Maybe he should just end it all tonight. There was nothing left for him anymore. The premiere had gone really well, but all the success in the world meant nothing to him if he no longer had Holly.

Josh sighed, then sipped his coffee.

I'll just wander out onto the highway and get flattened by one of those huge trucks. It'll hurt a lot less than what I'm about to go through. "Fat, Old, Washed-Up Comic Flattened by a Big Truck." *I can already see the headlines on CNN.*

Josh gulped down the bitter remains of his coffee.

No, no, that headline won't do. What about "Beloved Jewish Comedy King Dead from a Broken Heart"? Hmm, that's a lot better. Maybe I should tweet it to CNN before I do the deed.

Josh pushed open the car door, the cool night breeze blowing softly around him, and tossed the empty cup and its lid into a large garbage can. He glanced at the busy highway, covered with a steady stream of cars and heavy trucks, their bright headlights punctuating the black night.

He closed the car door and turned on the ignition. *Maybe I should just turn around and drive home to Los Angeles.* But if he did that, he would have to deal with a bunch of pesky calls from Paul, Greg, the studio, and everyone else. And he would have no excuses to hide behind. Josh knew that love was not an excuse, especially when a lot of money was involved.

He pulled his car onto the highway, and then, once again, pointed it toward Toronto.

He would just have to find out once and for all.

Chapter Twenty-Seven

Where am I?

Eric pried open his eyes, slowly and painfully, and peered at the small clock on the opposite wall of Holly's half-dark living room. It was nine thirty on Sunday morning. Maybe he had a few too many beers last night and had passed out on Holly's couch.

His head throbbing, he glanced at the coffee table, which was littered with a half-eaten sandwich and a colony of six empty beer bottles, a thick stench floating above them.

What happened after all those beers? I hit on Holly — I think — then she pushed me down onto the couch. Then I blacked out.

Eric looked up at the staircase, the clock ticking ominously in the background. He rose from the couch and walked slowly toward the front hall, his legs unsteady. *I'd better get out of here fast. I doubt Holly is in any mood to have breakfast with me. God, my back hurts like hell.*

A few minutes later, Eric backed his fiery red sports car out of Holly's driveway. As he steered it onto the empty street, the heady perfume of fresh spring flowers filling the air, he passed a small black car parked in front of the townhouse, partly concealed by the shadows cast by the weak morning sun.

Josh watched Eric stumble out of the townhouse and drive away. *It looks like Holly spent the night with that hunk.* He drove all night long, for hours and hours, just to see her, speak to her, hold her in his arms again ... and for what? Just so he could fall asleep in the car and wake up in time to see her lover leave her home.

Shivering in the brisk morning air, Josh pulled down the small mirror on the passenger side of the car. He looked horrible. Wrinkled tux, messy hair, bloodshot eyes. He groaned as he inspected his reflection. And he felt like crap. His back was stiff from sleeping in the car, and seeing that guy leave Holly's house made him sick to his stomach. It was a big mistake for him to come here. He should just go home. Holly had already forgotten about him, and if he tried to speak to her, he would only make a fool of himself.

Hands shaking, Josh thrust his key into the ignition. The engine sputtered for a few seconds, then coughed. Then nothing. He tried again. Nothing.

What the hell was he going to do now? Not only was he stuck in front of the house of a woman who clearly wanted nothing to do with him, he also had to pee. And Josh couldn't drive to a restaurant or gas station to relieve himself because he knew he would never make it in time.

Josh opened the car door and slipped outside. As unobtrusively as possible, he ducked behind a row of tall green hedges at the side of the house and started to unzip his pants.

"Good morning."

Josh, half-crouched behind the hedge, looked up into the eyes of an elderly man, his small body covered by a pale yellow nylon jacket and dark gray pants. He was accompanied by a small poodle with white fur, the panting dog's mouth curled up into a goofy smile, its beady brown eyes staring suspiciously at Josh.

Oh, great. Just what I need: some old busybody who's offended by the sight of my private parts.

Josh hastily pulled up his pants and drew himself up to his full height.

"I dropped something," he said.

The elderly man nodded. Without speaking another word, he turned around and steered the dog back to the sidewalk.

Josh stared at Holly's front door, his stomach uneasy. *Looks like I've only got one choice ... unless I want to pee my pants. I just hope she opens that damn door and lets me use her toilet.*

His bladder now uncomfortably full, Josh walked up to Holly's front porch.

He didn't want to ring the doorbell. He didn't really want to enter this house. And to be honest, he was afraid to face Holly.

Out of the corner of his eye, Josh spied a burly middle-aged man in a navy jacket, his graying hair and beard contrasting sharply with his brown skin, tossing rolled-up newspapers onto the front porches of the townhouses across the street.

It's only a matter of time before he gets to this house. And, heaven forbid, he might recognize me. Just try the damn door, Josh. That guy probably left it unlocked.

Josh twisted the brass handle. The heavy wooden door opened with a faint creaking. Entering the half-dark townhouse, Josh tiptoed down the front hall toward the bathroom.

Holly heard the soft footsteps from her bedroom on the top floor. *Shit, Eric's still here.* She pulled back the curtains only to be greeted by the harsh, unforgiving rays of the morning sun. Wincing, she drew them closed again.

It had been a really rough night. Eric wouldn't leave Holly alone. He'd kept grabbing at her, even though she told him that they were finished. Then he'd got drunk on beer and flopped down on the couch, his glazed-over eyes glued to some boring hockey game. At that point, Holly decided to leave him there and go to bed.

But the man she was really pissed off at was Josh. He never asked her to that premiere. He just acted like she didn't exist. Why did he do that to her?

Bleary-eyed, Holly glanced in the full-length mirror beside the bed and sighed with disappointment at the middle-aged, lined face that stared back at her.

I barely slept a wink last night, and it shows. Maybe I should get some work done on my face and then book a flight to a warm and exotic country to shop for a new young lover. That is, if I can actually force myself to do it.

The flushing of a toilet from the first floor interrupted her thoughts.

"I'll be right down, Eric!" Holly shouted as she threw on her bathrobe and stepped into her slippers. What did she have to do to get rid of him? She could pretend that she had an important breakfast meeting with a client. Yeah, that was exactly what she would tell him. Then he couldn't hang around here any longer.

Slowly and cautiously, Holly padded down the stairs, entered the living room, and flicked on the overhead light.

"Hello, Holly," Josh said, smiling sheepishly at her from the couch. His voice was weak and tired, his face was covered in black stubble, and there were dark circles under his bloodshot eyes.

Holly gasped at the sight of the unshaven Josh in his wrinkled tuxedo.

Am I dreaming? Wasn't Eric on this couch just a few hours ago?

"Your boyfriend just went home," he said, his eyes downcast. "It looks like he left your front door open."

"He's *not* my boyfriend. Eric's just a friend of my son's who fell asleep on my couch." She paused. "Why am I telling you this?"

"Holly — "

"My personal life is none of your business. Besides, you haven't exactly been crying over me. You took another woman to that premiere last night."

"Her? That was a blind date Greg arranged."

"Sure it was."

"I couldn't ask you. You weren't speaking to me." Josh rose to his feet. "I couldn't go to the premiere of my own movie alone. Besides, I didn't even want to be with her. In fact, I drove all night from New York just to get away from her."

"You did? Why would you do something crazy like that?"

Josh smiled. "Because I wanted to be with you." He sighed. "What's the use? You don't want to talk to me. You ignored all my messages for months." Tears filled his big brown eyes. "I shouldn't have come here." He turned around and headed toward the front door.

"Josh?"

Josh stopped walking and wheeled around.

"Please don't leave." Holly's voice was warm and relaxed. "Why wouldn't I want to talk to you? After all, you drove all night to be with me."

"Because," he began, trying to force the words out. "Because I wasn't very nice to you. Holly, about that club in Montreal. I never meant to hurt you with those stupid jokes. Believe it or not," he continued in an unsteady, ragged voice, "I planned a really romantic evening for us. I arranged a front row table for you with roses and champagne, but the club screwed everything up."

Tears filled her eyes. *I wish I'd known.*

"And I was so nervous, I forgot the special routine I wrote. I was tired, stressed out. I wasn't sleeping much, and I couldn't cope, so I ended up using a bunch of hoary old jokes." Josh paused. "I'm so sorry, Holly. Are you still mad at me, dear?"

"Of course not, Josh. I feel so awful. I should know better by now than to take your jokes personally."

"Don't feel bad, dear." Josh wrapped his strong arms around her small body, drawing her close to him. "I understand." Warmly and passionately, Josh kissed Holly on the forehead, nose, ears, lips, and neck.

"I really missed you, Josh," Holly said, kissing him back, as big tears coursed down her cheeks.

"Me too, baby. That's it — I'm never letting you go ever again."

"I love you, Josh."

"I love you, too, Holly," Josh said, stroking her hair. He paused for a moment and, with one hand, began rummaging through the pockets of his tuxedo jacket. "By the way, I have something for you. I'd better give it to you before I forget." Josh pulled out a piece of crumpled green paper and handed it to Holly. "Here, take this."

"What is it?"

"It's the check you gave me. I never used it — never even thought of using it."

"Oh," Holly said, taking the check from Josh's hand. "You should have used it to finance your movie."

"I didn't have the heart to spend it. It's too risky to invest in movies. I couldn't bear the thought of you losing your hard-earned money."

Holly smoothed out the check. A delicate gold ring adorned with a single peridot popped out of the folded-up paper and fell onto the carpet.

Holly bent down and picked it up. "Oh, look, a ring." She handed it to Josh.

Josh handed the ring back to her. "Why don't you try it on and see if it fits?" he asked her in a tender voice.

Holly looked at the delicate ring, now resting in the palm of her hand, then at Josh. "Is this … what I think it is, Josh?"

"What do you think it is, dear?"

"It looks like an engagement ring."

Josh smiled. "Well, if you think it looks like an engagement ring, then it probably is an engagement ring." Heart pounding, Josh placed the ring on Holly's finger. It fit perfectly.

"I meant to give the ring to you at that club in Montreal, but I left it in my hotel room by mistake. That's what made me so nervous. See, I'm not afraid of commitment," he smiled. "A joke is just a joke."

"I'm sorry I didn't trust you. I feel really silly now."

"I feel silly, too." He grinned. "Well, do you want the ring? Do you want … me?"

"Of course, Josh!" She threw her arms around his neck.

"You mean everything to me," he said, covering her face with soft kisses. "The truth is, I fell madly in love with you the moment I first saw you in that club in Toronto, even before you tossed your drink in my face."

"I'm so sorry," Holly murmured, burying her face in his big chest. "I should never have done that to you."

"But you were justified, so don't apologize. It was actually a good thing, a wakeup call for me." He nibbled her ear gently.

"I fell in love with you that night, too, the very moment you walked into the room."

"Oh?"

"Yes. Something about those big, kind brown eyes of yours." She paused. "Right away, I just knew I wanted you." She kissed Josh on the lips, deeply and passionately.

"But I haven't always been good at showing you how I feel," he said in a humble voice, his eyes downcast.

"Sure, you have. I know you care about me. You just tried to hide your feelings for me under one-liners and punch lines because you were afraid of getting hurt by another woman."

Just as Josh and Holly began kissing again, a loud groan ripped through the air.

"I think my stomach is trying to tell me something," Josh said.

"Have you had breakfast?"

"Would my stomach be protesting like this if I'd had breakfast?"

"I guess not." Holly headed toward the kitchen. "I'll fix you a nice big meal. You can't start off our life together hungry."

A few minutes later, the townhouse was filled with the pungent aromas of toasting bread and freshly brewing coffee. Josh peeled off his tuxedo jacket and tie, loosened the top buttons of his shirt, and flung himself down on Holly's couch, eyes half-closed.

"Mmm, smells so good," he said, sniffing the air. "I'll help you clean up after breakfast."

"No, honey, you're too tired," Holly said from the kitchen. "You should take a nap in the bedroom."

"You're starting to sound like a wife."

"I could sure use the practice. I can't believe we're getting married. What's your tour schedule for the next few months?"

"My ... tour schedule?"

"Yeah. We'll have to plan the wedding around it." She gingerly placed the hot toast on a plate. "When can we get married? Sometime next year? Or maybe in a few months from now?"

Josh drew a deep breath. "I know the perfect time. Let's do it after my show tomorrow night."

Chapter Twenty-Eight

<http://www.jsteinbergreality.com/blog>

Hi, everyone. It's really me, the one and only Josh Steinberg, the Jewish Comedy King himself. (Yeah, I know, it's quite a stretch for a moderately successful comedian like me to make that claim. Whatever.)

I started this blog a few years ago to keep my loyal fans up to speed on the latest developments in my less-than-illustrious career ... even though I only have about five fans left: my wife, my mom, my rabbi, and my two cats, who aren't exactly experts on stand-up comedy.

Right now, my career is doing "semi-well." My former agent, Greg Fanelli, abandoned me six months ago, with no warning whatsoever. Something about being burned out from spending too many months on the road, starting his own talent agency, and spending more time with his new partner, Jill Boudreau, and her newborn son, Gregory (I wonder where she got that name from?), whom she had with her former boyfriend, Mr. Good-For-Nothing Billionaire. Jill is my former protégée. She's currently taking time off from her stand-up comedy career. I don't think she plans to go back to it — the last time I saw her, a couple of months ago, she thanked me for helping to get stand-up comedy out of her system — but who knows what to expect from Jill?

Maybe Greg decided to quit as my agent because my dream comeback movie, *It Only Hurts When I Laugh*, wasn't the big success we were both hoping for. The movie made a decent profit for the studio and for Paul Cohen, its fledgling producer — the *only* movie producer in Hollywood who believed in my movie, and in me — and now Paul's services are in demand. Even the guy's uncle, big-shot studio head Ari Cohen, can't get an appointment with his own nephew. Good for Paul!

Paul kept me going when I wanted to give up — when almost everyone else in Hollywood wanted me to give up — on my movie. And when the movie was finally released, it was Paul, more than anyone else, who gave me the credit for its success. Thanks to Paul, the critics did the unthinkable: they actually fell all over themselves praising my performance in the movie and my script, calling the writing "sharp" and "witty."

But that "sharp" and "witty" movie, profitable as it was, did nothing to boost my sagging career. No lucrative offers to write or perform in high-profile movies have been dangled in front of me; it's almost like people have forgotten that I even exist. Instead, I'm now doing small but colorful character roles in sort of interesting, quirky, low-budget movies, and getting slightly more lucrative comedy club gigs. None of these jobs is making me filthy rich, but hey, there's more to life than money, right? At least that's what I tell myself.

Oh, I almost forgot, I did get one "important" offer from a big-shot director. The once-great-but-then-overrated-and-now-disgraced movie director Ivan Bronkov sent me a letter, raving about my latest cinematic triumph — from prison. He actually had the gall to suggest that even though my movie was great, it would have been even better if *he* had directed it! The man is so out of touch with reality that he asked me to star in his next movie, a comedy set in a prison. As he put it, "By pushing the envelope just a little, Josh, you can once again prove to the world that you're a powerful comedy force to be reckoned with." Um, I don't think so.

It would take a lot more than a desperate attempt at edgy comedy to rescue my career from life support. Once upon a time, I was a hot, young, hungry comedian with a brilliant future and more fans than I could ever count. Not so anymore. My original fans have forgotten that I ever existed and, judging from the box office receipts of my latest cinematic masterpiece, the teenage boys who buy most movie tickets aren't exactly flocking to theaters to catch the latest antics of a plump and balding fifty-something comedian.

I suppose I just have to be realistic, especially at my age. I've never been leading man material, even when I was young, and I never will be. I'm still insecure about my looks, but I've given up on the plastic surgery dream. If I get it, I'll just look like a plastic version of Josh Steinberg. And then I'll be even more washed up than I already am.

But it sucks to have so little control over my career. It also sucks to see how well the star and director of my cinematic masterpiece — namely, Jason Williams and Mike Labelle — are doing. The careers of those two assholes — I mean, men — are hot, while I, Mr. Nice and Decent, continue to struggle.

It's hard to see why, though. When my movie was recut, Jason's role became a lot smaller. Yet movie producers have been panting for his services, offering him more and more money for each new movie. The same puzzling thing happened with Mike. My movie was no longer "his" after it was recut, but the critics started calling it *his* masterpiece. Sometimes I wish that the movie hadn't been recut, because the original uncut — and crappy — movie would have shown the world, once and for all, how untalented these two jerks really are.

The only bright spot in my life is my wife, Holly. We tied the knot — or more accurately, eloped — almost a year ago when we got married in a civil ceremony. This beautiful, kind, and whip-smart lady has done so much for me. First, she sold her share of her event planning business to her former partner, Diana, and became my new agent (with a bit of coaching from Mr. Fanelli). Who knew that such a tiny, delicate-looking woman would turn out to be so tough and ballsy, especially with comedy club owners who refuse to pay lowly comics like me? Holly also sold her beloved townhouse in Toronto, leaving her long-time friends and neighbors behind in Canada just so she could move in with me.

Holly's family gradually warmed to me — sort of — once it became obvious that I wasn't going to go away. After several false starts, I finally bonded with Holly's son, Kyle. He and Holly's ex-boyfriend, Eric What's-His-Name, used to go to sports events together, so I decided to top him. On one single weekend last fall, I took Kyle to every sporting event in Toronto I could find: the Maple Leafs, the Argos, the racetrack, a badminton tournament at a high school ... a ping pong competition for senior citizens. He enjoyed them all. Holly's mom was a little harder to win over. Margaret, based on her "experience" as a fan of Woody Allen movies, once told me that all Jewish men are neurotic. Who am I to argue with such an expert? To get on her good side, I bought her an appropriate birthday present: two dozen movies and TV shows on DVD starring the best Jewish comedians of all time. As I wrote in my birthday card to her, "Here's proof that you're right!"

My mom — always an enthusiastic cheerleader for our relationship — was thrilled when Holly and I tied the knot. My father wasn't so thrilled, but his fraught relationship with Holly has gradually improved. Holly somehow managed to convince my father to sit through my act at a comedy club in New York ... on my birthday. I almost fell off the stage when I saw my dad (without his latest wife) with Holly, Margaret, and Kyle in the audience. Of course, my dad refused to laugh the whole time I was up there — all he did was scowl at me and shake his head — but I swear I saw him crack one tiny smile when my head was turned.

And he was civilized to everyone afterwards, even to Margaret (who had kept her hands cupped over her ears during my act to block out all the dirty bits) and to Kyle, who actually fell asleep while I was onstage. And, for the very first time in my life, my dad showered me with compliments, calling my act "fine," "okay," and "not bad." We shared a long-postponed pizza dinner with Holly and her family, although the pizza was cold, the crust was stale, the club was loud, and Margaret and Kyle had almost nothing to say to me.

Holly's relationship with my irascible comic alter ego has gotten better. As time has passed, she's become tougher and far better at putting him — I mean, me — in my place and less willing to swallow bullshit. One night last month, when I made fun of her shortness while performing my stand-up act in a club, she dashed onto the stage and snatched the microphone from my hand. She then told the audience, "I may be short, but my brain is full-sized, unlike the puny brains of some big men I know." Despite her sharp words, Holly knows how I really feel about her. She even told a reporter a few months ago, "Josh makes fun of me in his act because I mean something to him." Love is the ultimate punch line!

But there's one thing I still don't understand. Last week, while performing my act in a club, I asked her, "What exactly do you see in me, Holly? Do you go for the male pattern baldness, the big nose, the big belly?" And she said to me, "I love the big brain, the big heart, and those big, kind brown eyes of yours." All I could say was, "Lady, you have excellent taste in men. *Oy vah!*"

Above all, Holly made an enormous personal sacrifice for me, a sacrifice that none of the other women I dated even dreamed of making: she converted to Judaism. The rabbi tried to talk her out of converting three times, but Holly, after a year of study, wore the poor guy down.

Lately, however, she's becoming a bit too Jewish. Usually, when I'm on the road, I indulge in big, hearty breakfasts to keep up my strength: buttered toast, scrambled eggs, home fries, and bacon. The other day, when I asked Holly to recreate this feast for me at home, she said no. She actually told me, "I can't cook bacon. It's sacrilegious." I reminded her that I've been a Jew far longer than she has, but I got nowhere.

In the not-so-distant past, a more cynical me would have gotten angry at Holly. But this sweet woman — who I now show off at all red carpet events, by the way — has made me so happy, so loved, that I find myself chuckling over her wholehearted embrace of all things Jewish.

Why should I get mad at her? For the first — and probably the only — time in my life, I've found a woman I can trust, someone I can truly be myself with. Besides, Holly's transformation into the ideal Jewish wife is perfect material for my stand-up act.

I mean, it's great for a guy like me to love and cherish his wife … but we comedians still have to eat.

Thank you for purchasing this book. Now that you have finished reading it, I would be grateful if you would take the time to post an honest review of it on Amazon, Barnes & Noble, Indigo, or the sites of other online booksellers.

If you have an Amazon account, you can post reviews on Amazon, even if you purchased the book elsewhere. Your review need not be long; just a couple of well-chosen sentences can be enough to help a potential reader decide whether or not the book is worth their time. Your opinion is valuable to me.

I put a lot of effort into checking the manuscript before publication, but no book is perfect. If you notice an error, you can help improve future editions by emailing me with the page number and the line of the error so that it can be corrected.

Finally, if you found the book to be a "good read," please tell your friends about it, in person and on social media such as Facebook, Twitter, LinkedIn, and others.

Kathleen Jones
joneslepidas@bell.net

CPSIA information can be obtained
at www.ICGtesting.com
Printed in the USA
LVHW110110111019
633870LV00001B/27/P